A Lady's Journal of Love
(AND OTHER LEGAL MATTERS)

MOST IMPRUDENT MATCHES
BOOK SEVEN

ALLY HUDSON

Busy Nothings Books

This novel is entirely a work of fiction. The names, characters, and incidents portrayed in it are the work of the author's imagination. Any resemblance to actual persons, living or dead, events or localities is entirely coincidental.

NO AI TRAINING: Without in any way limiting the author's and publisher's exclusive rights under copyright, any use of this publication to "train" generative artificial intelligence (AI) technologies to generate text is expressly prohibited. The author reserves all rights to license uses of this work for generative AI training and development of machine learning language models.

A Lady's Guide to Abduction (and Other Legal Matters) Copyright © 2025 by Ally Hudson. All rights reserved. Printed in the United States of America. No part of this book may be reproduced in any form or by any electronic or mechanical means, including information storage and retrieval systems, without written permission from the author, except for the use of brief quotations in a book review.

Digital Edition ISBN: 979-8-9918384-4-3

Print Edition ISBN: 979-8-9918384-5-0

Cover design by Holly Perret, The Swoonies Romance Art

First edition

To my mom, who lived a thousand lives between the pages of books, but shared the best one with me.

Love that journey for me.

> — "THE DRIP," *SCHITT'S CREEK*,
> CREATED BY EUGENE LEVY AND
> DANIEL LEVY

A Lady's Guide to Abduction

Author's Note

Dearest Reader,

Welcome to *A Lady's Guide to Abduction (and Other Legal Matters)*.

If this is your first time entering the Most Imprudent Matches universe, you should know that events in my series are interconnected. Though the inciting of this book is directly caused by the events in *The Scottish Scheme*, it is not necessary to have read that book to enjoy this one. However, this story does contain spoilers for earlier books in the series.

Readers of the previous books will know that the the last three begin (more or less) at the same masquerade. My original vision was for each of the final four books to begin there. In fact, the first scene I wrote for this book was the masquerade. But, Kit and Davina had been interacting for years by the masquerade and the scene didn't feel right. So I wrote a scene further back. Then another, and another. Until I realized that I was headed in the wrong direction.

At long last, I settled on the beginning we have now. *In medias res* was absolutely the right choice for this story. But, I

AUTHOR'S NOTE

was left with a great number of hilarious scenes and nothing to do with them...

Which is where this author's note comes in. I polished up those scenes and have decided to treat them as little prologues. They're not necessary to the understanding or enjoyment of the story, but they are good fun. Readers can grab them all here.

I also created a map for readers to follow along with Kit and Davina, here.

All this to say, happy reading...

Best wishes and warmest regards,
Ally

One

HART AND SUMMERS, SOLICITORS, LONDON—
APRIL 10, 1817

KIT

The bell above the door gave a disgruntled *clang* of protest.

The contract I was reviewing was far too tedious to look away from if I didn't wish to get distracted and have to re-read it a fourth time. Barley trade agreements were hardly the most interesting aspect of my job.

When no tired greeting was forthcoming, I called out, "Welcome to Hart and Summers, Solicitors. I'll be with you in a moment," without glancing up from the parchment before me.

Light footsteps against the worn wood echoed through the empty office.

I finished reading the sentence before finally lifting my gaze. My jaw dropped at the sight before me and I found myself blinking several times.

When the vision did not change, I was forced to admit that this was real—or I'd broken too far from reality for my eyes to be trusted.

She was dressed as a pirate. A floppy, sea-blue tricorner hat sat jauntily atop her head. Everything else had clearly been stolen from her brother's wardrobe. The white shirt, emerald-green waistcoat, and tan trousers—all tailored for a man who dwarfed her in height and weight. Save the shoes; those were dainty black riding boots.

An attempt had been made to hide her identity. She wore the shadows cast by the afternoon light streaming in from the front windows like a cloak. A black domino mask concealed her cheeks and sharp, dark brow. The ridiculous hat topped a blond wig.

And the sword—that was plenty real. Sunlight glinted off the blade, blinding me momentarily as she brandished it.

"This is a kidnapping," she insisted in an affected masculine tone, infusing a hint of gravel to the words.

Lady Davina Hasket was nothing if not dramatic. Years of sorting her messes already in progress had left me with a curiosity. The beginning was nearly always a mystery to me. It seemed today was the day I would, at last, experience the full effect.

She strode forward, sword swaying in her lazy grip, to halve the distance between us.

"Get up," she added, weapon pointing vaguely in my direction.

I set my quill in the rest with a performative sigh before leaning back in my chair.

Her lips parted on a gasp and I bit back a grin. She clearly hadn't anticipated such nonchalance out of her victim.

Even swimming in her deceased brother's clothes, her breasts bound in a way I had no business noticing, she was lovely. All soft lips and creamy skin. The domino covered her dark brow, but I could almost sense it arching in challenge beneath the fabric.

"Get. Up," she demanded a second time, still rasping her lustrous alto tone. Her order banished the intrusive thoughts.

They'd been coming faster and sharper in recent months, and it wouldn't do to give them purchase.

I'd never understood before why *they* were always fooled. The gentlemen who frequented the gaming hells and failed to notice it was a lady who won every round. The milliner who so easily believed a duke's daughter to be a shopgirl. The sailors who urged her aboard and handed her a mop. And now, having seen the full effect, I knew with absolute certainty that they were buffoons.

There was no concealing the fiery essence of Lady Davina Hasket. Not behind a mask, not in a wig, and certainly not in some ill-fitting trousers.

Wordlessly, I slipped the contract I had been reviewing into my desk and rose as bid. She did, after all, have a sword pointed at my throat.

"Now what?" I asked, my hands raised in a half-hearted placation.

"This is a kidnapping!" she insisted.

"Yes, you mentioned that before. Also, it's technically an *abduction*. What would you like me to do now that I've complied with the first order?"

"Turn around so I can bind your wrists."

My gaze skimmed down her person. There was no rope obviously present, though her clothing was loose enough that she could have it tucked somewhere. Regardless, it wasn't an overly appealing prospect—at least, not for what I suspected she had in mind. "Is that necessary?"

"Yes," she insisted and stamped a tiny foot, abandoning the affected gravel in her frustration.

"What if I promise to cooperate fully? After all, you do have a sword and I value my life."

She paused, contemplating the options. "Fine, but any missteps and you'll be tied up!"

"Agreed, I won't put a toe out of line."

"Then you need to come with me."

"Where are we going?"

Her jaw clenched in irritation. *Hadn't been expecting questions, had you?* "That is not for you to know."

"Do you suppose we'll be back by tomorrow morning? I ought to leave a note for Will if I'll be late," I explained with a gesture toward my partner's empty desk.

Will and I had been sharing my office for months. That situation left the room cluttered, cramped, and, far too often, occupied by his distracting new wife. Since the attempt on his life left his office charred, it was the best solution. Even if I was left to trip over them all day long while they made eyes at each other.

"Fine," she replied.

I rushed to snatch a clean piece of parchment and scribbled a note to my business partner and mentor. A few words were all that was necessary to inform him that Lady Davina was "kidnapping" me and I wasn't certain when I would return. With that intelligence, he was unlikely to worry for at least a fortnight—neither of us were strangers to her escapades. That thought considered, I added a postscript asking him to water the plants at my apartments down the street.

I set it across his desk. The note stood in stark contrast to the uncluttered wood of Will's workspace. Marriage had left him a less dedicated business owner. He never had an empty desk before Celine.

"If you're all finished," she began, sarcasm coloring her tone, "we can set off." She must have realized it wasn't usual to allow the abducted to leave notes, at least not ones without ransom requests.

"How long will we be gone? And to where? I should probably pack a few things."

"You know, don't you?" she demanded.

"Know what?" I asked, biting back a smile and hoping the

mirth in my tone wasn't too obvious. It was a familiar sensation in her presence, one I'd grown quite comfortable with over the years.

She sighed before dragging the hand not holding the sword across her face in irritation. Her domino slipped with the effort and she rushed to right it. The display was amusing, particularly in light of the fact that she must be certain I knew her identity. Her sword hand was flagging again. The weapon was a great oversized thing that seemed much too heavy for her.

The reasonableness of my request must have struck her though, because she nodded.

"Where do you live?" Lady Davina had entirely forgotten to drop her voice that time and instead resorted to her usual bell tones.

"Half a block south. Do you want to wait here?"

She considered for a moment before nodding.

"Make yourself comfortable. I'll be quick."

She settled into my recently vacated chair as though she owned it and kicked her feet up on the desk. I shook my head and grabbed my great coat before I slipped out of the darkening offices, then rushed up the street to my apartments before she found some other trouble.

The brisk walk left me with more questions than answers. Lady Davina had kept her mischief to a minimum since her elder brother left for Scotland last summer. I'd thought her penchant for mayhem was dying down. There had been no gaming-hell incidents, no odd investments, no unexpected employment, and no petty thievery.

Her brother, the Duke of Rosehill, left me with strict instructions to rescue her from any scrapes she found herself in without regard to cost—a task that had fallen to me regularly before he left town. Now it seemed she was merely combining all her smaller misdeeds into one grand performance.

Once inside my apartments, I raced to the wardrobe and dragged free my father's old, dusty, formerly red portmanteau. I set it on the floor and yanked it open.

Years ago, I'd inadvertently torn a hole in the lining—now a feature, I stuffed a handful of coins from my pocket inside. I riffled through the wardrobe, gathering sensible shirts, practical waistcoats, and comfortable trousers with an unadorned cravat and set them in the bag.

I considered the portmanteau carefully before I strode to the desk tucked beneath the singular window. There, I snatched a few bills from the top drawer and added them to the lining leaving only a few coins in my pocket.

Rushing, I made for the basin I used to wash every morning and evening and grabbed an unused bar of soap and a clean cloth and tucked those away as well.

The kitchen revealed little. Only a few apples and a loaf of bread rested on the counter across from my sleeping area. I tossed those on top of my clothing.

A thousand different scenarios spun through my mind. There were untold ways Lady Davina could have found trouble. And it was entirely in character for her to choose this utterly absurd way out of it. I might have need of any one of a million different things to help her.

But I knew, deep down, that whatever mess she was in, I would never be able to guess it. And so I yanked the case closed, barely, and buckled it before I set off back to my offices and the chaos awaiting me there.

Two

HART AND SUMMERS, SOLICITORS, LONDON—
APRIL 10, 1817

DAVINA

This was a properly terrible idea. I knew that. Anyone with even the slightest bit of intelligence could see that. And Mr. Summers was a good man; he would almost certainly help me without the ruse. But...

That was the problem, the but. The what-if hung there in my head, floating ominously over the near certainty I felt of his assistance.

I could not risk Xander's secret, his very life, on a but.

Not until I was assured Mr. Summers had as much to lose as I did, as much at stake as Xander.

This wasn't the proper way to go about it either, kidnapping—*abduction*, apparently. For years my half-hearted disguises had bamboozled the *ton*. But I was fairly certain Mr. Summers hadn't been fooled for a second. His willingness to play along with my charade lent further credence to my suspicion that he wouldn't betray us.

With a sigh, I settled back into his usual chair. It was an ugly green shade, though more comfortable than the ones he left for visitors. Perhaps, when all this was finished, I could redecorate these abysmal offices. That might be a sufficient thanks.

I yanked the top drawer open. Nothing of interest: a seal and red wax, a stamp, some paste, and a few wrapped hard candies that *I* wouldn't be testing.

The next drawer was more interesting. Neatly labeled folders were packed tight, vertically, within easy reach. Some familiar names gave me pause, but even I could not bring myself to look at private documents that didn't belong to me. The one with *my* name, however, felt appropriate.

The Lady Davina Hasket folder was thick but neatly organized by date, beginning with my adventure at Decker's and ending with the evening at Wayland's last June, when I won a tidy sum. Behind that was the settlement Xander had prepared for my eventual dowry—not that I would ever need it.

What I hadn't known about was the living Xander had arranged. Dated a mere ten months ago, the document showed that Xander had arranged to provide me a living of at least £2,500 per annum when I reached the age of five and twenty. Mama, too, had an immodest £25,000 to live on in her lifetime. Anything remaining on her death would go to me. The settlement was separate from my ostentatious dowry.

How Xander had managed to keep the funds from me after I reached majority was most likely Mr. Summers' doing. But the efforts my brother had undertaken to ensure my comfort solidified my determination to help him now.

Xander had sacrificed a great deal for me. Money, property, dignity, the promise of love—all were tossed away in favor of my health, safety, and happiness. And now, finally, I could do the same for him.

Dressing up as a pirate and dragging a solicitor to Scotland was an easy price to pay for Xander. He'd undertaken worse for me, had done, in fact.

The irritating bell above the door jangled to announce Mr. Summers' return, as promised, overstuffed portmanteau in hand.

He took one look at me and sighed. "Tell me you're not sifting through private documents."

Before I could move to stuff the folder back in the drawer, he reached my side. He flipped the folder closed and slapped his hand atop it.

"What are you— Oh, that's fine," he muttered.

Indignation rose instinctively before the actual understanding did. "So Lady Davina is not deserving of privacy?"

The expression he shot me was so unlike him and so very like one I used for Xander when he was being particularly dense that I had to bite back a laugh.

Not fooled even in the slightest then.

"Must we continue with this ridiculous charade? The Rosehill carriage is nowhere to be seen, and His Grace would never hire staff that would encourage this nonsense anyway. Presumably you intend to hire a hack. How do you propose to do so dressed like this?"

"When did you figure it out?"

"Sometime between the bell ringing and the pronouncement that you intended to kidnap me," he replied, tone droll.

"And you went along with it?"

"It was amusing. I usually arrive after your adventures have gone sideways. I wanted to experience the entire effect."

"And?"

"You've reaffirmed my belief that the *ton* is full of dullards and dimwits," he said, his gaze flicking up and down my frame.

He tugged the hefty file from beneath my hand and returned it to the designated spot in his drawer. "We can dispense with the foolery. What, precisely, do you need my assistance with?"

"I cannot tell you."

"And I cannot help you if you do not tell me what you need help with."

"It's a secret."

"I'm a solicitor. Confidentiality is essential in my profession."

"I'm sorry, but I cannot tell you."

He sighed and leaned against the other desk. "Lady Davina, I've never once betrayed your confidences."

"No one would believe you even if you did," I retorted. His head tipped to the side, a singular brow raised in a strange sort of acknowledgment.

"Still, I won't help you, not without more information. And I'm not entirely certain *I* believe this is happening. I guarantee no one else would."

My teeth found my lower lip and gnawed on it in that way Mama always scolded me over. This was why I had formulated the ridiculous kidnapping plot in the first place. But it wasn't my secret, and the *ton* was already too eager for gossip about Xander. And this secret... There was a fate worse than ruin if the wrong person discovered it.

"If you won't help me, I'll find someone else who will."

"Who?" It was a simple question, demand really. And one I hadn't the slightest answer to, but there was something in his tone that left me flummoxed.

"That is none of your concern."

"Lady Davina..." The exasperation swirled with plea had me hiding a smile. He was giving in.

"Or, if I cannot find anyone, then I will go myself."

"Trying to find yourself ruined or killed," he grumbled. "Fine."

"Thank you! Thank you, thank you, thank you!" I could not contain my little hop of delight.

He shook his head and pointed at the door. "Come along

then. You need to change into something appropriate before you're arrested for indecency."

"That is not neces—"

"I'll wait outside."

"I have the carriage situation well in hand."

"How?" he asked, worry creeping into his tone.

In lieu of a response, I merely caught him by the forearm and dragged him back out beneath the annoying little bell.

Once outside, I waited for him to lock the door before pulling him around the corner where our conveyance was waiting.

Mr. Summers stopped short at the sight before him, jaw hanging slightly open.

"You cannot be serious," he protested, then stepped toward it with caution.

Three

LONDON—APRIL 10, 1817

KIT

IT COULD BARELY BE CALLED a carriage.

I preferred to repair rather than replace at every opportunity, but... this formerly red painted scrap heap should have been given to scrap a century or so ago. Instead of a box seat for the drivers, two whiskey barrels sat where the cushions belonged. No two wheels had come from the same vehicle. The door was stolen from some other conveyance and had been belted on with leather straps. And where there should have been a glass window, there was... nothing.

Sprawled atop one of the barrels was a scrawny lad of perhaps fifteen, with a pinkish-red stocking cap covering his head and a once-white shirt half-unbuttoned on his torso. It was not undone as a fashionable choice or to make a statement. Rather, the rest of the buttons were simply absent. A green waistcoat hung open over his shoulders. His breeches fortunately had no holes I could see, and to my astonishment, his boots were nearly new—and too big and much too fine for such a boy. Almost certainly those hessians served as this lad's salary for his role in this farce.

"Mr. Jack, yer carriage," he drawled, moving to hop off the barrel.

"Too late, Alfie. He knows," Lady Davina replied with no hint of her false masculine tone.

His brow twisted in confusion. "But ye said I was only to call ye Mr. Jack."

Something about the lady's sigh told me there had been a great deal of rehearsal on that subject. The knowledge tipped the absurdity of this moment from nonsensical to amusing.

"Call me whatever you like, Alfie. Alfie, this is Mr. Summers, Mr. Summers, this is Alfie."

"Pleased to meet ye," the boy said and thrust his hand down to me from his place on the footboard.

"Likewise," I replied, shaking his surprisingly clean hand with an internal sigh. "Is it just you, or..."

"Nah, ole Rory is here somewhere." He threw a thumb behind his back to indicate the missing Rory.

"Of course," I replied with a significant look to Lady Davina. "Wouldn't want to forget Old Rory."

"Yer right about that! She's the best smug—er, carriage captain this side of Slough, ole Rory is."

"Driver, carriage driver," Lady Davina added pathetically, her voice failing on the last word.

Alfie was either unhearing or uncaring as he returned to his barrel and dug through a crate between them and plucked out a strip of dried meat. He tore into it with a revolting kind of enthusiasm. I would wager everything in my pocket that the meat came with the boots.

I turned to her. "I take it you found these two outside the distillery?" I asked, recognizing the Bonnie Barrel Whiskey stamp on one of the barrel-seats.

The distillery had been another one of Lady Davina's

flights of fancy, an ill-conceived investment that turned out well for her—as they always did.

"Yes," she muttered.

"The *carriage* as well?"

"Yes."

"Please tell me we're not traveling as far as Slough? We may have the best smuggler this side of it, but we certainly don't have the best carriage."

"We're not going anywhere near Slough," she replied slyly. I pretended not to notice her careful wording.

One of the horses sighed and flicked its ear in an irritation that perfectly matched my own. The pair of sooty Cleveland Bays before me were nearly as decrepit as the coach they were tethered to.

"That's the last of the supplies, Mr. Jack," came a voice from behind us.

Instead of the weathered, elderly man I expected from a name like Old Rory, I spun to find a girl—young woman, in truth—hauling a heavy trunk. She was my age, perhaps a few years younger, with a messy, dull red braid and a nose that was slightly too flat for her otherwise delicate features. Her skin was clear and clean, and her form was slender beneath the tan trousers and blue waistcoat she wore. Unlike Alfie, her clothing was neat and well cared for.

"Just Davina, Rory. He figured it out."

"I told ye that he would," Rory snorted as she hefted the trunk to the back of the *carriage* and began to tie it down. She turned to observe me and her upper lip curled in a sneer. "Is his face always like that?"

"Yes," Lady Davian replied for me.

I fumbled to make amends for my certainly befuddled expression. "Apologies Miss Rory. I was just expecting someone—"

"With more impressive ballocks?"

I blinked dimly for a moment, before replying, "Well, yes. Also a bit older."

"Why's that?"

"Well, Alfie called you Old Rory."

"He would. I'm older than young Rory. And I'm much older than wee Rory."

"There are three Rorys?" I asked, regretting the question as soon as I asked it.

"There are five Rorys. Granddaddy Rory, big Rory, ole' Rory—that's me—young Rory, and wee Rory."

"Dare I ask why?"

"Firstborn in my family is always Rory," she said with a shrug, tightening the last strap before yanking the portmanteau from my hand. "Do ye want this on the back? Or in with ye?"

"With me," I said. "Forgive me, but isn't Rory a—"

"Lad's name?" She dropped the portmanteau by the door and it landed in the mud with a damp *plonk*. "What of it?" she questioned as she tugged on the straps keeping the door shut.

"Not a thing," I replied, finally coming to my senses. "Thank you for your assistance, Miss Rory."

"It's just Rory to ye. Ye dinnae ken any of the others."

"Right."

"That went well," Lady Davina murmured to me.

"You could have warned me."

"And miss this? Absolutely not." Mirth spilled from every note.

"Remind me to tell your brother that I've given up my life as a solicitor. I'm taking my rightful place in the House of Lords. Claiming my ancestral seat, as it were. He'll have to find someone else to sort out your misadventures," I muttered, acknowledging for the first time that there was a fate worse than the earldom I'd inherited. That fate almost certainly awaited me in that carriage.

"No, you're not. You'd rather eat Alfie's hat than make nice with the *beau monde*."

I gulped, eyeing the boy's head covering wearily. "No," I insisted. "I suspect whatever you have planned for me will be infinitely worse."

"Worse than the dancing? The endless dancing?" she retorted.

She was right, I really did loathe the dancing. "Fine," I snapped, just as ole' Rory successfully unfastened the door and heaved my portmanteau inside. I stomped in after it, not properly handing Lady Davina in as was her due. If she wanted to dress as a man, she could bloody well enter a carriage like one. All that besides, it was probably for the best that I tested the strength of this agglomeration before she got in.

It swayed dangerously as I settled on the rear-facing wooden bench before creaking ominously when Lady Davina followed and dropped primly onto the opposite seat before tossing her hat beside me. At least if the carriage collapsed, there was no piece of this jumble substantial enough to cause injury.

The carriage rocked as ole' Rory climbed up to the barrel beside Alfie's, the wood groaning in displeasure. With a jolt, it creaked forward, swaying threateningly as we clambered off down the cobblestone street.

Good Lord, what had I gotten myself into?

Four

LONDON—APRIL 10, 1817

DAVINA

MR. SUMMERS SWAYED UNEASILY with each divot the wheels found. And there were, unfortunately, quite a lot of them as we navigated the lesser-traveled side streets.

I had been confident in my plan, perhaps overconfident. Once I procured the carriage and Bonnie Annie had strenuously implied that our drivers needed to be elsewhere, Alfie out from underfoot and Rory out of London, everything had fallen into place.

That was, until Mr. Summers pointed out the structural inadequacies of our transportation.

I was fond of my little adventures, that was true. And it was also true that Mr. Summers had rescued me from more than one mishap they'd resulted in.

But truly, I only allowed people to think I went off half-cocked. In point of fact, it required a great deal of organization to purchase a naval lieutenant's uniform and sneak about one of His Majesty's vessels without detection. If I had put no effort into it, I never would have been able to board in the first place.

But in this instance, I perhaps could have considered more carefully—at least the carriage.

"Where the devil are we going?" Mr. Summers demanded, his usually pale complexion blanched to a ghostly grey.

"Nowhere near Slough," I teased, as I worked the pins free from my wig.

"I've packed for three days. Please, I am begging you, tell me I have brought enough clothing."

He hadn't, of course, but I'd brought the few useful things that still remained from Gabriel's closet. Alfie was currently wearing my deceased brother's long-untouched boots. Though, now that I had Mr. Summers in front of me, it was quite clear that he was smaller than Gabriel. Much smaller.

My late brother was, quite simply, a great oaf of a man, tall and broad in a way that the wiry, compact Mr. Summers was not.

"What do you know about tailoring?" I asked, tossing the wig atop my hat.

His thumb and forefinger found his eyelids as he grumbled, "I think I'm going to be sick."

"Because you don't know how to sew?"

"Because I get carriagesick," he replied before dropping his head to rest between his knees. "And you just implied that we would be in this death trap for more than three days."

My own stomach dropped dangerously. I had absolutely failed to account for all the variables.

"Well, sit here by the window," I insisted, scooting to the other side of the wooden bench. I nudged his portmanteau out of the way with my shoe. Most carriages had two windows. At one point even this one probably had. But the far one had been boarded up and the one at my side was little more than a neatly carved hole in the door that was strapped on.

"Can't."

"Why not?"

"It's not proper. Gentlemen sit rear-facing when ladies are present," he murmured pathetically to the floorboards.

"Gentlemen also do not cast up their accounts on a lady's boots." I caught his forearm and hauled him to sit beside me. He obeyed with a pathetic groan, resting his sweaty brow against the edge of the perpetually open window.

"This is a disaster," he groused to himself even as the color returned to his cheeks. His flush bloomed slowly while the dampness dissipated from his brow.

"Sitting beside me is that bad?"

"Stop being obtuse, it doesn't suit you," he snapped. "We're stuck in this great heap of junk for Lord only knows how long—well, I suppose you know, but you won't tell me. We're traveling only Lord—and you—knows where, to do only Lord—and you—knows what. I'm going to flash the hash at any moment. And you're entirely unchaperoned. If this carriage doesn't kill me, your brother certainly will."

"There's Rory."

"Rory is not an acceptable chaperone and you know it."

"I had actually thought of that. It's like that time you found me at Gunter's."

"What is like that time at Gunter's?"

"Reciprocal havoc."

He was silent a moment, probably recalling that incident, before finally turning to me for the first time since I hauled him beside me. It was years ago that he caught me unchaperoned enjoying an ice. At least, I was until an unwanted suitor wished to claim my attention. Mr. Summers' rescue—if it could be called that—had required a bit of imprudent familiarity and fibbing. We'd mutually agreed to refrain from discussing it with Xander. The accord ensured that I was not scolded for my brief unchaperoned foray into the world and he was not called out for impersonating my cousin.

Mr. Summers' countenance was much improved as he contemplated me in his usual, serious way, warm brown eyes searching mine for some answer. "I won't tell anyone because I don't want your brother to have me hanged. What've I got on you?"

I offered him a little smile. "You really worry about that too often. Besides, Xander cannot have you hanged, you're an earl now."

"Barely," he grumbled, lip sinking lower into his regular frowning pout at the reminder of his newly acquired title—the one he'd spent months studiously pretending he hadn't inherited.

"It's simple. You won't tell anyone because if you did, we'd be forced to wed. And that, I'm certain, would make you even grumpier than you usually are." I poked his shoulder with my index finger to emphasize my point.

"Right," he agreed, swallowing.

"And I won't tell anyone because I have no interest in marrying you or anyone else."

"And you think your brother will just accept that."

"I do," I said simply. "Xander would never force me to wed, even at the expense of my reputation."

"I suppose we had better both pray that you're right."

"You seem to be feeling better," I observed.

"Facing forward helps."

"Even though it's improper?"

His eyes slid shut in that way they did when he couldn't decide whether he was annoyed or amused by me. "Even though it's improper. Don't suppose you can tell me where we're going?"

"Not yet," I said, peering around him and out the carriage

window. The streets of London were thinning out, but we weren't nearly far enough for me to be certain he wouldn't put an end to this entire scheme.

"And what we're doing?"

"You're helping me with a legal matter."

"The abduction charges?" he asked, one corner of his mouth ticking up in a half smile. It was one of his better ones.

"*Other* legal matters," I corrected in a prim tone.

He huffed once with a note that could have been a chuckle.

"Besides, it was hardly a crack abduction. You knew it was me the entire time." I pouted.

"You used a sword," he whined, nudging it with his foot where it rested under the far seat.

"Not a very sharp one."

"Well then, charges dismissed," he retorted.

"Are there?" I asked. My stomach flipped unpleasantly at the sudden recognition of the severity of what I had done.

"Are there what?"

"Charges?"

He huffed a laugh. "Not for you."

"What do you mean?"

"You do realize you're an heiress?" he asked.

"No! It had escaped my notice!"

"The daughter of a duke with a dowry to make most men blush goes missing, later to be found dressed in ill-fitting men's clothing. She is traveling northward in a dilapidated carriage with a solicitor. Who do you suppose they're going to believe abducted whom?"

"But I—"

"There's not a soul alive, save perhaps your brother, who would believe *you* abducted *me*. Especially not if we're heading where I think we're heading."

"Where do you think we're heading?"

"Scotland."

I left his unasked question unanswered, considering him for a moment. "I wouldn't let them hang you, you know."

"You would have very little in the way of choice."

"We're not going to be caught."

"Of course."

"We're not. I sent Mother to Bath with Cee's Mama and friend. Cee is still a newlywed, she rarely comes up for air. And Xander is in Scotland. No one will be looking for me."

"The servants will notice your absence."

"All in my debt, or I know their secrets. Every single one."

His gaze was heavy, thoughtful. "You're a terrifying little thing. Did you know that?" There was nothing in his words or tone, nothing in his eyes nor the downturn of his lips that lent itself toward my interpretation, but his words felt like a compliment.

"I'm taller than you."

"Everyone is taller than me," he said with a one-shouldered shrug. "I think we're the same height anyway."

"Do you need spectacles as well?"

He huffed another half laugh. I'd earned so many and our journey had barely begun. Perhaps I would receive full-throated laughter before we reached the border. "Probably. Only from too much time spent trying to read all the documents in your folder."

"You should really make improvements to your penmanship."

"I'll take it under advisement." He glanced out the window once again. We'd finally abandoned the rutted cobblestone city streets for the worn dirt roads between London and Edmonton.

This part of the journey was familiar to me. It had been years since I'd visited our ancestral home in Yorkshire, since before Father passed at least. But in my youth, we made the journey there and back at least once a year.

"Can you tell me what you had planned for coaching inns and the like? Or is that a secret as well?" he asked, still contemplating the road ahead.

"I never said we would stop at coaching inns."

"So you don't intend to stop at the Old Bell in Enfield?" Reading my surely astonished expression, he continued, "I'm from Lincolnshire, remember? I've made the journey a fair few times."

"I thought to call you my brother?"

There was no discernible movement in his face, yet it seemed as though his frown deepened. "It might work. But closer to Grantham there might be folks who recognize me."

I raised a questioning brow.

"Clergyman's son. Or, more specifically, clergyman's wife's son. Mother dragged the three of us all about the county with her on visits."

"Oh, well, we have quite a bit of time before that becomes a concern."

"I don't suppose you packed anything to eat?" he asked, then tipped his head back against the wooden seat.

"I did, actually," I replied with a grin.

When I didn't offer any additional information, one eye peeked open. I tugged free the trunk that was hidden beneath our bench seat and unlatched it.

At the sight of two little fairy cakes resting neatly at the top, he perked up and shifted forward in his seat.

"Hudson's?"

"Is there anywhere else to get them?"

My question had been rhetorical but he replied, "Not anywhere worthwhile."

"I got you one of the chocolate ones you're always pestering Will about."

"Thank you," he said, reaching eagerly for his fairy cake. "I take back at least seven percent of my grumbling today."

"Then you may have seven percent of your little cake thing," I replied with a teasing grin.

He froze, fairy cake halfway to his full lips. "I'm willing to go as high as thirty-four percent."

"Then you may eat thirty-four percent of your fairy cake. That may be a full bite."

He sighed, dark lashes flickering between me and the fairy cake in his hand. "Fine. This plan of yours is brilliant. You've done absolutely nothing wrong, ever, in your entire life," he said, just before he took a massive bite out of the decadent dessert.

An indecent groan spilled from his chest and his eyelids fluttered shut. A chocolate crumb caught on his lower lip and his tongue darted out to catch it in an entirely ungentlemanly display.

"If—" I broke off to clear my throat. "If I'd known all it would take to end your whining and to acknowledge my exceptionalism was a little cake thing, I would have given you one at our every meeting."

"Thought you didn't want a husband," he said, not glancing away from his fairy cake.

"I don't."

"Giving a man a fairy cake at every meeting is an excellent way to end up with one."

I could do nothing more than blink slowly at him as he decimated every last crumb of the cake before popping his fingers in his mouth one after the other.

Five

NORTH ROAD—APRIL 10, 1817

KIT

As soon as the sugary confection left my hand, my head caught up with my mouth.

"Not me, of course," I tacked on to my entirely inappropriate proclamation.

"Right," she agreed kindly, leaning across me to peer out the window. "I think we're almost to the Old Bell."

Much of her hair had come loose from her coiffure when she pulled the wig off, and a few loose strands kissed the back of her neck. Those curls were darker than the rest, unaccustomed to the sun's touch.

A wheel hit a divot, rocking the carriage and causing her shoulder to knock into mine, her delicate, sweet and spicy scent brushing over me.

Desperate for a less enticing breath, I cleared my throat. "Did you want to go into the inn?"

"I thought to, yes. These places always have the best sorts of people," she said, something eager in the tilt of her arch brows.

"And were you going in as Mr. Jack?"

Startled, her gaze dropped to her form, and she plucked at her oversized shirt with surprise. Apparently, her attire had slipped her notice. "I suppose it would make me less recognizable."

"And attract more notice."

"I attract plenty of notice in my gowns, thank you very much," she informed me with a little smirk.

"I'm aware. Do you have something simple? That dress you wore at Decker's, perhaps?"

The day that had started it all—my very first rescue of Lady Davina Hasket. Minutes after my promotion from Will's clerk to his partner, Rosehill strode in, fretting something fierce about his sister, who had managed to find employment at a milliner's under a false identity and had been accused of theft.

Will, ever the bemused employer, volunteered me for the retrieval mission.

"You remember that?" The astonished note was an irritant.

"Remember? It was my first day! I was sure Will would demote me or sack me. And besides, it's not as though I have other clients involved in that sort of mischief. "

"That was your first day? But you were so... so..."

"Unprofessional?" I supplied.

"Gallant," she corrected. "Mary still talks about that day. The way you swanned in and growled at Mr. Decker."

"I do not growl," I muttered, recalling the moment I'd seen the bruise the bastard had left on her ivory cheek. A duller version of the fury that had overtaken me rolled through my frame. Even if she had stolen, which I was now confident she hadn't, there was never an excuse for striking a woman.

Much of that day was a blur—overwhelmed as I was by

irritation and terror in equal measure. Bits and pieces returned in flashes at inconvenient moments in the years since. I remembered convincing the other shopgirl that I was Lady Davina's—Lucy's, as the shopgirl knew her—brother, threatening Mr. Decker, and dropping the pennies and farthing on the floor for the scoundrel to scramble after in pathetic, disgraced desperation.

Her chuckle was bemused. "Of course not," she agreed with false solemnity. "It was the sort of thing Gabriel would've done—the way you tossed the missing payment on the ground."

"Do not compare me to your reprobate brother—I cannot survive the insult to my honor. And I remember swearing to myself that it was the last time I would come to your rescue."

"I did not require rescuing then. And you are not rescuing me now. I've abducted you." Lady Davina's hands danced in front of her in the same way Rosehill's so often did—hers a little more controlled than his. The sight had a smile playing at the corner of my lip. Something in the education they gave young ladies must have taught her to dampen a little of the visual reminder of her enthusiasm in a way that school hadn't for her brother. But every once in a while, her instinct broke free and she was so overcome that she forgot herself. It was enthralling.

Instead of acknowledging that rather inappropriate thought, I retorted, "You've abducted me for the purpose of solving some sort of problem. Some might call that a rescue."

"Some might, but I would not."

"Call it whatever you like," I said, setting the teasing aside for the moment. "I did not know Mary remained with you, though." Mary had been the other shopgirl working that day, and Rosehill had seen fit to employ her in the household, but I had no idea she was still there—or thinking of me.

"She's my maid. And she fancies you. After every ball and adventure, she asks after you."

I hummed, tucking that thought away never to be perused again. "That was the first time I acted as your brother. Almost as though nothing has changed at all."

"A bit has changed," she insisted.

"I'm still reluctantly sorting out your mischief. You're still gallivanting about in disguises. And I'm still pretending to be your brother or cousin. What, precisely, has changed?"

Her dark eyes considered me and I could almost hear the thought, *You're an earl now*. But ever the surprise, she said, "My gallivanting has taken us out of London. That is new."

"Your gallivanting nearly took us to France."

"That ship was headed for the Caribbean," she retorted, a grin sliding onto her full peachy lips.

"You do realize that is not materially different for the purposes of my argument?"

"It is though. The weather is better there than in S—" she broke off, wide brown gaze eyeing me warily.

"Scotland?" I finished.

"Slough." She crossed her arms definitively and tossed her chin back in an effort to seem more intimidating.

A huff escaped from my chest. "All right," I said between chuckles. "Well, I hear they're easily scandalized in Slough, so you'd best find that dress."

Lip caught between her teeth, she shifted the extra fairy cake aside in her trunk. There she unearthed a simple, familiar, peachy-coral frock.

She pulled it free, exposing a flash of white lace and silk beneath it that had both chuckles and breath abandoning me.

"Mr. Summers?" Her voice was soft, lower than her usual alto—calling my gaze back to hers.

"Yes?"

"How—that is—have you any idea how to go about this? You know, changing in a carriage."

Well damn.

Six

NORTH ROAD—APRIL 10, 1817

DAVINA

Mr. Summers' eyes widened in a way that was actually quite comical, flicking erratically between me, the trunk, the roof of the carriage, and his own lap.

When he finally remembered how to speak, it was with incredulity. "How should I know how to dress a lady in a carriage?"

"You've never... you know... in a carriage?" I asked.

"Of course not!"

I rolled my eyes. "You do not need to be cross with me. I thought it was something every gentleman did at some point."

"When? When do you suppose I would have time to find someone to tup in a carriage? I spend all my time chasing after you."

"Well, I don't know. It was on the list of places Gabriel told me I must never be alone with a man. Or a man and another woman. Or two men."

"He... What?" Mr. Summers' jaw hung loose as he blinked

rapidly. "Never mind. Your brother was the most notorious rake in the country. I doubt there was any place that wasn't included on his list."

"It was quite extensive," I agreed.

"And you thought to compare me to him?"

"I thought that all young men... sewed their wild oats. Not Xander, of course, but other young men."

"I don't know what all young men do, but I am more of His Grace's mind on this." Annoyance was written across his brow before he pressed his thumb and forefinger to closed eyes. The exasperated expression was familiar. "If your brother warned you against being in a carriage alone with a man, why on earth did you abduct one?"

"I didn't abduct a man. I abducted you."

"That's... Once again, you do see how that is not actually different?"

"Are you planning on compromising me?"

"Not in a way that either of us would enjoy," he muttered.

"Then I fail to see the problem."

"The problem is the same as it always is. You throw yourself into danger at the first opportunity without a care for how anyone else would feel if something happened to you."

"This isn't dangerous! You're not any man. You're Mr. Summers."

"I don't—what does that mean?"

"You fix things."

"What?"

"When I have problems, you fix them."

He sighed, irritation heavy in his tone and on his brow. "If you plan to change into your frock, you'd best figure it out now. We're getting close."

Without explanation, he shifted to strip off his weighty woolen greatcoat. And then he held it up in front of him, and out, covering his view and the one functional window in one move.

It wasn't an ideal changing room, there was no doubt of that. It was, however, more than satisfactory. He may have scoffed, but he *was* solving the problem. Or at least part of it.

I tucked my hat and wig in the trunk before I set the dress across from me and gathered the necessary accessories, plopping them on the vacated rear facing seat. Then came the trickier bit. A glance at Mr. Summers confirmed that he was still demonstrating his gentlemanly qualities and his face was well hidden by the coat.

Removing everything was easy, if nerve-racking, until I reached the bandaging pressing against my breasts. That was a bit more challenging but not impossible.

I managed to don chemise and stockings with relative ease as well, only knocking into his coat with an arm or elbow twice.

Then I came upon the first significant obstacle. While Cee had spent years espousing the benefits of half stays *à la paresseuse*, of course I hadn't listened. And across from me lay the evidence of it. My everyday corset—the one that laced entirely in the back.

With the quietest sigh I could muster, I slipped it overhead and settled the straps into place. Simple. Then I reached back to grab the lacings and that was where everything went wrong.

My elbow met something hard and linen-covered and a grunt broke from Mr. Summers' chest.

"I'm sorry!"

"It's no matter," he wheezed—rib cage then.

I tried again, reaching with the other arm. That time, my elbow met with the carriage wall, finding that peculiar spot that always hurt more than it ought to have. Biting back a curse, I caught the lacings and pulled.

One tug and I recognized the calamity I'd caused. I hadn't

found the loose lacing, instead finding one in the middle that should have remained in place. The corset tightened awkwardly around my belly, loosening around my waist and bust. *Damn. Damn, damn, damn.*

"Mr. Summers?"

"Yes?" Weariness clung about the word, as though he knew precisely what I was about to ask and he was already dreading it.

"I require your assistance. If you would be so kind?"

I heard him swallow before he replied. "How indecent are you?"

"I'm still more undressed than any other woman you've shared a carriage with," I quipped, earning a chuckle.

The coffee-colored curls appeared first as he studiously faced the window while he moved around the coat. Carefully, he tucked it along the seam between the loose door and the carriage, cloaking us in shadows and hair-thin sunbeams.

His shoulders were surprisingly broad under that coat. I'd once spent the better part of an evening staring at the back of him. Though I hadn't known it was his back at the time. Those shoulders hadn't looked like *that* at the time. I would have remembered the sharp blade edge and tight curve.

Task finished, he turned warily, gaze firmly planted on his lap.

"Your vision may be required for this, I'm afraid."

He inhaled sharply before lifting his gaze to me. There was an unreadable quality to his expression. None of his usual frown lingered. Instead his eyes felt ponderous, poignant. His lips were parted but only just. "Wh-What do you need?"

I shifted on the seat and offered him my back. "The lacings," I whispered.

"How do I—where do I start?"

"At the top."

A soft, ghosting breath teased my loose curls, brushing

them along the back of my neck. My spine prickled. Heat radiated from the hands hovering likely no more than an inch or so from my skin. I'd never been aware of anything the way I was of his not-quite-touch. But it wasn't an unpleasant awareness.

And then, without warning, I felt a tentative tug at the lacing near the top. Then the corset narrowed at my bust. Finally, the familiar taught sensation settled along my ribs before he moved down another row.

"You can—a little tighter is fine."

"I don't want to hurt you," he rasped.

"It doesn't hurt. A little tighter sits better, otherwise it will chafe." He returned to the top and pulled the laces in to fit more snugly. "That's better, thank you," I added, a strange, inexplicable trill in my voice.

Row after row he tightened and finally reached the bottom. The tension was uneven, and it was looser than I usually wore it, but it would do.

"Now what?"

"You can just lace that through the bottom row again."

Through the gossamer fabric of my chemise, warm fingers worked at the edge of my corset. He fumbled, slipping once, twice, before I heard the unmistakable sound of the lacing pulling through the eyelet.

"Now you can just slipknot it."

"I don't—"

"Oh, make a loop with the extra and slip it under the last row, then pull it through." I felt him scramble for a moment before making some sort of knot. "Tuck the extra under?"

Fingers brushed against my back as he followed my instructions. When I turned back to him, I found him still wearing that unnamable expression.

"I'm quite sure I mucked that up. But it should hold."

"You did well. Do you mind helping with the dress as well? It buttons in the back."

He merely nodded, a furrow etched between his brows.

Carefully, I shrugged into the petticoat and gown, only knocking my knee against the opposite seat once. Mr. Summers managed the fabric-covered buttons of my floral day dress without instruction.

Satisfied with his efforts, he yanked his coat free from the door, bathing us in the setting sun. Instead of donning it again, he balled it up and plopped it onto his lap.

He studied the front of the carriage with more interest than I'd ever given anything, his throat bobbing under the edge of his cravat. In the newfound light, I noticed that the tip of the one ear I could see was bright crimson.

"Thank you."

In response, I received only a curt nod and a grunt. Apparently, he found the crack along the front wall too fascinating to spare me a glance.

I had only just settled back against the seat when the carriage creaked to a stop.

Before either of us could move, Alfie's face filled the open window.

"The two of ye finished with whatever ye were getting up to in here? We're at the inn."

"We're not—yes," Mr. Summers replied.

"Stepping inside?"

I nodded at the exact same moment Mr. Summers shook his head. He refused to so much as turn toward me, and I was forced to climb over him to escape once Alfie unstrapped the door. My reticule smacked against his knee in punishment.

Rory appeared at my side and tucked her elbow into mine as soon as I stepped out. She peered inside only to take one look at Mr. Summers before laughing. "Dinnae worry yer head. I'll keep her out of trouble for ye."

Mr. Summers shot her a look—yet another one I couldn't interpret—that had her tossing her head back in a full belly laugh.

"I think ye broke the poor lad," she said as we walked into the inn.

"I've no idea."

"Oh lassie, if ye dinnae ken, I'll not explain it."

Seven

OLD BELL, ENFIELD—APRIL 10, 1817

KIT

As soon as they were out of sight, I allowed my head to hinge back and clunk dully against the back wall with a satisfying thump.

She still hadn't confirmed we were bound for Scotland, but she'd also never denied it outright. Since I was more than positive her aim wasn't Gretna Green, we were most likely going to her brother.

I couldn't recall precisely where his Scotland estate was—Will had managed that transition—but a flight to Gretna Green was usually a nearly four-day endeavor. I'd had one desperate client manage it in two, but that was with a proper carriage, with proper coachmen, and proper horses. In this one... perhaps five days to Scotland and maybe another day to His Grace's estate.

Five or six days with an erection could not possibly be healthful.

It had to be that damned peach frock. She couldn't have packed one of her thousand others, all silky and impractical, ethereal. No, it was that simple cotton one that got me into this mess in the first place.

I'd known Lady Davina for years. And save that one instance at Decker's, she had merely been the silly, frivolous sister of a duke. Ornate and unapproachable, she wore the latest fashions made of fabrics that would crumble to dust if someone looked at them wrong. I'd known she was beautiful —a person would have to be blind to miss it—but it was the beauty found in paintings of deities and queens. It was a beauty that could be seen but not known.

And then, at the worst time of my life, she waltzed into Hart and Summers, Solicitors in that exact peachy-coral frock. There was nothing particularly alluring about it. It was modestly cut to her collarbone and the sleeves kissed her wrists. In fact, it may have covered more of her skin than any other dress I'd seen her wear.

But the effect was a kick to the gut. It was—she was— breathtaking. Breathtaking and real. That day, she had foregone the fashionable, face-framing ringlets and elaborate twists in favor of a simple knot. Free from the distraction of overdone curls, her eyes seemed bigger, brighter. Her lips were fuller than I'd ever noted, and heart-shaped, just like her face. Without the lace and ribbon frippery, there was nothing to distract from her graceful curves.

She was tangible.

I was a self-aware man. I knew her allure that day probably had less to do with the dress and more to do with my newly changed situation. In our previous meetings, I had been Mr. Summers, clergyman's son and solicitor. At that meeting, less than a fortnight after my father, uncle, and cousin passed in one wretched accident, I was an earl—Lord Leighton. And entirely without warning, I went from a background character of her life, to a potential suitor. Though I had no intention then of keeping the title as soon as I found a way out of it—

that knowledge hadn't been enough to keep my breath in my body.

Which would've been all well and good, except it didn't go away. The flood gates had been opened that day and now irritation and adoration warred every time she crashed into my life, wreaking havoc.

She'd drawn that reaction in mere hours. What would be left of me at the end of six days?

"Mr. Summers?" A bright voice came from the open door. I turned toward him, rolling my head along the wall.

"Yes, Alfie?"

"Mr. Jack says we should eat here. Do ye want to come in? Or did ye need a few more minutes?" There was a cheeky quality to his grin, indicating that he was entirely aware of my predicament.

I sighed, then stepped out of the so-called carriage. "It's Lady Davina, Alfie."

"Mr. Jack said I can call her whatever I like."

I shrugged, eyeing my great coat warily before setting it on the seat. "Are you staying here?"

"Ole Rory is bringing me a plate."

"Very good. Do you mind buckling the door?" The words were even more ridiculous when spoken out in the world than they had been in my head.

"Not at all."

After setting off into the courtyard beneath the high stone archway, I rolled my shoulders slowly, trying to ease the first strains of ache. It would only be worse from here. Unending days in a poorly sprung carriage would be the end of my spine.

The inn opened onto the tea room. The yellow walls were wideset, spacious, and filled with the tempting scents of hearty soups and baking pies. The oak floor creaked beneath my black hessians, protesting the addition of my weight.

Movement from the far corner caught my gaze. Lady

Davina had selected a table for two near a bay window and waved me over.

"Where's Rory?" I asked as I sat across from her.

"She's seeing about getting Alfie a plate. I ordered you the shepherd's pie. I hope that is to your taste."

"It's fine. I've only changed horses here, never stopped for a meal. It's nice."

"I hope it is. It certainly smells as though it is."

No sooner had she spoken than a plump, rosy-cheeked maid set two plates before us. The potato topping was perfectly caramelized, and she was right, the pie smelled incredible.

We nodded our thanks before digging in without a word. The meal was delectable, the vegetables retained a firm bite and the meat was seasoned to perfection. Fresh herbs complemented the flavors without overpowering.

"This is quite good," Lady Davina murmured between bites when we were both nearly half finished. Her cheeks were pinked with a pleased flush.

For a brief flash, I could see it. Day after day, returning to a cozy little house, sitting across from her at a round table with a blue-checkered tablecloth, enjoying an excellent meal and secretive smiles.

But that wasn't real. That life wouldn't happen. I would have to forsake everything I'd worked for, everything I was, and accept the damned title—not that she would agree, even if I did.

I was a self-made man. It was the source of my greatest pride. I hadn't leveraged my grandfather's title to enter the law. I earned the position as a clerk at Will's on my own merit. I worked day in and day out for years on a pittance. Admittedly, it was a slightly more generous pittance than other offices in the area, but a pittance nonetheless. And I impressed Will day after day until he made me a partner. My father was a clergyman of no particular import. And no one gave a damn that I was the grandson of an earl.

Until they did.

Suddenly the world decided I was different, even though I was precisely the same man I always had been.

"Mr. Summers?" And there it was, the one person in the world who had never, ever called me Lord Leighton. I remained Mr. Summers to Lady Davina alone.

"Yes? Oh, yes. It is very good."

"Are you quite well? You're a little flushed."

"I—it has just been quite an eventful day," I replied, then added under my breath, "It's not every day that I'm abducted."

"I like to ensure your days are exciting."

"Exciting? I suppose fits of apoplexy are exciting."

Her laugh was full and bright. "Are you almost finished? We need to be onward to the next excitement."

"I'm not certain my heart can take much more, but yes." I tossed a few coins on the table and nodded at the serving maid a few tables away.

Lady Davina rose and slipped her hand into the crook of my elbow as she allowed me to escort her out.

Back in the courtyard, Rory and Alfie were prepared for the next leg of our journey. Our horses seemed as rested as they were capable of. At the sight of us, Alfie hopped off his barrel and moved to unstrap the door.

As we settled back in our respective seats, the lad buckled the door again with an ominous, "Good luck."

It was then that I realized the last rays of the sun were kissing the horizon out my window. New understanding left me wary. There were no lamps inside the carriage, not that I was overly confident in the safety and efficacy of the ones on the exterior. Darkness would soon fall, and with it, the last vestiges of propriety.

Eight

NORTH ROAD—APRIL 10, 1817

DAVINA

There was something *intimate* about the near blackness that I hadn't considered in my plan. Even with the beat of the hooves and the unintelligible murmurs of Alfie and Rory up ahead. The carriage's interior was its own little world, Mr. Summers and I the only inhabitants.

"Should have saved the fairy cake," he whined into the darkness, breaking the silence.

"Would you believe I had forgotten that I did save mine."

"Yes. I was debating trying to sneak it without you noticing.

I gasped in mock offense. "Mr. Summers! You would steal from a lady?"

"No, not from a lady." I heard the shifting of fabric and felt more than saw him turn toward me. "But from you…"

"Well, I never!"

He huffed a breath in that way I was coming to understand was his version of a chuckle. "My Aunt Prudence's missing snuffbox says otherwise."

"What snuffbox?"

"The one you pilfered from my aunt at Katie's wedding. While you were pretending you hadn't been eavesdropping."

"You remember that?"

"My sister's wedding to the numbskull? I have a vague recollection, yes," he insisted in the darkness.

"You were so determined to help Kate. You would have burned the entire house down to get her out of the marriage if she'd asked. It was... admirable." And it had been.

I'd watched through the crack between door and frame as Mr. Summers begged his sister to leave. Swore he would manage an annulment. It wouldn't have been easy—but if anyone could manage it, I believed he could've.

"She's my sister. And Hugh is an ass."

A startled laugh escaped my chest at the blunt assessment. "She seems happy enough."

"Katie makes the best in any situation. She may have decided to love him, but that doesn't mean he deserves her."

"You cared more about your sister's happiness than her reputation." Xander would do anything for me. I was certain of it. But an annulment would've been a stretch—especially a marriage to a peer.

"Of course," he said, so matter-of-factly.

"You have no idea how extraordinary that is, how rare."

"Your brother would do it for you. Though this escapade may test that theory."

"I know. That's what I'm doing. That's why I need your help." The words spilled out of me, safe in the darkness.

"This is about your brother?"

I nodded. I doubted he could see the motion, but he seemed to sense it.

"He needs my help?"

Another nod.

"Da—Lady Davina—I can help you both much better if

you tell me." His voice was gentle and warm in the swaying carriage.

"I'm not being stubborn or contrarian. It's not my secret to tell."

"But you're not in any danger? You're not in trouble?"

"No."

He released a heavy sigh and shifted once again on the seat. "All right then."

"That's it? You aren't going to press me?"

"No. I just wanted to be sure you were safe," he whispered.

"Truly?"

"When I'm cross with you, you know that is why, right?"

"What do you mean?"

"You throw yourself headfirst into danger. I'm terrified that one day I'm going to be too late. Sometimes I have dreams, horrid dreams, of that day at Decker's. I still see that bruise on your face."

Two surprisingly soft fingers brushed my cheekbone, the one Mr. Decker had struck. The pain was gone—had been for years—but Mr. Summers' fingers knew the precise location of that long-forgotten ache.

Remembering himself, he jerked his hand back and I heard a heavy swallow. "Apologies, that was inappropriate."

"No..."

"I'd never wanted to hit a man before that day. There've been a few since, but nothing like that. Not even Hugh, not even when Katie ran away from him. I've never felt... out of control like that."

"I... Thank you. For always helping me. Even when it's my own fault."

"I'll always help you. All you have to do is ask."

"So I didn't need to kidnap you?"

"Abduct—kidnapping is for children. And no. I would

have insisted on a proper carriage and chaperone. And an actual explanation. But I will always help you."

Something in my chest tightened strangely. It wasn't new information. Deep down, I'd known all along that he would help. But to hear it so plainly...

"We're going to Scotland," I supplied. It was a pathetic concession, but he deserved the answers I *could* give him.

"Yes, I'd figured that out."

"When?"

"Around the time we joined the North Road."

If I couldn't offer him information, there was but one thing left. "Do you want to share my fairy cake?"

The question earned me a full laugh, a rarity from him. I wished there was some light in the carriage, I wanted to see if his smile was a match. "Do you really need to ask?"

"No, I know very well the answer to that question. You adore fairy cakes."

"I do."

~

KIT

A trusting woman, she handed me the fairy cake while she dug through the trunk for something else. Whatever it was, she pulled it out with a triumphant, "Aha!"

"What is it?"

"Whiskey," she retorted, holding the bottle up with a glee I could sense in the darkness.

"You didn't..."

"I did." She uncorked the bottle and took a swig before plugging it back up. "Is my little cake thing in one piece?"

"By virtue of my honor as a gentleman only."

"Hand it over."

The tree cover lightened or the moon had risen above it because the carriage brightened a little and I caught sight of her expectant hand. Reluctantly I handed over the treat.

The little sound she made when she bit into the delicacy made me grateful for the remaining darkness.

Distractedly, she passed the bottle of whiskey to me. "We're sharing this as well?"

"Not if you don't want to…"

The taste was familiar, a gentle caramel burn—her pirate whiskey. "So you're still investing?" I asked.

She froze for a second, fairy cake raised to her lips. "How did you know?"

I shook the bottle at her in response. "Also, your friends up front. Oh, and I've an agreement with Annie and Grace."

"You— What sort of agreement?" Lady Davina's voice was high and tighter than usual—suspicious.

"I just wanted to be sure they'd treat you fairly. And a solicitor on the up-and-up lends legitimacy to their distillery."

I saw the exact moment she took my meaning. "You! You're in business with pirates."

"So are you," I teased.

"Yes, but I've been told I'm a rebel."

"Oh yes, positively anarchic."

"You, Mr. Summers, are far more interesting than I would have credited you for," she acknowledged, tipping her fairy cake toward me in a facsimile of a toast. Entirely too charming for her own good.

"Kit," I blurted before I could stop myself. Damned whiskey.

"What?"

"You can call me Kit. If you like."

"Kit," she tested, tasting the word on her tongue, seeing how it blended with the floral fairy cakes she preferred. I heard the rustle of skirts before I understood that she had tucked her knee against the seat to face me fully.

"Only if you wish to," I added.

"I do. It suits you. Kit and Kate, your parents liked the *K*'s and *T*'s."

"Christopher and Katherine, actually. And the family calls her Katie. So not that similar, in truth. But Katie couldn't say her *s*'s when she was little. So Christopher became Kitopher, which is absurd. So Kit."

"Kit," she said once again. It was intimate, visceral, hearing a woman using my Christian name. And Davina using it, with her low, rumbling, rasp... I felt it lap over me, waves licking at my skin. My chest tightened at the sensation. "Davina—if you'd like."

My heart took that as permission to stop for a second before racing to catch up. "Davina," I repeated. It wasn't the first time I'd said the word, not by any measure. But dropping the title... It was musical, like one of Katie's piano melodies, but less showy. "Not Dav?"

She shook her head. "Davina. I prefer it."

"Then why does your brother call you Dav?"

"I suppose he always has, long before I could object, and I've just... never corrected him."

She held out the final third of fairy cake in her open palm. "Really?" I asked eagerly.

"Quickly, before I change my mind."

Never one to pass up a sweet, I finished the proffered treat in a single bite. Lady Davina—*Davina*—preferred floral and herbal flavors in her sweets. I liked them, but I would choose the chocolate every time. This one was lavender and lemon, which swirled together into something light and refreshing, rather than the rich, dark chocolate one I'd decimated earlier. It was breezy and bright, like her.

I chased it with another sip of whiskey, even smoother on the second sip.

She made a grabbing motion with her delicate hand, now bereft of fairy cake. I passed her the bottle, watching as her lips found the neck. Christ, the inside of my head was beginning to sound like Will's whenever he looked at Celine.

"Whiskey calls for a game," she insisted, her tongue dipping out to catch an amber droplet from her lip.

"What sort of game?" I croaked before holding a hand out for her to pass the bottle.

Her dark gaze cast about the carriage for a moment, searching for some sort of game as I savored the burn of another sip.

Suddenly, she perked up, snatched her reticule from the far seat, and tugged it open. Her hand slipped inside and dug around far more thoroughly than such a tiny bag ought to warrant.

Her spine straightened and she pulled out a pair of dice, holding them between thumb and middle finger triumphantly. "Hazard?"

"Lord, no."

Full lips twisted into an exaggerated pout but I held firm. "Fine," she relented. "I know! If we roll even, you tell me something I don't know about you. Odd, I tell you one."

I saw disappointment cross her face as reluctance crossed mine. Unable to bear the forlorn expression, I sighed, nodding.

Her answering grin was full and bright. She slipped the dice into her palm and rolled them about before dropping them to the seat between us. Five.

Davina considered for a moment, briefly catching her lip between her teeth. "Oh, I know, the dice—they're Gabriel's. He gave them to me before he passed. They're lucky."

A laugh broke from my chest. "That was not the sort of secret I was expecting out of you."

"What were you expecting?"

"Some sort of elopement tale with the crown jewels of a foreign nation. Perhaps, a history of spying for the military."

"I wouldn't be a very good spy if I told you, now would I? And our family's jewels are much more impressive than anything a nation, foreign or otherwise, could provide."

"Of course," I agreed with solemnity, fighting the corners of my mouth as they threatened to turn up.

She rolled again, this time landing a six and four.

"My turn then..." My mind was suddenly impossibly blank, refusing to offer a single secret. At least one that wouldn't be dreadfully dull to my vivacious companion.

"Don't rush to tell me anything," she teased.

"I'm thinking... I'm not as interesting as you. Oh, I once added red cabbage to the laundry. Turned my sisters' underthings permanently purple."

"You didn't!" She laughed.

"Oh, I did. Lizzie wouldn't speak to me for a week. Kate likes purple, though. She thought it was fun."

"Mischievous, Mr. Summers," she said, tipping the bottle to me in a toast.

"I try." Quickly, I snatched up the dice between us and rolled again. Two and a four. "My turn again."

"So it would seem."

My gaze tossed around the carriage, searching for an idea, before landing on her. "I admire you, the way you handle yourself on your adventures. Even though they're often foolish and dangerous. You're so confident, brave, even when everything has gone pear-shaped."

"I've never done anything foolish or dangerous in my life," she retorted with a smile that belied her words. "And it's easy. I know you'll be by to sort out whatever is wrong in short order."

"Davina..."

"Roll the dice, Kit."

I did, then snatched the whiskey from her hand and took a swig before they landed. Seven.

"Your turn," I retorted with yet another sip. I would need to stop soon, the poorly sprung carriage would not be improved by an excess of drink.

"I admire how dedicated you are to your work. You're confident in that way. And incredibly knowledgeable and creative," she whispered.

My heart gave a tiny jolt at the compliment. I knew I was good at my work. My results spoke for themselves, as did our general success. But from her lips... "I thought you found it all to be a bit dull."

"If I had to study it, it would be. But that's why we have you," she added. I couldn't determine from her tone if it was a compliment or not.

Her hand slipped between us, a silent request for the bottle. I passed it over without comment, transfixed as her lips curled around the neck, pursing there. I was a half-drunk letch. That was the only explanation for my fixation.

"We should be almost to the next posting inn," I tossed out, desperate for a subject that wasn't the other places her lips could touch.

"Yes."

"Did you have a plan? Are we changing horses? Or taking a room?"

"I thought to leave that decision to Alfie and Rory. It's probably less costly to change horses," she opined.

"Cost isn't a concern."

"It's not?"

"I thought we may need some funds."

"You did? What else did you bring?"

"During the usual packing time before an abduction?"

"You do not need to tease me. They don't teach young ladies the practices of abduction."

"I would never be able to tell," I said, a grin pulling at the corners of my lips. "I didn't pack any fairy cakes, I must admit."

"None at all?"

"No, just clothes, a few apples and some bread, coaching schedule, that sort of thing. I had little in the way of both information and time."

"No whiskey?" I could hear the smile in her voice.

"Alas, I did not think that far ahead. But fortunately for us both, you did."

"That I did. Gabriel taught me well—always bring your own dice, stab enemies with the sharp bit, and never begin a journey without sufficient drink for the return."

"Of course he told you that. Taught you hazard, too, if I recall. Are there any vices he didn't impart? Did he take you to that brothel of his as well?"

My stomach lurched when my head caught up with my mouth. Discussing brothels with a lady—Rosehill would have my head. Did she even know of her late brother's habits? Bound for hell, I was.

"No," she replied primly. "He thought to leave that particular vice for my future husband." Tension left my gut at her teasing note. I hadn't scandalized her—of course, I hadn't.

"Good. I don't even want to imagine the trouble you could get into over there."

She waited until the precise second I took another sip before asking, "You spend a great deal of time imagining my comings and goings at brothels, do you?"

Naturally, I choked on the whiskey—hacking, racking,

heaving coughs shook me to my soul as I tried to dislodge the liquor from my lungs while she giggled beside me.

In my struggle to breathe, I didn't recognize that the carriage stopped until the door swung open beside me. "All right, Mr. Summers?" Rory asked.

"He's fine, Rory. Merely scandalized."

Rory shrugged, disinterested. "We're at the Green Dragon. The road's clear and dry, and the moon's bright. We thought to change horses and carry on through the night. Ye all right with that?"

"That's perfectly well."

Finally, I managed to clear the whiskey from my chest and nodded, not trusting my voice.

"We'll set off soon if ye want to stretch yer legs."

Davina climbed over me, slipping from the carriage first again. I followed after her, still trying to catch my breath. I handed Rory a shilling, then watched as my traveling companion stretched her shoulders in the courtyard. The lamplight left her silhouetted, long elegant legs too apparent through the thin fabric of her dress. The curve of her neck sloped down in a tempting curve. And her other curves—no, I was a letch.

The reality of the next several hours washed over me. It was going to be a long, long night.

Nine

NORTH ROAD—APRIL 11, 1817

DAVINA

I was surprisingly comfortable when I woke to the gentle chirping of nearby birds. Or I was comfortable until the moment I realized that my head was in Mr. Summers' lap. Well, resting on the coat he had placed on his lap.

He'd been odd after we returned to the carriage, quieter, more formal. The jest about the brothel may have been a step too far, in retrospect.

I couldn't recall the precise moment I fell asleep, but it could not have been long after I abandoned my efforts to coax him into more conversation and more whiskey.

Warily, I pressed myself up to a seated position, then glanced over at him nervously. A relieved sigh escaped when I saw that he was asleep. Given the coat's placement, it was entirely unlikely he had missed my unconscious familiarity, but I could only hope.

His forehead was pressed against the seam where the carriage and door met. At some point in the night, he had loosened his cravat, leaving the ends to hang down his chest.

He'd rolled up his sleeves as well. His forearms were bare and surprisingly intriguing.

In all my mischief, I'd never seen a man dressed so informally, at least not one who bore no relation to me. Mr.—Kit's arms were stronger than I would have guessed, not bulky, but definitely not delicate like mine. The muscles there were corded, defined, and he had a trail of dark hair that ran along the backs of them. His fingers, curled around the black wool edge of his coat, were long and squared at the tips. His nails were neatly trimmed and clean underneath but for the middle one of his right hand. Ink-stained, that one, and seemingly permanent. They were nice hands, strong, probably dexterous.

I wasn't sure why the sight fascinated me so. I'd never once considered a man's arms or hands, unless they were remarkably long, or worse, notably short. But I hadn't seen them before either. It was probably the novelty.

That was how I assured myself when my gaze traced up those arms to his newly bared inches of chest. There was a divot in the precise center, and a carved line of muscle began just below. His collarbone, too, seemed to be etched in a way mine wasn't. And then there was the dusting of dark hair, just barely peeking over the neck of his shirt.

More intriguing, though, was the beginning of a beard that had sprung up overnight. The beard *fit* him in a way I couldn't quite define. If pressed, I would have called him attractive without it. With it... he was devilishly handsome. It defined his jaw and drew the gaze to his full lips, shaking off the boyish quality.

Whatever pomade he used to tame his hair had forsaken him. Kit's hair was *curly*. Very curly. The dark, almost black curls kissed his loose collar, escaping from behind his ear. The locks were messy and poorly defined, spilling from the off-center peak in his forehead. How had that escaped my notice before? It was charming.

His eyebrows mimicked the V in his hairline, a disorganized revolution in the center before falling over in line as they went along. They sat above impossibly long lashes. Men always had the most lovely eyelashes and it was entirely unfair.

A breeze whispered in from the—perpetually—open window, brushing a curl across his cheek. His nose scrunched adorably before I recognized a fact that had entirely escaped my notice since I woke. We weren't moving.

A glance out the window held the answers. A thick blanket of fog carpeted everything as far as the eye could see. Now that the outside world had caught my attention, it was impossible to miss the great sawing sound emanating from outside. Alfie, no doubt, if the register was any tell. He was lucky Rory hadn't stabbed him for that racket.

It was impossible to guess how far we'd made it before they had to pull off or risk a calamity, but it would be some time before it warmed enough for the fog to dissipate.

And that was when I recognized a more pressing issue. Distracted by our position upon waking, Kit's intriguing wardrobe changes, and the fog, the needs of my own body had been pushed aside. Now they were back in full force. And I was quite trapped.

Kit slept between me and the only door. And the only door had to be belted on, which meant even if I woke him, I'd have to wake Alfie—or more likely Rory—overtop the sound of Alfie's snores.

I shifted back on the hard seat, already lamenting the loss of my pillow. Inappropriate it may have been, but it was also quite comfortable. There was nothing for it. I would just have to ignore my discomforts, all of them.

No sooner had I made up my mind than movement caught my attention out of the corner of my eye.

My body recognized the danger before I did—releasing a scream that startled even me.

Suddenly, a board smacked me across the chest and I was shoved unceremoniously behind Mr. Summers. Or... not a board. His arm.

"What is it? What's wrong?" he demanded, head swinging back and forth rapidly. His body coiled tight in front of me, shielding me from the danger.

Reluctantly, I raised a finger from behind his back, pointing to the enemy across from me.

"A spider?" he questioned, voice hoarse. "That screech was over a spider?"

"It's massive!"

"What is it?" cried a winded voice from the window—Alfie. From my perch behind Kit's shoulder, I could see Rory in front of him, guarding his back.

"She saw a bloody spider," Kit replied.

"'s just a spider, Rory. Ye can stand down," Alfie repeated as though the lady in question could not have heard Kit.

"It's not just a spider," I insisted. "It's a gigantic, bloodthirsty demonic spider."

Rory peered around Alfie's shoulder to see inside. "It's a wee lil' house spider. Damn near pissed myself over a wee lil' house spider."

"Can you unbuckle the door please, Rory?" Kit asked, dragging a hand through his hair.

"Why haven't you killed it yet?"

"Because I'm not going to. I'm going to let it out of this damned hell."

"What? Why?"

"Because neither of us deserves to die in this pile of junk. And while I have no choice, there's still time for him to escape."

Flabbergasted, I watched as he shooed the spider onto his hand. The comparison did make the beast look a little more manageable, but still. He just... picked it up, biting back a smile as I scrambled to the opposite end of the coach, and took it outside.

Through the open door, I watched in horror as he set the creature on a tree trunk.

"You cannot leave that there, it will get back in."

"Perhaps you should have considered that when you selected this carriage," he retorted, then made his way around the tree and into the woods beside us. Presumably he was taking care of the same need that had seemed much more pressing before the unwanted guest.

I crossed my legs against the discomfort.

"Where are we anyway, Alfie?"

"Few miles south of Peterborough. Had to stop on account of the fog."

"And when do you suppose we can be on our way?"

"Another hour mayhaps."

I weighed the desire to avoid another encounter with Beelzebub in arachnid form against nature's call.

Rory appeared at the door. "Yer not going to want to wait, lassie. Come on, I'll even check for spiders."

Reluctantly, I followed her deeper into the little woodland beside us, in the opposite direction of both Mr. Summers and the "wee lil' house spider." Liars, the lot of them.

Ten

NORTH ROAD—APRIL 11, 1817

KIT

I clenched the hairpin in my left palm, letting the sharp edge dig in, but the effort was hardly necessary. Not like it had been last night.

In the dark, my senses dulled by decent whiskey and exceptional company, I'd needed every reminder of our differences I could find. Lungs filled with lavender frosting and lemon curd and the unmistakable amber spice of her, it was difficult to keep my head. And when she slumped into my side, her silken curls brushing my cheek, I couldn't resist brushing my lips across her crown.

But then she'd started to lean forward, and bound for hell I may have been, but I couldn't let her sleep like that, all curled awkwardly against me. And my coat was right there, a perfect pillow.

As she nuzzled into my coat, for just a moment, I considered it. I let myself believe it could be real. That every day could be filled with laughter and fairy cakes and what I was fairly certain were flirtatious comments. She could fall asleep against me every night. I could run my fingers through her hair.

Without thought, my fingers had done just that, catching on a pin. It tugged free without waking her and I examined it in the moonlight. It was simple, nothing special about it, except I was almost positive it was made of gold. And wasn't that the sum of it. Davina may act as though she were not a duke's daughter, but she wore gold in her hair.

Lady Davina could drink whiskey and flirt with the solicitor, but she would return to her fine wines and suitable suitors.

And for the first time last night, just for the moment that the cool ribbon of her hair slipped through my fingers, I wanted to do it. I wanted to say yes. I wanted to forsake the law offices and the life I'd worked so hard to build. I wanted to abandon everything that made me Kit Summers. I wanted to accept the inevitable and wear the title of Lord Leighton. I wanted to be a man she could say yes to. It was so breathtakingly easy, I could taste the word on my tongue.

I fell asleep that way, visions of a life I'd never wanted dancing in my head, and the heavy warmth of a woman, lovely and tangible, on my lap.

And I woke to a lady screeching her head off. Over a damned spider. I didn't know what ladies did, but I knew clergymen's daughters handled spiders in one of two ways: with the bottom of their shoe, as Lizzie did, or with a teacup and a piece of parchment as was Katie's practice. Lady Davina wasn't real, she wasn't tangible. I couldn't abandon my entire life for her. And she hadn't asked me to.

I made it back to the carriage while she was still off with Rory and tucked the pin into the pocket of my waistcoat. There I made a thorough inspection for any more "bloodthirsty demonic spiders" and the regular sort. Finding none, demonic or otherwise, I slipped one of the apples out of my portmanteau and took a bite.

The sun was breaking through some of the fog cover and we could be on our way soon. Another day—this time a full one—trapped in a carriage with Lady Davina. A day in which I would absolutely not forget myself this time. I wouldn't be distracted by silly plots, flimsy chemises, tempting whiskey, or glossy curls.

I settled back in the carriage, facing the rear as was proper, and thought to pray for the sweet oblivion of unconsciousness. The apple did little to sate my hunger, and I was ravenous when I tossed the core out of the open door.

I heard her footsteps before I saw her, dainty little patters in the underbrush. She peered in the open hole where the door belonged with a wary brow.

"There's no spiders—demonic or the usual variety. I already checked."

Something about my statement confused her because she stared at me, head cocked to the side for an eternity before she replied, "Thank you," and stepped in. "Why are you sitting all the way over there?"

I opened my mouth as she clambered overtop me, prepared to give my speech about appropriateness, propriety, and all the like, and it just... wouldn't come. How could it when her eyes were so soft and warm and every strand of her dark hair was rebelling against the remaining pins? Such a speech was impossible in the face of skin that looked softer than the finest velvet, just barely flushed in the morning fog. No man could be expected to maintain distance from such a perfectly heart-shaped mouth.

And so I brushed my knee against hers and said, "Just stretching my legs."

The lie seemed to satisfy her and she straightened hers out as well, our bodies forming a perfect V in the carriage.

"Are you hungry?"

"Not enough to send you foraging," she said with a smile.

I kept the corner of my lip sternly tucked down. I may not be able to disappoint her, but I ought not encourage her. "It wouldn't be a long forage." I held up an apple.

"Oh, then yes, please."

I tossed it to her unthinkingly as I dug for the others, then winced the second I recognized what I had done. Instead of the distressing *thunk* of fruit meeting skin, I heard the *smack* of a catch.

My gaze flicked up just as she took a delicate bite. Were there etiquette books on the subject? How to catch and eat apples to entice the reluctant solicitor one had abducted.

I shook the thought away and called out the door when I found the final apples that had slipped to the bottom of my portmanteau. "Oi, Alfie, Rory, are you hungry?"

"Oi?" Davina questioned between bites.

"If you wanted proper English, you should have selected a proper carriage."

"Are you planning to let that subject drop any time soon?"

"Perhaps when I'm dead and buried."

She *humphed*, before taking another bite of her apple, this time maintaining a challenging glare. It reminded me of the disgruntled barn cat of Lizzie and Sidney's, five pounds of righteous fury in an adorable body.

"What've ye got?" Alfie asked, appearing in the open-door hole and leaning against it.

"Apple."

"Na, thank ye though."

"Alfie," I heard Rory call from somewhere near the front of the carriage. "Eat the apple. It's good for ye."

"Ye're not my mam," he called back.

"And I thank God for that every day. Eat the damn apple."

"If I remember my Bible right n' proper, it's not God who said that."

"Alfie, if ye get scurvy I swear I'll take ye over my knee," she retorted, appearing behind him in the doorway.

"I'm a man grown. You can't do that."

"Grown men eat their damn apples wi'out complaint."

"It's true," I replied, holding it out to him. The boy merely glared before snatching the apple from my outstretched hand. He took a massive, performative bite, before chewing very, very slowly.

"Good lad," Rory replied, then took the last one from me.

Alfie merely grunted in reply, glaring at the apple as though it had personally offended him, before stomping off. He was almost certainly going to toss the rest of it into the woods.

When I finally glanced back to Davina, she was examining me in a way I couldn't quite name. "What did I do?"

She shook her head and replied, "Nothing."

"Fog is lifting. We'll be off as soon as that one finishes his apple."

I heard the unmistakable *thunk* of an apple core—or more likely an apple with a singular bite out of it—landing on the ground.

"If I find an uneaten apple in the dirt, I'll feed it to ye myself," Rory called. She disappeared, followed by the shuffle of feet in the leaves, a kick-like thump, then the rustling of leaves as a once-bitten apple rolled down the hill. "Yer getting six more at the inn."

A plaintive whine of Rory's name earned an eye roll from the lady herself as she returned.

"Ye ready to set off?"

Davina nodded and Rory buckled the damned door. I

leaned back, tipping my head against the wall, and praying this time would be different when I heard Rory climb onto her barrel.

The carriage jolted forward. We'd changed horses overnight at least once while Davina and I slept, and these two were far more up to the task than the ones we'd set off with. While that was good, it also meant their trot was somewhat more impressive and my stomach twisted uncomfortably.

"You're sitting over there?"

I nodded, not glancing her way. Given half an opportunity she would manhandle me back to her side and I'd never manage to extricate myself again.

"If you're sick on my skirts, I shall never forgive you."

"Noted."

"You're acting strangely this morning."

"Forgive me, I'm not aware of the proper protocol of waking to a she-demon's screech over a spider in a carriage-shaped lump of wood with my abductress."

"Abductress?" she questioned, laughter in her voice.

"Feminine of abductor."

"Is it really?"

"No. I made it up," I deadpanned, finally opening an eye to look at her.

"Well now I really cannot tell."

"Good, quiet now. 'M trying to sleep."

"But—"

"Hush, little menace. It's time for quiet."

"Menace?" she whispered in between the croaks and groans of the unhappy carriage.

~

DAVINA

"Menace..." I couldn't decide whether I liked that.

His entire body rocked with the motion of the carriage as he feigned sleep.

With no other form of occupation, I was left to observe the *sleeping* Mr. Summers—Kit—again. Somehow, without my notice, he'd become a rather an attractive man. True, his nose was a little too big and too straight, but the stubble distracted from that. And yes, his lips were perpetually downturned, but they were incredibly full and seemed rather soft. Perhaps his form was too wiry and his frame too short. But the combination was strangely beautiful, a masculine beauty, of course, but beautiful.

I could see it now, why that woman he'd been with at Gunter's years ago was so eager to win his affections—before I ruined their outing.

If I were a better person, I might feel badly for her loss. But I wasn't a better person and I did not.

Because I knew now, Kit wasn't just the least objectionable option for a woman of a certain situation. He was kind, noble, and roguishly handsome—at least with the hint of a beard. I had no interest in marriage, not ever if I could arrange it. But if one had to wed, they could do far worse than Kit Summers. It was even possible they could do no better.

That, however, was not a thought I was going to entertain any further. First, because I had no need to wed anyone. Second, because he would certainly never wed me. And third, because Kit was turning that odd shade of putrid green again as he sat there, resolutely pressing his eyelids closed in the rear-facing seat.

"Are you ready to give up yet?"

"Don't know what you mean," he grumbled, the corners of his mouth dipping down even farther.

"You're positively chartreuse."

"'M fine."

"Are you sure about that?"

"I'd be better if you stopped asking about it."

So whoever he married would be saddled with a particularly stubborn husband. One couldn't expect to find perfection in a single soul.

Eleven

BELL AND CROWN, STILTON—APRIL 11, 1817

KIT

My desperate attempt to cling to the hint of propriety I'd wrenched from this situation was a bit of a disaster. It took less than a mile before my stomach protested the swaying of the so-called carriage.

I was left to maintain propriety from her side. My efforts were certain to go as well as they had yesterday.

My hand dipped into my waistcoat pocket, and I tightened my fingers around Davina's hairpin. The edges of the metal bit into my palm—a sharp reminder.

Meanwhile, we'd made surprisingly good time, particularly given the state of the couldn't-really-be-termed-a-carriage, and we were perhaps a half day's journey from my sister's farm.

I trailed Davina inside the inn pathetically while Rory veered off to the stables, leaving Alfie to re-buckle the door.

Unlike the inn where we took supper, the furnishings of the Bell and Crown were well worn, too well. Every table was scarred from many previous patrons and coated with a thick, tacky layer of something I didn't wish to consider that shone in the morning light even through the grubby windows. The housekeeper, a short, stout woman wearing an ugly pink cap, grunted a greeting, and Davina took that as permission to seat ourselves, with a raised brow at the sticky oaken table.

Wordlessly, the housekeeper deposited a plate of bread, no butter or jam, and two teacups.

"Do you have coffee?" I asked.

"No," she growled.

"Tea it is then."

"Butter?" Davina pressed.

The woman grunted again and walked away. I turned, wide-eyed to Davina. "Is she coming back with butter?"

"I think that was a no."

"Well, with such exceptional bread as this, I can see why she wouldn't want to ruin the flavor with butter," I whispered, then plucked a piece off the plate and held it aloft, peering with one eye through one of the massive holes.

Her giggle was bright, bell-like. "How do you suppose they managed to get it like that?"

"Under-risen dough," I explained, sniffing it hesitantly.

"How do you know that?"

I glanced up at her and attempted to hide a wince. No wonder the housekeeper was curt. Davina's hair was spilling from her remaining pins. I'd have assumed it was mussed from a lover's caress if I hadn't known better. "Not everyone's father was a duke," I replied.

"Your grandfather was an earl," she retorted.

I shrugged, giving her credit for a point well struck. Tentatively, I took a bite of the bread, regretting it almost immediately. "Or there's sawdust in the dough, that would lessen the rise."

"That bad?" she asked, disappointment written across her face.

"Worse."

"Ugh, I was hungry too."

"I've got a bit of bread in my bag. We can stop at the next inn," I offered, taking a minuscule sip of tea. It was, perhaps, more unfortunate than the bread—it may have seen a tea leaf in its lifetime, but it certainly hadn't been touched by one, too bland even for the name.

She nodded, eagerly accepting my offer.

"We'll be off," I called to the housekeeper.

"It's three shillings," she shouted back.

"I beg your pardon?"

"You heard me."

"One shilling, no more," I replied. "It was barely edible," I added under my breath. From my periphery, I saw Davina catch her lip between her teeth and bit back my own answering smile.

"Are you insulting my cooking?"

"Yes," I muttered, and Davina covered a chuckle with a dainty cough. "Merely the price of it," I added louder. I tossed a shilling onto the table, still far too much for such fare. "One shilling. We didn't finish it and I'm certain you plan to serve it to the next unsuspecting patron. They can pay your three shillings."

Davina's hand slipped into mine and tugged me along before the housekeeper and I could get into a more expansive discussion about the legalities of her business.

As soon as the door swung shut, she broke away and burst into bubbling laughter. One hand found her chest, and her head tipped back, glee etched across her face.

Behind her, I caught Alfie peering from around the barn door. "It's all right, Rory. She's laughin' not dyin'," he called out.

"Not that I don't appreciate the enthusiasm, but it wasn't that funny," I said.

"No, it was just—" Giggles erupted again. "Your face," she added between chuckles.

"Well, now I find the enthusiasm a little more insulting."

"No, I've just never seen you look anything other than sullen. I've started categorizing that thing you do with your lip that I believe is your version of a smile. But your face when she said three shillings..." She curled up one lip and squinted the eye above, furrowing the same brow in some absurd sort of mimicry.

"I make that expression every time your brother arrives to tell me of another one of your exploits."

"I've been responsible for that expression?" There was too much excitement in her tone. "That may be my greatest accomplishment."

"Oi," Rory called, pulling my gaze to the newly readied carriage. "Thought ye were breaking yer fast."

"Trust me, you want to wait until the next inn," I replied as she sidled up to us.

"That bad?"

"Worse, three shillings worse."

"Three shillings? That's highway robbery. And what's got her cackling?"

"My face, apparently."

She cocked her head to one side, squinting. "'Tis a funny one, it's true," she retorted, setting Davina off again.

"I'm getting back in the carriage now," I grumbled with a performative frown.

Davina trailed after me, not in any particular hurry and in short order the door was buckled back on.

Having learned my lesson, I sat next to her in the place I'd occupied yesterday, and the carriage rumbled across the cobblestones.

Davina wore her amusement all over, in her crinkled eyes, in her upturned lips, in the occasional full-body, silent huff.

"You don't really believe I look sullen all the time, do you?" I asked.

"I'm sorry, I didn't intend to offend you." Her grin belied her sincere tone.

"You didn't. I just... you think I'm sullen?"

"Sometimes, you're downright surly."

"I'm—that is just the way my face is."

"Perhaps," she agreed with some hesitation.

"Tell me."

"The day we met, in Hyde Park?" At my nod she continued. "You were laughing and teasing your sister when we came upon you. Of course, the dowager Lady Grayson was herself and insulted you both. I think that was the last time I saw you smile, truly smile."

"I smile," I protested.

"You do, but they're half smiles. Or the ghost of one."

"I suppose I'm usually cross with you. Often you've flung yourself into danger."

"Yes, but if I didn't fling myself into danger, you would have no employment. And then where would you be?"

I felt the corner of my lip lift instinctively. "Less likely to die in a fit of apoplexy at the youthful age of six and twenty."

"Six and twenty? Such an old man," she tutted, sardonic. "No wonder life has lost its joy."

"Is it so different from one and twenty?"

"You would know better than I. Though I suppose one's gender must play a greater role."

"I feel older, since my father passed."

"I didn't feel much of anything when my father passed," she said, then dipped her gaze to her lap.

"No?"

"Perhaps relief. He was—he made life difficult."

"How so?"

She sighed, her lovely dark gaze meeting mine. "Did you know Gabriel?"

∼

DAVINA

The question hung between us for a moment, or perhaps that was merely Gabriel's ghost, lingering over the entire family to this day.

"By reputation only," Kit said.

"Then you did not know him. He wasn't always... Will and Gabriel were nearly the same age. And Will... it's much easier to impress someone who has absolutely no expectations of you. But father had every expectation of Gabriel. He learned early that he would never meet them. So he simply stopped trying."

Kit's eyes were warm and thoughtful in the dim of the carriage.

"Father held them up in comparison, and Gabriel was found wanting. Always. Eventually, not trying became actively courting father's disapproval. My brother, he pretended he didn't care. But father's disapproval bothered him until the day he died."

"I think I understand—"

"It wasn't just Gabriel though. It was all of us."

"Father broke Xander as well. But Gabriel had already disappointed Father. And Xander hadn't years to learn to manage the weight of expectation."

"He seems to have managed well."

"He—if Father could see him now... He hasn't managed well, not by Father's definitions. And Xander knows it."

"His Grace is more generous and caring for you and your

mother than any other gentleman who works with us. The estate is in exceptional condition. What could there be?"

"A duchess. One would think Father would have treated his own duchess better, given the importance he placed on the concept. In some respects, I suppose he did. Mama loved him at one point, I know she did. She would insist that she does to this day. But he crushed her spirit."

Kit considered me, lips pursing and gaze roving my face. "And you?"

"I love Xander. He is the best of brothers. And he's certainly more suited for the role than Gabriel was. But in many ways, Gabriel and I are one and the same. Faced with pressure, Xander will give and give until there's nothing but dust left. Gabriel and I, we push back."

"And that is why..." he trailed off, searching for the words to describe me. I liked that, the way he couldn't find the words for me. I was undefinable.

"I get into all my mischief?" At his nod, I continued. "Partly. It's also just fun."

Kit's lip curled into one of his quarter smiles. That one always felt indulgent in nature. That quarter-smile made me want to tell him, to give voice to it.

Xander knew nearly all, especially after our last conversations before he journeyed to Scotland. Celine, too, suspected, that was certain. Mama, she rarely had even the slightest idea of what I was up to.

But this was Mr. Summers... And something about his dark, warm eyes always made me feel safe. "And there's the practical aspect."

He raised a brow.

"I have no intention of ever marrying. In fact, I've worked hard to ensure no one ever wants to wed me."

Kit's lips parted on a gasp, his eyes narrowed. He was a

beautiful study in contrasts: pale skin, dark features, soft lips, and knowing eyes.

"All this time," he breathed. "All your adventures... Your brother has worried himself half to death because you don't want to wed. *I've* nearly done the same. You could have simply told him."

"Where would be the fun in that?"

"Davina," he whispered. One hand came up, forefinger and middle hovering over my cheek. He was so close I could feel his warmth. Then he blinked and it was gone. His hand fell back to the seat between us.

Without pausing to give it consideration, I set my hand beside his. Our littlest fingers brushed against each other.

His dark gaze flicked down to our hands. Instead of pulling it away as I expected, Kit merely left it there. Something about that choice, so deliberate, left me conscious of the contact, my skin tingling in a way that was too extreme for the simple touch.

Kit swallowed and caught my gaze once more. "I worry about you. I worry about the day that I'm too late. I worry about the day I cannot find a way out."

"I don't."

"What?"

"I don't worry. You're Mr. Summers. There's no problem you cannot solve."

"Davina..." The way he said it, low and musical, tripping on each note... I'd never been so glad I'd insisted someone use all three syllables before. "There are a great many problems I cannot solve, no matter how much I may wish it."

Entirely of its own volition, my little finger curled around his. The only indication that he noticed was his barely audible inhale.

"I have faith in you."

He sighed, his head swinging back and forth in so small a motion it was nearly imperceptible, shaking away my faith. But he couldn't shake me so easily.

Twelve

WHITE HORSE, NORMAN CROSS—APRIL 11, 1817

KIT

"I have faith in you," she insisted, so sure.

How long had it been since anyone had faith in me? Since I had? Before Father passed, certainly. Probably before I failed to free Kate from a wretched engagement. Those words, so misplaced, were a balm on my psyche.

It was far too early in the day for such earnest compliments from such a devastating source.

"Your faith is misplaced."

"We shall have to agree to disagree then." Her reply was so pert in tone. At some point I would disappoint her. It was inevitable. What would her tone be then?

"Why don't you wish to marry?" I asked. It was a desperate grasp for distance from the certain tilt to her brow and set to her spine. Carefully, I pulled my hand from where it lingered against hers. After dipping it into my waistcoat pocket, I clenched my fist around the stolen hairpin.

"Why should I? I'm a lady of independent means. I can

live a life most women only dream of, and I've no need of a husband to do it."

"What if you fall in love?" The question slipped from my lips.

She laughed gaily, but there was a false, tinny quality to it. Though that may have been only in my head. "There's not a man on this earth who could love me, precisely as I am."

"You've decided a great deal on behalf of a man you've yet to meet."

She sighed and leaned back against the seat. "I've met them all."

"You've met every man in the world?" An incredulous note slipped into my question.

"Near enough. There are the rakes. Those men are adventurous and might be able to abide my independence. But they'd never support me while I cared for my mother. The dandies, they might appreciate my mother's style, but they'd never approve of my adventures. And a dandy can never be seen with a woman more handsome than him. And I'm always more handsome than them." She offered me a teasing grin with the assessment, her eyes dancing.

"Then there are the scholars. They find the entirety of me an irritant, the ones with political aspirations too. The new moneyed are too infatuated with my mother. And the old moneyed know that my mother is absurd. The gentlemen, well I've yet to meet a gentleman who *actually* warrants the name."

You've forgotten the solicitors. I barely managed to bite back the argument. That would certainly be enough to shatter her faith in me.

"No," she continued. "Until I find the man whose company I find more agreeable than my own, I see no reason to marry. And, as you know, I'm delightful."

"You are." The agreement was as easy as breathing, if entirely inappropriate.

Her answering smile was quiet, almost shy. It was an odd expression on her—different from her usual bright, unshakable self-confidence.

Suddenly, a drop landed on my hand from the open window. I stared at it, uncomprehending, as another landed right beside it.

"What is it?" she asked.

A third found my cheek. "Rain," I replied. For the first time in some hours, I wondered if our surprisingly good luck would hold.

"It's raining?"

"That's what I said."

"But we have no window!"

I turned back to her with a raised brow. "I noticed."

"You do not need to be snippy."

"You abducted me in a decrepit carriage. I have a right to be a tiny bit snippy."

She crossed her arms over her chest with a huff in the same manner she used when she was cross with her brother.

"I'll allow a bit of snippiness if you provide a solution."

With a sigh, I snatched my coat from the opposite bench and tucked it haphazardly into the door once again. I'd be lucky if the garment survived the trip.

"Fine, you may be as churlish as you wish."

"Thank you for the permission." I eyed the poorly built corners of the carriage with some trepidation. I wasn't at all confident my coat would be sufficient.

"Do you suppose we're nearing the next inn?"

"I hope so, if only for my empty belly. And perhaps we can find a more effective solution to the window there."

I fussed with the coat, trying to keep the worst of the rain off my person when she asked, "You intend to marry, do you not?"

Not particularly interested in traversing this path with her,

I gave a half-hearted shrug hoping she would take that as a sufficient response.

"Kate is trying to make you a match," Davina added.

"Oh?" I asked, resolutely facing the window, hiding my wince.

"You know she is," Davina retorted. "She's not subtle and you're not a simpleton."

"If I remember correctly, she thrust *you* in my direction as an option the night of the masquerade."

"*That* was a desperate attempt to keep me from the gaming tables."

"You're not wrong." At last, I turned back to her. She'd been observing me, her head tilted curiously like a puppy. "Still, I'm sure she wouldn't attempt to dissuade you if you took a liking to me."

"And you?" she asked, glancing distractedly at the seat beside her where a few raindrops found their way through the cracks in the wall.

"Oh, Katie has little use for my opinion. In this or any other matter."

Davina gave me a little laugh. "It is good that you are aware of your own irrelevance."

"Of course. If anyone should have the final say in my future marital bliss, it is Katie."

"Quite right."

"Does His Grace take your opinions into consideration? I imagine his choice would impact you more than mine would impact Kate."

"Xander considers everyone's wishes except his own in that respect."

"Oh?" I asked, wondering at her careful wording. Unfortunately, the ground beneath the carriage shifted from dirt to an uneven cobblestone, signaling our arrival at the next inn.

DAVINA

Distracted by our arrival, Kit carefully untucked his coat from over the window. The rain had slowed considerably but was still pattering away on the roof. He settled the coat overtop my shoulders. The damp hadn't penetrated the wool to the soft fabric satin and I was grateful for his effort. Then, after fetching the bonnet I'd abandoned as soon as we'd entered the carriage, he plopped it on my head just as Rory began to unbuckle the door.

She wore an oversized men's great coat and an expression of irritation.

"Do you want to wait for the rain to clear?" Kit asked her.

"We'll see whether it's finished spitting when yer finished eating. Might have to wait a bit."

Alfie appeared at her side, equally drowning in his own great coat—the one I'd stolen from Gabriel's things. He tugged the pink stocking cap off his head and shook his damp curls like a dog in Rory's direction.

Kit urged me out of the carriage and inside with a chuckle when my reticule smacked against his side. With a wry grin, I switched it to the outside hand.

The White Horse was busier than our last stop, and homier. A young lad rushed right between Kit and me and out the door without a word.

That was when I finally looked at Kit. The rain hadn't been significant enough to soak him. But the damp must have slipped around the coat because the fabric of his white shirt clung to his left side. It was just his shoulder and arm, but it was interesting. The way hints of ruddy skin shone through where it stuck to him left little to the imagination. His curls clung to his forehead in an entirely flattering way. There was absolutely no denying the realization that had been steadily building for the entire trip, perhaps even before. Kit Summers was an attractive man. And Cee hadn't been lying about inexplicable solicitor musculature.

I shook that thought away as we were led to a table. Much improved from our last stop, we broke our fast with contentment. A table full of gentlemen nursed the aftereffects of drink in one corner. A couple chatted quietly beside us while three little ones raced circles around their table. A few other couples were scattered about. Though nothing exceptional, the toast and cold meats were simple and hearty and left us satiated.

Just as Kit tossed a few coins from his waistcoat and rose to go find Rory and Alfie, a woman at a nearby table cried out, "Little Christopher Summers? Is that you?" Her voice had a distinctive, nasally pinched quality to it and I knew the second Kit recognized it because his eyelids slipped closed in preemptive exhaustion.

After a fortifying breath, he turned to face her. "Mrs. Lanaham, how good to see you."

She was a tall, spindly woman with yellow hair and a beaked nose to match her small, avian-like eyes. Kit positioned himself between us, blocking her from my view.

"Why, I thought we would be seeing more of you after you became a fancy lord."

I could not hear his response—only noting the tightening of his shoulders. Then he asked, "How is your husband, Mrs. Lanaham? Does he still suffer from gout?"

"Oh, yes, he does. Poor man, and a touch of the rheumatism. I left him with our daughter while I was visiting my sister."

"I'm sorry to hear that. When I was last here, I heard you two went to take in the waters for his health."

"We did, but it turns out the waters didn't agree with

Martin. And it was too much sun for me. Oh, I was a wretched, pocked thing after only a few moments."

"I'm certain that wasn't the case, Mrs. Lanaham."

"What are you doing here, my dear boy? Visiting your poor, lonely Mama?" she asked, a scolding tone in her question.

"I'm headed north on business."

"And that business, does it involve an anvil and the pretty young miss back there?"

That was the moment my stomach dropped. This woman clearly knew Kit. I could not serve as his sister. A cousin could be tricky as well. If I couldn't conjure an excuse, and quickly, this situation could become messy.

I rose, stepped to Kit's side, and slipped my arm into the crook of his. The fabric of his shirt was still damp under my fingers. I opened my mouth, praying desperately for something, anything other than the singular idea ringing through my mind to escape. But it was no use. The words I tried to trap between my lips slipped free.

"Lady Leighton, it's a pleasure to meet you."

Her mouth fell open, hanging there like an unflattering beaked shelf before she slowly, consciously closed it. "Oh, that's wonderful! I hadn't heard the news. Congratulations indeed, my Lord."

He offered only a pinched smile. For as rare as his smiles were, I wasn't happy to see this one.

"It's new," he gritted between clenched teeth.

"We're traveling to see my brother to share the news in person," I added, my voice high and nervous to my ears, but she didn't seem to catch the false note.

"When was the happy day?"

"Just last week," Kit supplied.

"Oh, your mother must be so happy. She's always telling

me about Katie's boy and Lizzie's brood. Soon you'll have little ones of your own."

"We wouldn't want to get ahead of ourselves," I interjected.

"No, we wouldn't want that," Kit bit out.

"You're a beautiful pair. You'll be blessed with such lovely babies. I'm sure your mother will keep me abreast. Unless, are you finally going to take up the estate? You know, young man, there's nothing like country air for raising babies. And it would be so wonderful to have you closer. Just like when you and my boys were young."

"We haven't made any definite plans yet, Mrs. Lanaham. I'm sorry, but we need to be off. It was lovely to see you. Travel safely."

"Oh, you as well, dear. I'll give your mother your warm wishes. Stop and see her soon, will you?"

"Of course, Mrs. Lanaham."

"Let's go, *darling*," Kit growled, as he dragged me along with him. My heart threatened to pound out of my chest.

He found our carriage quickly in the drizzle and shoved us behind it and out of sight. Alfie lay sprawled across the seat, boots hanging out of it.

Kit banged on the wall, jolting the sleeping boy awake. "For the love of all that is holy, tell me the weather is fine enough to travel?" he demanded.

"Aye, what's got a bee in yer bonnet?" Alfie asked as he climbed out.

"My *wife* and I ran into a neighbor."

"Yer wife?"

"Yes, Lady Davina and I are husband and wife now. Was that news to you as well?"

"Er... yes," Alfie tried tentatively, unsure of how to manage the fuming man beside me.

"I couldn't think of anything else," I added unhelpfully. Alfie's gaze bounced between the two of us with interest.

"Let's see, you could have chosen not to abduct me in the first place. You could have brought a proper chaperone along with us. Hell, you could have not done whatever ridiculous thing you've done that required my assistance in the first place. Literally anything other than proclaiming me your husband did not occur to you?"

"It's for Xan—"

"Xander, I know," he finished, rolling his eyes. "That woman is the biggest gossip in the county. It will be all over Lincolnshire that I've wed. And Mr. Kit Summers didn't wed. No, it was Lord Leighton."

"I didn't—"

"My mother! She will tell my mother that I've wed. Without informing her. Do you know what this will do to my mother? If your brother doesn't see me hanged, she will."

"If we just explain—"

"There is no explaining. How do you not understand that?"

"Christopher Summers, you will stop interrupting me right this instant!"

He blinked slowly, stupidly for a moment before making a hand gesture that I generously chose to interpret as permission to continue without interruption.

"I am sorry this did not go as planned. I am sorry for what I told her. But you weren't offering her any answers either, and don't deny it. And I am sorry that I abducted you, but to be quite frank, you didn't put up much of a fight."

He crossed his arms and leaned against the carriage, silent.

From behind me, I heard the crunch of boots on worn cobblestones. "Are ye ready to set off?" Rory asked.

Kit said nothing and Alfie was stuck, staring wide-eyed at the two of us, so it was left to me to nod.

"What's wrong with him?" she asked me when Kit slid into the carriage before me in a huff.

"I may have accidentally implied that he was my husband."

"Ye would think a man would be happy about a thing like that. What with the way he looks at ye and all."

"I beg your pardon?"

"Never ye mind, lassie. He'll get over himself."

I nodded distractedly and slipped in beside him, wincing as Rory buckled the door, sealing us inside.

This trip just became infinitely longer and more unpleasant.

Thirteen

NORTH ROAD—APRIL 11, 1817

KIT

I HAD NEVER, not once in my entire life been so furious. Not two hours before, Davina was declaring that she would never take a husband. And now she'd all but ensured I would be hers.

It was the needling possibility that sank into my very bones during the morning. Even before Mrs. Lanaham, I had struggled to see a path through this abduction forest that didn't include a ring and a shotgun. Now... Davina's path was still whatever she made of it. But if my mother left me in one piece, I would be a pariah in Lincolnshire. The rumors might stay there, it was possible. But unlikely.

No, I had a wife now. Or as good as.

"I really think that if you just explain what happened, everything will be perfectly well," she said, settling beside me in my coat, which was far too big for her.

In a fit of pettiness, I chose not to say anything.

"It was just a misunderstanding. A lark. That sort of thing." Her lower lip found its way between her teeth, trapped there while she stared with wide, dark eyes. "Do you not think?"

"Am I allowed to speak now?"

She huffed in irritation. "Yes, obviously."

"Because I wasn't certain that you were—"

"Stop being obtuse," she insisted.

I swallowed for a moment, considering her crossed arms and the pert twist of her lips. "You've quite possibly ruined my life. You do know that?"

"You're being a little dramatic."

"How do you propose I return home—ever—unwed. The whole of the county will know of my marriage by sundown."

"You said that already," she retorted, quieter than she usually managed.

"Davina, we're in a bit of a situation at the moment. And you seem unaware of the gravity of it. Your brother would be well within his rights to force us to wed. And I would not blame him for a single second."

"Xander wouldn't. He would never force me to wed."

The throbbing behind my eyes returned acutely. "And perhaps you're right. But you've just destroyed my reputation as well. My future. Mrs. Lanaham has no idea who you are. You can disappear into the wilderness of Scotland. You can join a pirate ship's crew and sail away to the Caribbean. You can do whatever you'd like. But now, as we speak, the entirety of my acquaintances are being informed of my wife."

"I didn't mean to."

"Well, you did. I cannot divorce you, one because we are not actually wed, and two because that would ruin me. I cannot wed, and any children I had would be bastards."

"We'll think of something," she insisted, her tone pitiful enough that I was certain *she* wasn't to be the one to think of it.

"I need you to desist with the unearned optimism, please. At least until you have an actual suggestion."

"Because frowning at me and insisting your life is ruined is so helpful?"

I was so, so angry that words abandoned me and I merely let out an irritated grunt before turning to face the wall. It didn't help that I was away from the window and my stomach was revolting against both my predicament and the damned carriage.

Out of the corner of my eye, I saw her finally heeding my request. She crossed her arms over her chest with a huff and turned to face the window.

∽

We continued in a similar vein for several miles. Her staring out the window in irritation. The various causes of my nausea warring for prominence while I struggled to keep my accounts where they belonged.

The rain dripped slowly but steadily overhead. If I were any sort of gentleman, I would have switched seats with Davina. And if I were less stubborn, I would have asked before my insides rebelled. But I wasn't a gentleman, I was a solicitor, and an obstinate one at that. At least she still wore my coat.

Davina was right, I hadn't a better idea. But, Christ, hers did complicate my life. This wasn't one of her usual mishaps, easily solved with a few bank notes or a handful of documents. And I wasn't separated from it.

In a time that was either an eternity or only a few minutes, we arrived at the next coaching inn. A glance out the window told me what I'd already known. Ancaster, we were in Lincolnshire. We were less than five miles from Lizzie's. And Mrs. Lanaham was barreling toward her home, ready to share my "wonderful news" with anyone and everyone. Including my mother.

"Do you want anything inside?" Davina asked, tentative as Alfie unbuckled the door. She shuffled out, then peered back in at me, dwarfed in my coat.

"No, thank you. But there are a few shillings in the pocket of my coat. Help yourself to whatever you'd like."

She slipped her hand in the pocket and pulled it out empty. Then the other. And then her eyes met mine, wide, and I knew.

In a flash, I remembered the precise moment it happened. So quick and so subtle at the last inn when the boy ran between us. Damn it all to hell and back.

I dragged a frustrated hand through my messy curls, keeping the litany of curses silent. It wasn't everything, I wasn't that dimwitted. But it was enough to miss, certainly.

My head hit the wall with a solid, satisfying *thunk*. I repeated the process for good measure.

"It's all right. I-I have pin money," she stammered, holding up her reticule as I slid off the seat and out of the carriage.

Wordlessly, I yanked my portmanteau out from under the seat and tugged it open. I dug through it, found the hole in the lining, and handed her a few shillings with a sigh.

"You don't have—"

"Take it," I growled, shoving it in her palm. I had to forcefully clasp her fingers around it then grasp her by the shoulders and spin her toward the entrance with a gentle push before she moved. I put a few more shillings in my waistcoat pocket.

Alfie wandered off to tend the horses and I decided to take the opportunity to freshen up while the carriage was my own.

Just as I was yanking a clean shirt over my head, I heard a soft, "Oh," from the doorway. A quick glance showed the back of Davina's thin frame, her neck flushed.

"Apologies," I grumbled as I pulled the fresh linen into place and tucked it into my breeches. "I thought I had a few more minutes."

"No," she answered in a strangled tone. "No matter, I was trying to be quick. I didn't think..."

"You can turn around now," I said, settling the waistcoat on my shoulders.

She did so slowly, hesitantly. Her cheeks were flushed when I finally saw them.

"I didn't intend to scandalize you."

"No, I know." She clung to the last syllable, her lips pursed in a perfect O. When the expression finally abated she straightened her spine and pulled her shoulders back. "And as your wife, I've certainly seen more scandalous parts of your anatomy," she added with a hesitant smile.

Against my will, a chuckle escaped, her bright laughter joining in a moment later.

I clambered out of the carriage, then gestured for her to go in first. "I need the window, if you don't mind."

"You could have said."

"I was being stubborn."

"And grumpy," she added, settling primly in my former seat.

"I've been reliably informed that I'm always grumpy."

"I really do think it will all turn out."

"We'll have to agree to disagree on that," I retorted, while Alfie buckled the damned door again. The rain had slowed to a dreary drizzle during our stop, which was something of a relief. Outside, I could hear the horses snort, eager to set off.

Davina hummed, fussing with her skirts before moving to slide the coat off. "Keep it," I insisted.

"How much did he take?" she asked quietly.

"A few pounds. I brought more, but much of it is in bills. Which are more complicated to change out here."

"It was quick thinking, splitting the money."

I shrugged off the compliment. "What were you planning? When you abducted me?"

"I think we have established that I did not plan particularly far in advance."

"Good thing you allowed me to pack, then."

Tentatively, she pulled a handkerchief from the pocket of my coat. Tucked inside were a dozen or so confections in varying colors. "I got you some candied fruit that they were selling. I wasn't certain which you'd prefer so I got a bit of everything."

I settled my hand beneath hers to steady it against the rocking of the carriage. "Thank you, you didn't have to do that."

"I am sorry, you know," she whispered, looking up at me through dark lashes.

"I know. And you're right, I didn't have any better idea of what to say."

I pulled my gaze away from her.

"Which do you prefer?" I asked, nodding toward the candies.

"Pineapple, but they didn't have it."

"No, they wouldn't," I replied as I plucked and bit into an apple slice.

"Once, Mrs. Ainsley made a fairy cake with pineapple. It was the best thing I'd ever tasted," she said, eyes lighting at the memory. "She had rum with it."

The carriage trundled along as we munched on candied fruits, and I tried not to think on Mrs. Lanaham's location.

"I never had the chance to try that one. She didn't want to keep them on the menu?"

"Too difficult to get fresh pineapples. She tried a few more times but they arrived rotten."

Through the window, I could hear the *snikt* sound as the

wheels trudged through the mud. A glance outside confirmed that the rain had been heavier in this area and the roads were caked in viscous muck. The scents of petrichor and sweets drowned out Davina's spiced notes.

"You should ask your pirate friends to help her out," I replied with a half grin.

"Do you know, I think I will."

"That was not a serious suggestion."

"No, it is too late. Immediately on our return, I shall visit Grace and Annie to see about a pineapple agreement." She wore her smile in her eyes, teasing.

"My wife doesn't consort with pirates," I grumbled.

"She does if she is me," she countered with a prim little wiggle, straightening her shoulders.

"Well then, it is a good thing that—"

Crunch!

The unmistakable sound of cracking wood was followed by a disgruntled squeal from the horses up front. Shouts from our drivers joined the cacophony outside as the carriage jolted to the side.

Davina slid into me, elbow colliding with my rib cage. Candies flew about, raining down on us.

I caught her against me, holding her tight as we both tensed, waiting for more. My breath caught in my chest and refused to leave as the seconds ticked by.

And then I heard it, the creak of another wooden bit on the carriage protesting its newfound weight.

Davina's terrified eyes met mine, and I pulled her even tighter, bracing her. No sooner had I done it than I heard the final snap, and everything went dark.

Fourteen

NORTH ROAD—APRIL 11, 1817

DAVINA

"Kit?" I whispered into his chest when the carriage stopped crumbling around us.

When I received no response, I recognized that his grip about my waist had loosened.

"Kit!" I demanded, pulling away to look at him. There was a cut along his temple where his head must have hit the frame of the door. My chest tightened painfully as I unwound myself from his embrace. He slumped against the door while gravity made it difficult to extricate myself without crushing his prone form.

Carefully, I shook his shoulders. I couldn't risk further injury to him or what was left of the wrecked carriage. A soft groan came from his chest and air filled my lungs.

"Kit? Can you hear me?"

A wince crossed his face but he didn't open his eyes.

"Kit?"

He grunted. Blood poured freely from the cut on his head. The amount left me more than a little concerned.

"Are you hurt anywhere else? Can you move?"

"'S loud," he grumbled in his usual disgruntled tone.

Relief pooled in my chest. "I know, but I need to know how badly you're hurt."

"'M fine," he insisted, lashes fluttering now.

"We need to get out of the carriage before it collapses entirely. Can you move?"

"Carr-ge?"

"We were in a carriage accident. Do you remember?"

His eyelids opened, revealing panicked and unseeing beautiful brown eyes. The arm around my waist tightened almost to the point of pain. His breath was rapid and harsh against my chest.

"No, No. We're all right for the moment. But we need to get out."

Just outside, I heard Rory call, "Davina? Mr. Summers?"

"Here," Kit called back, swirling with my own agreement.

"We'll get ye out. Might want to brace yerselves though. We're gonna cut the door open."

"'S fine," Kit replied but his tone was weak.

I wriggled against him, struggling to free myself.

"Stop tha', what're ya doin'?" he slurred.

"I don't want to land on you," I protested.

He merely grunted, tightening his grip even more. I wasn't sure where he found the strength to hold me as firmly as he did. It would've been suffocating if it weren't so damn comforting after the unnerving, unending moments of stillness before he awoke.

I heard the knife against first one, then another of the straps and then we tumbled out of the carriage into the muck.

Kit's only response was a pained huff. I scrambled off him while Alfie and Rory pulled him away from the remains of the carriage.

"Stop it. I can move."

"You're bleedin' something fierce," Alfie grunted as he and Rory dragged Kit to the base of a nearby tree. I stumbled to my feet only to collapse to my knees in front of Kit where they'd propped him.

Quickly, I found another handkerchief in the pocket of Kit's coat and pressed it to his forehead, careful to keep my dirty fingers from his wound. His hiss was sharp but he didn't pull away.

"Head wounds bleed a lot. It's fine," he protested, batting ineffectually at my wrist.

"Where else are you hurt?" I demanded.

"I'm fine. There'll be some bruises, that's all." The improvements to his speech gave me some hope. When his eyes opened again, clear, piercing chocolate pinned mine, my hope turned to something like elation. "Are you well?"

"Just muddy," I insisted. "Rory? Alfie?"

"We're well. Just a bit shaken up," Rory answered behind me.

Tentatively, I pulled the handkerchief away, breath caught as I waited. Blood immediately pooled before dripping down toward his eye. I struggled to catch it with the handkerchief once more, earning another wince.

"What day is it?" I asked

"What?" he demanded, irritable.

"What day is it?"

"April something. We've been in that blasted carriage for so long that time has ceased to have meaning."

I tried to pull the handkerchief away again but was forced to press it right back to the wound. Rory's hand appeared over my shoulder with another that I snatched in my free hand.

"What is your name?"

"Kit. You're Davina. That's Rory, the old variety, not the wee variety, and there's Alfie."

Carefully, I switched the handkerchiefs, keeping pressure.

"Where did we meet?"

The question earned me an eye roll, but I was mostly pleased to see that the handkerchief didn't immediately soak with blood, instead transitioning more slowly.

"You were eavesdropping. And stealing at my sister's wedding."

I tried again to lift the handkerchief away. Ten, perhaps fifteen seconds passed with even less bleeding. I caught his hand, brought it up to hold the handkerchief in place, and I pulled away. He caught my wrist in his free hand and interlaced our fingers.

"Where are you hurt?" he pressed again.

"I'm unharmed. Truly. But you're going to need stitches. Keep pressure."

He merely groaned at the thought.

"Stay here for a moment," I said, squeezing his hand gently before rising and turning to Alfie and Rory, noting for the first time that the horses were nowhere to be seen. "The horses?"

"They were all a-fright. We had to cut them free so they didnae tear the thing to pieces. They'll be round here somewhere," she replied.

I nodded, not ready to sort out frightened horses. "Can you two help me get the trunks?"

"Of course," Alfie said.

"Be careful," I urged, as he scrambled under the haphazardly perched carriage to lean inside. On the outside, Rory and I steadied the frame to prevent it from collapsing.

Alfie shoved first Kit's portmanteau out and slid it away. My reticule followed, tossed atop the larger bag. Then I heard the shifting of my trunk which he pulled free with a grunt before crawling free of the wreckage.

While he collected himself, I helped Rory pull the trunks from the back rack, the frame creaking irritably.

"What do you suppose happened?" I asked.

"Hit a rock in the muck. We didnae see it and it cracked the wheel." She nodded toward the fractured wheel, crushed into at least three pieces.

"Where are we?" Kit called from the tree. When I turned, he had already found his way to a knee and was trying to press himself up.

"Absolutely not." I stomped over to him, my feet squishing in the muck, and shoved against his shoulder until he collapsed back down with a petulant groan.

"Davina," he snapped, but didn't fight me. "Rory, where are we?"

"Few miles north of Grantham, I expect."

"Did we pass Foston?"

"Not yet," she called back.

"That's good," he mused to himself, trying to stand against the weight of my hand.

"Kit, stop. We've just slowed your bleeding."

"We need to get help," he insisted.

"Someone will be by soon."

He shook his head, then flopped back against the tree again when I wouldn't relent my counterweight. "Would you stop that?"

"No. Now sit still. I need to clean that cut."

"With what? Mud?" he asked, catching my hand again and waving it in front of my face. True, I wasn't much good like this.

Considering for a second, I supplied, "Whiskey."

"Oh, hell. I'd do better to drink it."

"Not with a head wound."

He rolled his eyes but released my hand so I could ferret out the whiskey from my trunk. Using a bit of our water, I rinsed my hands before digging for the drink and a couple clean handkerchiefs.

"Ye had whiskey this whole time?" Alfie grumbled. "Fancy folk never share."

Ignoring the grumbles from the boy, I handed Kit the water skin. He took a heavy slug before rinsing his own hands. I dampened one handkerchief then wiped away the worst of his dried blood. His forehead was beginning to swell but no fresh blood escaped.

I repeated the process, dampening a new cloth with the whiskey. Only when I turned to face him did I hesitate at the sight of the angry, reddened flesh. "This is going to hurt," I offered, wincing with sympathy.

"Never would've guessed," he retorted.

If I hadn't caught the clench of his jaw as he ground his teeth, I would've snapped back. Instead I pressed the cloth to his wound, slowly, gently.

I felt Kit's breath catch and his eyes pinched shut, but he made no other sound. Delicately, I dabbed the whiskey-soaked fabric.

"You need stitches," I whispered again.

He shook his head without opening his eyes. "Not here."

"Where then?"

"We're near my sister. Lizzie lives about two miles east."

"Oh."

"I'll go an' borrow a wagon or something." He tried once again to stand. This time I allowed it and rose with him. My hands hovered, useless, over his shoulders in case he needed someone to steady him. He was surprisingly sure on his feet for the amount of blood he'd lost.

"I'm coming with you," I insisted.

He rounded on me with more strength than I'd credited him. "You're staying right here. You can help Rory watch the supplies."

"You have a head wound," I reminded him.

"Yes, and yet, you're the greater pain."

"I'm not letting you walk two miles alone. You could swoon and die," I explained, perfectly reasonably.

"Men don't swoon, and it's a scratch. I'm hardly at death's door."

"There is nothing inherently feminine about the verb. And I'm quite resolved."

He looked beseechingly at Rory.

"I'm on the lass's side on this. Sorry. Besides, we need to find the horses."

I caught the edge of a curse under his breath before he set off to the left.

"I thought you said she was east?" I called after him.

Another muffled curse and he whirled around and stomped off, this time to the right.

"Are you coming?" he yelled over his shoulder.

I nodded at his back, grabbed the water skin and my reticule, then tripped along after him. He slowed for a moment, waiting for me to catch him up.

~

KIT

My head throbbed like the devil and it seemed I was to spend the entirety of our journey trying not to cast up my reckoning.

The formerly sticky mud was drying on my back and side like crackled wallpaper paste. Davina had fared little better, though the worst of the muck was on my coat. Of course, I had not packed a second.

It was good fortune that we found ourselves so near to Lizzie and Sydney. In our present state, and with our impressive transportation, no one of repute would have stopped to assist us.

Davina had the good sense to remain silent as we stumbled

across an uneven field, but as we found the road that led past Sydney's farm, she could restrain herself no longer.

"How are you feeling?"

"Fine."

"Do you need to rest?"

"No."

"Do you want some water?"

"No."

"When you hit your head, did you forget all words of more than one syllable?"

"Yes."

She huffed a chuckle beside me and I allowed the corner of my lip on the side facing away from her to turn up.

"So, your sister?" She tried, more tentative this time.

"Lizzie."

"Lizzie. If she's anything like Kate, I imagine she'll have a few questions..."

"More than a few."

"And how will we be answering those?"

I turned to face her and slowed to a stop. I waited until her gaze met mine. "You're my wife, aren't you?"

Something unreadable crossed her face before she replied, "Right, yes."

"You're my wife. We're traveling to tell your brother. We were going to stop to see her and my mother on the way back to London as a surprise."

She blinked in astonishment. "That will work. But, Kit, I don't have a ring. Mrs. Lanaham would have missed it, but your sister won't."

"Mother's ring."

"What about it?"

"My wife would get my mother's ring."

"Oh, but that should be something special, for your wife."

I merely raised a brow in answer.

"Which... is hardly a more significant concern than the fact that I've proclaimed myself your wife," she finished with a self-deprecating note.

"Precisely. Besides, we're not visiting my mother. You'll have to live without the ring," I said, starting off down the road again.

I brushed at bits of dried mud clinging to my arms and it flaked off in little sheets. It would've been satisfying if a layer of dirt didn't remain.

A needling thought danced in my mind, even though I didn't want to give voice to, didn't want to disgrace Davina by speaking. But I knew her. I knew her family. I knew her financial situation. And I knew she'd likely never been in a home such as Lizzie's.

"Davina... Lizzie and Sydney, they're not... He makes a good living. They're comfortable. But it's not... it's not what you're used to. And I hope that—"

Her hand caught my wrist and yanked me back to face her. "I know you're not asking me what I think you're asking me."

"I just... They're my family."

"And you think I would insult your family?" Incredulity slipped into her tone.

"Not intentionally."

"You're the one who turned up your nose at my carriage."

"Your carriage was a safety hazard. As evidenced by our current predicament." I gestured to the fields surrounding us.

"Any carriage could have struck that rock!"

"And collapsed in on itself?"

"Fine. I'll acknowledge that, perhaps, the carriage was somewhat lacking. But do you truly believe I would snub anyone who invited me into their home?"

"No, no. I just... We're about to impose quite significantly, and I wanted to be sure you were prepared."

"Noted," she replied sharply, turning back to the road.

"Davina…" I sighed. "I didn't mean to imply that you would be uncivil. I didn't—don't—think you will be. But in my experience, occasionally members of the gentry do not recognize their privileges."

"And you think *I'm* like that?"

"Your brother once handed me £150 to rescue you from that milliner's shop. Like it was nothing. He was concerned it wouldn't be enough. It was also more money than I'd ever held at one time."

"That doesn't mean I don't know how to act."

"Davina, I'm sorry. You're right. I should not have said anything."

"No, no. It's good to know what you think of me."

My head gave an angry throb to accompany every single heartbeat. "I'm sorry—"

"If I am frivolous, it is because there are no other options available to me. But I have never been accused of being oblivious, or worse, cruel. And I thought, of everyone, that you— Well, I thought you saw me differently."

"Davina, please. You know that is not what I intended. I have a head wound," I tried, wincing at the pathetic whine in my words.

"If you do not stop talking, you will have another one," she snapped before stomping ahead.

With a few curses under my breath, I jogged after her, my head pounding with renewed vigor. We continued in terse silence for more than a mile before we reached the familiar plots of Sydney's land. He'd begun to plow the fields and hadn't done any of the plantings yet—probably anticipating a final frost.

Up ahead, I could see the turnoff for the house and relief settled in. I may be having a spat with my *wife*, but at least there was a bath in my future.

"This way," I directed, pointing to the turn. I could only

hope Sydney had a wagon that wasn't in use. Perhaps the rains had kept him inside today.

Davina strode along at my side, righteous indication rolling off her in waves.

"We're newlyweds, remember," I offered.

"Are you sure you want me for a wife? I might give insult to your family."

Irritation settled through me once again. "You're not my wife. You don't even wish to be a wife, let alone mine. But you'll need to pretend because, as mad at me as you are, this is your mess that you've gotten me into."

"Of course, *darling*," she snapped, sarcasm dripping from her words and disdain written in the set of her mouth and the fire in her eyes.

"Wonderful, my little fairy cake." I watched for the exact moment the endearment registered and she struggled not to laugh. "Too much?"

"You tell me, they're your family. But I didn't see you as the endearment type."

"I've never used one before. I suppose we'll find out," I said as we approached the little white house Sydney built for my sister, then stepped up on the wrap-around porch that was her only request.

With a fortifying breath, I knocked on the red door I'd helped repaint the last time I was here.

Behind the door, I heard the commotion of Lizzie's brood arguing over who got to open it. And then a voice that had my stomach sinking to the wooden boards beneath my feet. "I'll get it, little loves."

It swung open. And there stood my mother.

Damn.

Fifteen

EARNSHAW RESIDENCE—APRIL 11, 1817

DAVINA

There was no question in my mind who this woman was. She was tiny, like Kate, but her curls were tight like Kit's, pulled back in a loose chignon with a hint of grey at the temples. The delicate lines on her face spoke of a happy life with many reasons to smile. Wearing a simple, dove-grey mourning dress, Kit's mother was the picture of elegance.

Around her skirts, a little girl with similar dark curls peered at me inquisitively. It took her but a second to recognize her uncle, covered in mud, and cry his name and wrap herself around his cleaner leg.

Her shout was enough to send three additional children running to greet Kit. They scrambled over one another, each trying to find a bit of him to cling to.

"Christopher," his mother began. "This is a surprise. I would hug you, but…"

"I'm covered in mud."

"Yes, dearest."

"Children, let Uncle Kit and his friend inside, please."

"You can just... a rag out here?"

"Oh no, I suspect this is a lengthy story. I haven't seen you in such a state since you were a boy."

"All right, Mum," he said, leaning over several children to press a delicate kiss on her cheek then step gingerly inside. He was careful to avoid mussing her. He turned back to me with a questioning, "Davina?"

I followed him in wordlessly, taking in my surroundings. The house was simple and open, the kitchen, dining, and living areas all in a single room. There was a staircase at the back that likely led to the sleeping areas. The floor was a well-loved oak, scarred and worn. The furnishings had been carved by hand with function and not style in mind. The stone hearth took an entire wall, with only a counter left for meal preparation. The dining table was long and rectangular, with eight mismatched chairs lining it, four on each side.

In fact, nothing matched. And there was color everywhere. Yellow curtains that were clearly remnants from two separate dresses hung over the windows. Cushions adorned each chair, one sewn from old tan breeches, another made from a blue gown. Another window had green curtains with pink floral sashes. The walls were lined with children's paintings of Lord only knew what.

The effect was garish. Garish and *home* in a way I'd never known.

"Davina?" Kit asked again, shaking me out of my reverie. His brows furrowed deeper than usual in concern. At the reminder of where he believed my thoughts lay, irritation snapped back through me.

I tossed him the most genuine smile I could muster through my annoyance. He swallowed heavily before turning back to his mother as a small boy tried to climb his arm.

"Mother, this is Davina Summers, Lady Leighton. My wife."

Her expression of shock was familiar to me. It was nearly identical to the one Kit wore on the occasions I managed to surprise him. But hers melted away, softening into something sentimental. Her eyes welled with tears and she threw her arms around her son, heedless of the mud and children trapped between them.

"Oh, my sweet boy." Her voice was thick with emotion. "Your father would be so happy." She pulled away, wearing some of Kit's filth, and moved to me. She caught my hands in hers. "You are so welcome, darling. We're delighted to have you in the family."

A knot formed in my throat, twisting into something hot. "Thank you," I forced out.

"Lizzie!" Kit's mother called out.

"What?" A feminine voice shouted back from upstairs.

"Come and see!"

Lizzie could have been Kate's twin—save her eyes and the boy of two or three braced on her hip. The eyes were Kit's. And the boy, I was almost certain, looked exactly as Kit had when he was the same age, with a dark mop of curls and a petulant frown.

"Kit! What on earth are you doing here? And why do you look like you've slept with the pigs?"

Kit ran an embarrassed hand through his hair before kneeling down to distract himself with the pile of children clambering for his attention.

"Never mind that! Look, he's brought a girl. He's married," Mrs. Summers said.

Sharp brown eyes found mine, astonishment filling them. "Christopher," his sister turned to him. "When did you get a wife?"

"It's new," he muttered. A little boy climbed atop his back and a little girl clung to his neck.

"Lizzie Earnshaw," she said to me by way of an introduction. She was shrewder than her mother, more discerning. And I couldn't help but wonder why he was so worried about his mother when this formidable woman ran the house.

"Davina," I replied with a curtsy.

She turned back to Kit. "Where'd you find her? The palace?"

"Lizzie!" Mrs. Summers protested.

Kit rose, children still wrapped about him. "She's not like that, Liz." I resisted the urge to point out that he'd considered me exactly like that a mere half hour ago.

"I expect you'll both be wanting a bath?" she asked by way of response.

He sighed, which would've been more impressive were he wearing less mud and fewer children. "Yes, please. And the use of a wagon if you have it."

"Syd's got it. He'll be back before supper. I'll get the water on," she said. "Staying for supper as well?" She wandered over to the kitchen and added a few logs to the fire with one hand, babe still resting on her hip with the other.

"Please, and we've two others with the carriage."

"They're a mess as well?"

"Yes."

She added another log without comment. "Simon, run down to the well if you please. Take Sarah too." And the two oldest children broke off Kit's legs and moved to the door, where they slipped through with ease.

"Oh, I can, if you just point the way," I offered, gesturing to the door.

"Oh no!" Mrs. Summers insisted. "The two of you have clearly been through an ordeal. You should sit. I'm sorry, Lizzie's completely forgotten her manners. What on earth happened?"

"Carriage accident," Kit explained, moving to untangle himself from the still-clinging children.

"What?" his mother cried. "Is that blood on your forehead? I thought it was mud!"

"We're fine, Mum. I'm going to help with the water," he explained, batting ineffectually at her fretting hands.

"He hit his head," I informed her, and he shot me a look when his mother immediately increased her fussing. She directed him to the table and pressed him into a chair. "I was going to stitch it," I added, "but it seemed better to clean it first, if we could."

Mrs. Earnshaw approached with a bowl of water and a clean cloth balanced in one hand. "Did you do this before or after you married without telling your family?"

"After," Kit replied, not rising to the implied insult. His sister wandered off upstairs wordlessly.

I settled across from him and dipped the cloth in the water and then dabbed it to his cut. When I dipped it back in the water, the basin quickly swirled a terra-cotta brown.

"Was anyone else hurt in the accident?" Mrs. Summers asked, still fretting on Kit's other side as the remaining children claimed chairs to watch.

"Kit took the worst of it," I replied. "Just a few bumps and bruises for the rest of us."

Mrs. Earnshaw came back down the stairs carrying a box of sewing notions in one hand, the child still resting on her hip. "I don't have anything for the pain." She settled the box before me with an expectant brow.

I'd never actually stitched flesh. But it couldn't be so terribly different from fabric. Could it? Besides, this was clearly a test. One I was almost certain I could pass. I would pass. I had to.

"Shouldn't have left the whiskey in the carriage, should we?" I asked, teasing.

"Mum can do it. It wouldn't be the first time," he said.

"Oh?" I asked, then shook off Mrs. Summers'

outstretched hand. "I wouldn't have thought you accident prone."

The corner of his lip quirked up in what I considered to be the biggest smile he was capable of. "You've forgotten the sight of me on the dance floor?"

Mrs. Earnshaw huffed behind him, but his mother's soft, dreamy sigh overpowered it.

"You managed to refrain from maiming my feet. You merely require proper direction."

As expected, his sister broke into a single laugh while their mother giggled. Kit took my teasing as intended, pulling a good-natured frown.

I knocked through Mrs. Earnshaw's notions looking for something fine enough for sutures, finally happening upon a bit of silk thread and a needle. She brought over a lit candle, and I heated the needle over the flame for a moment.

"What did you do as a boy that required stitching?" I asked, trying to distract him, and myself, as I lined up the uneven bits of flesh between my fingers.

"There's a creek near the house I grew up in. I'd try to catch frogs and put them in Katie's bed. I slipped and fell on the creek bed. Ripped my breeches and my knee."

I didn't do him the disservice of warning that my efforts would hurt. Instead, I pressed with the needle—hard. Skin was more difficult than fabric, much more. And more disgusting, squishing together in a most disturbing way. Kit pressed his eyes and lips closed, hard, against the pain while I swallowed back my nausea. I understood his carriage sickness much better now. After the thread was through both sides, carefully, I knotted it off, trying to keep the tension even, and then cut the ends.

"I need to do a second one," I said, trying to keep my rolling stomach from my voice. He nodded, finally opening deep brown eyes to meet mine. "Why didn't Mrs. Earnshaw earn a frog?"

"Older sister," she replied for him. "He knew I'd make him regret it."

"I only have older brothers," I said. The second stitch was every bit as vile as the first, and Kit hissed his way through it.

"You must have had your share of amphibians then," Mrs. Earnshaw said.

"Not a one." I tied off the second stitch. "Gabriel was much older, and of the two of us, I was far more likely to give Xander a slimy friend than the other way around."

"You hid a frog in your brother's bed?" The little girl asked.

"I, too, have difficulty believing that," Kit added, lip tipped higher than I'd ever seen it. "Especially after the spider incident."

"Oh, hush you. Frogs have a perfectly reasonable number of legs. And eyes. And absolutely no fangs to speak of."

"Don't like spiders?" Mrs. Earnshaw asked, a hint of derision in her tone.

"Not particularly," I answered. There was a note of weariness, wondering if I was going to regret it.

"Why'd you put a frog in your brother's bed?" the little girl asked.

"Oh, it was actually a newt in his wash basin."

The children gasped in unison, staring at me wide-eyed. "What did he do back?" the girl questioned.

Xander had convinced Cook to switch salt for sugar in all of my desserts for a month. But I rather thought that answer wouldn't endear me to this family. I suspected desserts were a luxury not to be tampered with. "Not a thing. I convinced him our eldest brother was the culprit. He's furious to this day."

The children giggled with delight, just as the eldest two

returned with the water buckets and carried them upstairs at their mother's direction.

"I can't heat the water and cook supper," Mrs. Earnshaw said. There was no apology in her tone, and I rather thought this was another test. "You'll have to make do. I assume you'll need to borrow some clothes as well?"

Kit nodded on our behalf, for which I was grateful. "I'll make sure Davina has everything she needs," he added as he stood. I followed him up the stairs, just as the two eldest raced down. "Oi!" he called after them.

At the landing, he guided me into what appeared to be the Earnshaw's bedroom, where a tub waited behind a screen. It was half filled with tepid water.

"I'll get you a cloth and find some soap," he murmured. "Is it just the gown? Or do you need the underthings as well? Because I don't expect much of anything that fits Lizzie or Mum will fit you."

I'd had a similar thought and was grateful that my chemise and corset had survived the ordeal. The petticoat's hem and the entirety of the dress were worse for the adventure. "I can do with only a dress, just until we can use the wagon to fetch our things. I expect I might scandalize everyone with my hemline though."

"I doubt it very much."

He searched a wardrobe, then settled a plain brown day dress on the bed. It was well worn and had been reworked more than once to accommodate changing fashions. "Is this one all right?"

"It's perfect."

I expected him to slip out the door, down the hall, and back downstairs. Instead he hovered, staring at the dried mud on his boots. His curls fell over his forehead in an endearingly boyish fashion that reminded me very much of the eldest boy downstairs.

"Can I help you with something?" I asked, confused by his lingering presence.

"I assumed you might need assistance with the buttons. And the corset. I can leave you to it if you can manage."

"Oh! I suppose I do. But it would be improper—"

"You're my wife. Remember?"

"Oh," I repeated, stupidly. "Yes, of course." I turned, offering him my back. I had to tug the tangled waves of my hair, long having forsaken the hold of any remaining pins, over my shoulder.

He was less tentative this time as he worked the buttons down my back in a perfunctory manner. Still, I could have sworn his breath felt ragged against the nape of my neck.

Once the dress gaped enough to pull free from my body, he backed away while I stepped out of it and my petticoat. All that remained were the corset and chemise. He loosened the corset with more confidence than he'd tightened it, until it pooled on the floor.

I heard his receding footsteps, then the scratch of the screen against the wooden floor, before the rustling of bed coverings.

"You're... You're staying?"

"I thought you might need help putting them back on. But you can just call for me."

"You're right. Stay close?"

"I'll just be outside the door." He opened and then clicked it shut again.

I pulled off my chemise. With a deep breath, I dipped a toe into the single coldest bath I'd ever had, trying desperately to hold back my whimper.

KIT

I let my forehead thump softly against the door as I dipped my hand into my waistcoat pocket only to find it empty.

And wasn't that a lark. Her hairpin—my pathetic talisman—my desperate attempt to remind myself of propriety, of integrity, lost to the muck and mire by the side of the road.

"What are you doing Uncle Kit?" Little Sarah asked behind me. I hadn't realized anyone was upstairs, but I couldn't bring myself to stand upright. The nine-year-old was hardly concerning company.

"Questioning my life choices."

"Did you need to be alone to do that?"

"No, sweetheart," I said, rolling my forehead until my gaze met hers. She was beside me now, peering up from against the wall.

"You got married."

"I did."

"I would've come. I didn't get to go to Auntie Katie's wedding, and now yours too."

And wasn't that enough to make me feel like a right arse in spite of the fact that there had been no wedding to attend. "I'm sorry for disappointing you, sweets."

She nodded in that too wise, forgiving way that she had. "Is it 'cause you're an earl now?"

I turned, pressing my back against the door before sliding along it to sit on the floor. She plopped herself beside me. "Sarah, if it had been possible for me to have you there, you would've been my flower girl. You know you're my best girl. It was the biggest disappointment of the day."

"Do you mean it?"

"Swear it."

"Your wife is very pretty."

"She is," I agreed easily.

"Is that why you had to marry so fast?"

"What? Where did you hear that?"

"That's what Momma said. That you lost your head and your honor over a pretty girl and you had to rush to the altar."

"You shouldn't eavesdrop. It's not polite."

"Neither is being in such a hurry that you forget to invite your family to your wedding," she retorted. "So did you?"

"No."

"Then why didn't you wait for us?"

And wasn't that the sticking point? How to explain the reasoning for rushing a non-existent wedding to a child. "Do you remember every summer when the first raspberries appear on the bush out back?"

"Of course, it's like torture."

"Right. So when they first appear, they're small and brown. Then they turn a yellow white. And then a light pink. But you can't have them then, because they aren't ready yet. Right?"

"Right."

"So once they turn the perfect red, you've been waiting for days, and you can't even wait to get them to the kitchen."

"So you waited days for Miss Davina?"

"Years," I breathed, the truth of the word settling into my spine.

"Uncle Kit?"

"Yes?"

"That sounds a lot like losing your head and rushing down the aisle. You just used more words."

My chuckle brought a smile to her little heart-shaped face. "When did you get so smart?"

"It's the raspberries," she grinned.

We were interrupted by the clump of boots and the excited cries of the children still downstairs.

"Papa!" Sarah cried as she jumped up and raced down the stairs, abandoning me to my vigil.

It was only a minute before the heavy steps made their way up the stairs. I scrambled to my feet, feeling the stiffness of the day setting into my joints.

"Kit!"

"Sydney," I replied, shaking his proffered hand.

"What the devil happened to you?"

"Carriage accident."

"And your *wife*?"

"She was in the carriage too."

He raised a single brow at my evasion. "Sarah dragged you out here to interrogate you?"

"Yes, but I deserved it." I felt the truth of those words settle in the depths of my chest. The weight of this lie threatened to drown me and I struggled to keep it from my face.

It must have worked because he merely tipped his head in silent agreement with my assessment. "Lizzie said you need the wagon?"

"I imagine she said a great deal more than that," I muttered, then added, "but we need to gather our things and our drivers if you can spare it."

"Of course. I can send Jacob now if you can give me direction."

"That would be much appreciated. It's about three miles north of Gonerby. Just shy of the main turnoff. The drivers are Alfie and Rory, and no, I cannot explain the state of the carriage or drivers."

"Are you in danger?" he asked, trepidation in his tone.

"Not physically," I said, dragging a hand through my hair before remembering the caked mud that fell like grotesque snow about my person.

"Ah, wives'll do that to you." He clapped me on the shoulder, then stomped back down the stairs, presumably to give his farmhand the directions.

"Kit?" A tentative voice called through the door.

I slipped back into the room and found Davina silhouetted in the afternoon sunlight wearing only a chemise.

I was bound for hell, or perhaps already in it. That was the only explanation for the torture before me. Sheer white fabric clung desperately to every curve, the light peering into the room ensuring that every elegant line was illustrated in perfect clarity.

Today's fashions may not have been shy about a low-cut bust, but ladies' legs were left a complete mystery. Until now. Long and lithe and meeting in a place I had absolutely no right to consider.

"Can you help with the corset again?" she asked, tone meek.

I could only nod, fearing my voice would break the way it had when I was a lad.

She tugged it up and over her chest before I had the time to devote to its study. Her haste was a travesty I could not give voice to. Then she spun, offering me her back.

Her curls were wet and clung to her back desperately. Wordlessly, she tugged them over her shoulder, leaving nothing but soaking white linen pressed to her skin.

Carefully, I tugged the laces the way she'd shown me, trying not to brush against the threadbare chemise. I felt a blush wash over my cheeks and up to the tips of my ears. My breath was harsh and uneven against her skin, but I managed to sort out the laces properly.

"Do you need help with the dress as well?"

"No, it buttons at the front," she explained, then stepped into it and twisted the buttons into place. She smoothed her hands down the front before turning to me with an expectant look.

For a few seconds, I was able to restrain the laugh. But once it escaped, I was done for. The dress sat at least six inches above the hem of her chemise. From there, it fit well enough until it hit her chest where it hung loose and sad. It would only sit on one shoulder at a time, the other falling free.

Her affronted expression melted away when she turned to the mirror and collapsed into giggles of her own. "It seems what I lack in bust, I compensate for in height."

Privately, I had never seen anything lacking in her bust, but she wasn't actually my wife, and it wouldn't do to give voice to the thought.

"I cannot wear this," she added.

"Sydney has sent one of his hands to meet the carriage with the wagon. They'll be back within the hour."

"I cannot go downstairs dressed this way. Your sister already hates me."

"She doesn't hate you."

"She certainly doesn't like me. And her opinion won't be improved if I show her husband and children my underthings."

"Well, you're not wrong about that."

"I'm staying here until our things arrive," she insisted.

I sighed and ran a hand through my filthy curls before remembering my state again. "Davina, I need a bath. The mud is beginning to itch."

"I'm not stopping you. I'm simply not leaving this room."

She was actually trying to kill me. It was the only explanation. "I cannot bathe with you in here."

"There's a screen. I promise I won't look."

"Davina..."

"Kit..." she teased. "The way I see it, you have two options. Wait until my things get here, or..."

The thought of spending another second in this grime was

enough to have me desperately scratching at a bit of muck on my neck.

"You will not peek around this screen. I do not care if the house is on fire. Am I clear?"

She raised a brow, before dragging her gaze from the top of my head to the tips of my toes. I took it for an affirmation and began digging in the side chest of drawers for a shirt and breeches I could borrow from Sydney. He was quite a bit taller than I was, but we had a similar build. They would have to suffice.

I took one last moment to fix Davina with a stare. She rolled her eyes. "I promise."

Once behind the screen, I undressed efficiently and with much less care than I usually did. It was entirely probable that these clothes were beyond salvage. I stepped into the tub without examining the water too closely. Sarah and Simon didn't need the extra chore to refill it.

Tepid water had never been such a relief and I sank all the way in, dipping my head beneath the waterline.

In spite of the relief, my bath was quick and perfunctory. I wasn't willing to linger with Davina just on the other side of the screen, probably growing restless, and only took the time to scrape the filth from my skin and hair.

In short order, I was shucking on Sydney's shirt and breeches. As predicted, I had to cuff the bottoms several times, but they would at least cover me before Davina became listless and found some new adventure.

When I stepped around the screen she chuckled at the sight of my bare feet and cuffed breeches.

"Laugh when your underthings are covered."

"Well struck." Something about the sight of her perched on the end of a bed, fresh-faced and pinked skin, chemise and lacy edge of her corset on full display, hair wild and free, was arresting. And less amusing than it had been a few moments before. Much less amusing.

Even my sister's ill-fitting dress wasn't enough to detract from Davina's charms.

"Kit?"

I shook away the imprudent thoughts. "Sorry. I've a head wound, remember?"

"You'll have a scar," she replied.

"Celine finds Will's to be rakish and handsome. What about you? Should a man have scars?"

Dark eyes considered me. "It's an improvement. You're too pretty."

"I beg your pardon?" I choked out.

"You're too pretty. The scar helps. The beard as well."

"I'm too pretty?"

"Yes. It's the lips, and the eyes, and the hair. I know more than one lady who would never dream of wedding a man more beautiful than her."

"Truly?"

"Yes," she said, as if that were sufficient explanation.

"Every time I think I understand you, you prove me wrong."

"I try," she chirped.

"I'm going to help Sydney with the wagon. It should be here soon. Try to stay out of trouble, will you?"

"I make no promises."

"You never do," I replied, then set off out the door and down the stairs.

~

DAVINA

The heat refused to leave my face. It was his nudity. I'd never been that close to *any* undressed man. Surely, the effect would be the same regardless of the man, not merely brooding solicitors turned earls with unfairly soft seeming lips.

Except that not every man spoke to me, teased me, in the way Kit did.

Even my irritation with him was lessening. Because he was right. My life was luxurious by any standard. And the occupants of this well-loved farmhouse had no notion of such indulgences.

I'd noted the worry that melted into frustration in his sister's eyes when she considered the prospect of four additional mouths to feed.

He was still wrong, though. I would never dream of insulting anyone in such a manner. But the reminder hadn't been unwarranted.

Not every man would have lied to his family, a family he clearly adored, for my benefit either. I'd listened through the door as even the young girl in her hurt received a lie. He'd fibbed for me before, but those had been breezy white lies delivered to strangers. Now, he was destroying his own reputation to save mine. Not with inconsequential acquaintances but with his own mother, sister, nieces, and nephews.

The sound of the wagon pulling up outside soon broke me from my reverie. I watched from the window as Kit, Rory, Alfie, and a man who could only be Sydney pulled our trunks off the cart. Mr. Earnshaw was tall—which had been obvious from the length of his trousers—with close-cropped, dark-blond hair. And he was very handsome. I could see why an earl's granddaughter would wed a farmer.

Kit grabbed my trunk and hauled it inside where I heard the *thunk* of his feet on the stairs. I met him at the door and ushered him inside. He set it in the corner and I rushed over to dig out one of the dresses I'd brought. They were all simpler than I usually wore, but the one in a heap on the floor was the plainest.

I found the tan day dress with ruching on the bust and pink rosettes dotting the cotton. It had a bit of embroidery on the hem, little swirls and flourishes, but nothing I would consider extravagant. It would have to do. The dark blue and the bright pink were too ostentatious for the setting.

"Can you—the buttons?" I asked and Kit nodded.

"Do you own any apparel you can don yourself?" he teased, not recognizing the truth of his question.

As he began with the line up my back, I wavered for a moment, wondering if I should let it pass. "Ladies do not dress themselves. It's a point of pride. That is why we wear white so often as well. It's difficult to maintain."

"Oh. Is that something I'm supposed to notice? With the title?"

"I'm certain the ladies vying for your affections would appreciate the effort. And there are men who would. But no, it's for other ladies to notice. You're only to appreciate the effect."

"I like the dress you were wearing before. Not Lizzie's, the other one." He finished with the last button and smoothed his hand along them in a way that had my breath catching.

"I'm afraid we may have seen the last of that dress. But it's austere, I'm not sure what you see in it," I replied as I turned to face him.

He was closer than I'd thought, inches from me. And there was something I couldn't name in his gaze. "I think I prefer it because you were wearing it the first time you looked like a person."

A breathless laugh escaped me. "What does that mean?"

"It's like you said before. Most days, you're a lady—too pretty, like a painting."

"And in that dress, I'm..."

"Tangible," he supplied, eyes gentle and warm when they met mine with a hint of shyness in the curve of his lip.

Something was different about this moment. Somehow, in the breath between my unspoken question and his answer, everything had changed. Kit hadn't stepped back, hadn't looked away, hadn't brushed aside the sentiment in jest. And even stranger, I couldn't find that I wanted him to.

Tentatively, his hand found my shoulder and brushed the hair aside. Then, impossibly slowly, he traced fingertips down my sleeve-covered arm and caught my elbow. He swallowed, throat bobbing above the open collar of his shirt, drawing my gaze.

"I like this one too. Still tangible," he whispered, drawing my gaze back to his.

His fingers trailed to my wrist, then brushed across my palm before tangling with mine. My heart tripped over itself when he raised our locked fingers. He tugged them up to press against his chest, right above his heart, his hand resting atop mine.

I wasn't versed in medicine, I didn't know what an appropriate heart rate was, but I was certain that his, even beneath the thin fabric, was too fast and too erratic to be unaffected.

"You too," I breathed. "Not a painting."

"No."

"Kit?" I asked.

He swallowed. "Yes?"

"I don't know what this is..."

His tongue darted out, dipping between his lips. "It's ev—"

"Kit," a masculine voice called through the door, startling me. Our hands broke apart, and I pulled back, my knees smacking against the edge of the bed. "I've got your portmanteau out here."

"Thank you," Kit replied in a strangled tone, looking every bit as flustered as he sounded.

"Are you two almost finished cleaning up? Lizzie's fussin' to put supper on."

"We'll be right down."

"I'll let her know," Mr. Earnshaw said.

"I need stockings." I fled to my trunk to find them. "And my hair, it's a mess."

"All right," he said, sighing. I didn't turn to look at him, I couldn't. But there was something heavy in his tone and it pressed against my chest. "I'll dress in the boys' room."

I heard the creak of the door and the *snikt* of it latching into place again as I pulled out mismatched stockings. I pulled on another pair, knotting them around something else in my trunk before they came free.

They were white and silk, too rich for the dress and the situation, but I couldn't bring myself to care as I raked them up my legs.

Faced with only one, still muddy, pair of boots, I had no other ideas but to clap them together out the window, knocking the worst of it off. I yanked those on with no care whatsoever and snagged the stocking with an audible rip.

I cursed under my breath at the sight of the hole. Unable to do anything else, I set about ignoring it.

I found Mrs. Earnshaw's settee, tugged my half-dry curls into a severe knot at the back of my head and jabbing the few pins I'd managed to locate into my skull. It was only then that I allowed myself to take in the entire picture.

My cheeks and chest were flushed an unbecoming carmine shade. And my hair was stern and unapproachable. But my dress, another *tangible* dress, was still a warm, inviting tan, with delicate pink roses dotted about to draw the gaze. It gathered in feminine pleats across the bust. The fabric was a sensible, soft—touchable—cotton. And I couldn't take it off, couldn't change it.

Not without Kit's gentle hands, warm breath, and whispered words on my back.

And *that* was out of the question.

Sixteen

EARNSHAW RESIDENCE—APRIL 11, 1817

KIT

I'D BEEN POSSESSED. It was the only explanation for the last five minutes.

I dragged my own clothing onto my body, then pulled on a waistcoat and cravat as well. My boots were worse for wear and I'd need to see if Sydney had any polish.

My chest still burned where Davina's fingers had lingered. The impossible possibilities lingered in my head. Would it have been a kiss? A slap? Something else entirely? Davina never did what I expected.

It was no matter, because I didn't know what those heart-shaped lips tasted like and I never would.

I strode downstairs, the presence of my nieces and nephews certain to shake me from this fog. At the foot, I found Maddie staring wide-eyed and awestruck at Rory. When she noticed me, she ran over to me and tugged at the leg of my trousers so I would lean down.

"Uncle Kit! She's dressed like a boy!"
"I know."

"That's so amazing!"

I laughed. "Why don't you ask her how many Rorys there are in her family?"

She turned to me, eyes alight with wonder, before running off to Rory's side where she leaned against the kitchen counter. She was peeling carrots while Alfie washed potatoes. Mum and Lizzie bickered over the hearth.

Sydney appeared at my side and guided me over to the table. "Everything sorted?"

"Yes, though I may be corrupting your daughter."

"Impossible, she's the corrupting influence on everyone. I know you said you couldn't explain about the carriage and the drivers, but..."

I sighed, overwhelmed with the prospect. "I really cannot."

"It's not illegal?"

"No, nothing like that," I assured him before reconsidering. "At least, I don't think."

"That's not the comfort you think it is."

"You wouldn't believe me if I told you."

"All right then. What brings you this way?"

"We're headed north to tell Davina's brother the news in person. We were going to stop here on the way back to tell you all." The easiest lie slipped off my tongue with a practiced tone I didn't like.

"I didn't even know you were courting anyone."

"Davina and I have known each other for years. She's a friend of Katie's," I explained. At least in this I was not lying.

"And you finally decided to press your advantage now that you have the title?"

"Something like that."

"Does that mean you've decided to stop searching for a way to escape it, the title?"

"I don't... know."

Lizzie wandered over, a bowl of peeled carrots in one hand, paring knife in the other. "If you two have time to talk, you have time to chop."

"Yes, ma'am," we replied in unison. I took her proffered knife while Sydney pulled a small, foldable one from his pocket.

"How big?" I asked.

She gestured with two fingers about a quarter of an inch apart before returning to Rory.

Simon settled on the chair next to me, supervising as I cut the vegetables. I suspected this was usually one of his tasks and he was trying to avoid his mother's notice before she found something less pleasant.

"How am I doing?" I asked him.

"Little smaller."

I nodded and focused on making my pieces more even. "This for nan's stew?"

"Yes." The boy had grown half a foot since my last visit, but he was no wider than a string bean. His formerly dark-blond waves had darkened to a solid brown, and his jaw had lost a bit of the boyish softness.

"You got married?" he asked.

"I did," I said, bracing myself for another disappointed not-so-little one.

"What did you do that for?"

"Simon!" Sydney admonished over my laughter.

"Because I wanted to," I said by way of explanation. It was as good as any other.

"But wives make you cut carrots and wash dishes," he complained quietly so his mother wouldn't hear him.

I didn't know how to explain to him that Davina had probably never seen a dish washed in her life, let alone found herself in a situation to order a husband to do the washing. "I think you're confusing wives with mothers."

"So?" he asked.

Just then, Davina came down the stairs, quiet as a mouse. And she was every bit the duke's daughter. Her spine was rod-straight, and her hair was back in a harsh knot. Entirely unapproachable.

I sighed, turning my attention back to the carrots lest I aim the knife at a finger and require more sutures.

"Someday you'll understand the difference. And I'll be there to tease you about that comparison."

He *humphed* and slunk down in his chair. At least he wasn't upset about missing a non-existent wedding.

Davina stood by the stairs, looking a little lost. I wanted to go to her, to help her, but if her countenance was any indication, she wasn't interested in my assistance. Under lowered lashes, I watched as she approached my sister, uncertainty slipping into the deepened curve of her spine.

She must have offered to help because Lizzie set her up with a few onions and a bowl on the counter, then walked away. And Lizzie and I both knew precisely how that would go.

I waited, hoping Davina possessed some heretofore undiscovered chopping skills of which I was unaware. It was not to be though. She stared at the unpeeled allium with trepidation in her brow before plucking the knife from the counter. At least that, it seemed, was an instinctive hand position. Of course, then she grasped the onion in her left hand and began to plunge the tip of the knife into the center of the bulb.

I was out of my seat before I'd made the choice. From the corner of my eye, I caught my mother also rising from her spot by the hearth.

I caught the wrist of Davina's knife hand before she could bring it down on her thumb. "Whoa there, little menace."

My other hand found hers as well and spun the onion so

the root was on the chopping block. Her back nestled against my chest. She stiffened briefly, then settled against me.

"No stabbing. That's for highwaymen and ruffians, just as Gabriel taught you. We're slicing, then chopping." I rocked the knife hand against the board until she got a feel for it. "You want to cut off just the ends, then we need to peel off the paper."

She nodded and let me guide her through the movement before setting the knife aside and stripping the dried layer off.

"Now, cut it in half from the root end. Watch your fingers." She followed my instruction, my hands only resting atop hers. "Good."

I called back to Lizzie, "Diced or sliced?"

"Diced, please," she replied.

"All right, we're going to slice vertically toward the root first. Try not to cut through it." I demonstrated on one half, her hands resting on the blade beneath mine. "Then we turn and slice the other way."

She nodded, the silk of her tightly woven hair brushing against my chin. Once I'd successfully diced half of it, I added, "Your turn."

Davina replicated my motions, less evenly and with less surety, but it was more than sufficient for Nan's stew.

"Better?"

"Yes," she whispered, something unsure in her tone.

I pulled away and caught Mum's attention then tipped my head toward Davina. She nodded and spun on her stool by the hearth.

"Liz, may I speak with you?"

"Yes?" she asked with false innocence, coming to my side.

"Outside," I added and started for the door without waiting for a response. I heard the sharp snap of the door closing behind her before Lizzie's steps followed me into the graveled drive.

"She asked if she could help," she began, not waiting for me.

"And you decided to give her a task you knew she had no experience with. And you gave her no instruction whatsoever." I whirled around to face her.

"If she had questions— She could have asked."

"You've been so kind and welcoming. I wonder why she did not?"

"How was I to know she didn't know how to do something as simple as chopping an onion?" Lizzie crossed her arms the same way she used to when we were children and she thought she'd won an argument.

"You knew damn well she'd never done that."

"Did I?"

"Don't play the fool, Lizzie. It's beneath you."

"I'm not the one who married someone incapable of even the most basic tasks. And then brought her around to judge from on high."

"Davina has been perfectly pleasant. The only person I see judging anyone is you."

Her eye twitched, the only hint that my point was struck. Instead of answering the accusation, she pivoted. "Your entire life you worked to be a solicitor. And you're giving that all up for what? The wealth? The title? A pretty girl? That's not the Kit I know."

"I haven't decided anything," I insisted.

"You did, though, the moment you married her. Do you think that girl in there is suited to be a solicitor's wife?"

"*That girl* is my wife. You will treat her with the respect she is due. I understand that we've inconvenienced you. I am aware that you're displeased with my choices. But Davina has done nothing to deserve your ire. She hasn't disparaged you or your home. She has quietly patched up my wound, cleaned up, and offered to help you make supper. Meanwhile you've varied only between being cold and outright hostile."

"I have done no such—"

"You have."

"For all that you complained about Hugh and Kate, I thought you would make a better choice," she snapped.

"Davina is not Hugh. And I am not Katie."

"She had you wed her without your family. You were traveling right past without stopping."

"It's planting season. Are you suddenly able to leave for a fortnight? And we planned to stop on the way back down."

"You're forsaking everything you are for her. You've changed," she insisted.

"I changed the moment Father passed. My life changed forever that day."

"Well, I don't like it," she mumbled to the ground.

"Neither do I," I agreed, approaching her cautiously. She tucked herself up under my arm, hugging me back.

"I miss him," she whispered into my shoulder.

"Me too."

"I'm sorry I was mean to your wife. She's not been like Hugh at all."

"Much as it pains me to admit it, Hugh isn't entirely awful."

"No?" she asked.

"No. He took his sweet time about it, but he loves Katie. And their boy. And he's helped me a bit with this title."

"He wasn't wretched when they came for the funeral either."

"I still don't like him," I insisted.

"No one could deserve Katie," she agreed, remaining pressed into my shoulder.

"Certainly not."

"No one could deserve you either."

"I know, I'm a treasure."

"I take it back, let the *beau monde* have you," she said, pulling away. She wiped her eyes quickly but there was a suspicious damp spot on my shirt.

"Well, I was going to suggest that I begin to visit twice a year, rather than the once. But if you've washed your hands of me, I suppose I'll have to see if Davina's family will have me."

"I suppose you may visit twice," she said, feigning nonchalance.

"What if I brought Katie and little Henry?"

"What about Hugh?"

"He can remain in town."

"That seems a fine plan."

"Are we all right then?"

"Yes, you'll have to forgive me," she insisted, then settled on the bench beside the door, patting the space beside her. "In fact, consider it payback for the way you treated Sydney when he was courting me."

I sat beside her with a humph. "He deserved everything Katie and I threw at him and more."

"I'll never agree to that."

Seventeen

EARNSHAW RESIDENCE—APRIL 11, 1817

DAVINA

I WORKED on the onions with false confidence, feeling tears perk. My showing was an utter failure and Kit's sister was outside surely convincing him to orchestrate an annulment. I didn't like to fail at anything, certainly not something so simple as onion cutting. My tears weren't because I was still rattled from Kit's overwhelming presence and the subsequent vacuum of his absence—they weren't.

Suddenly, I felt a warm body by my side. "Oh, dear. Onions get to me as well," Mrs. Summers said. "I keep a damp rag nearby and that seems to help some." She set one on the board beside me.

Through the open window in front of me, I caught bits and pieces of the argument occurring outside. It seemed the only thing they could agree on was that I was incompetent.

"Don't mind those two. They've been spoiling for a fight since their pa died."

My gaze slipped to hers, the same warm wood shade of Kit's. "I am so sorry for your loss, Mrs. Summers."

"Rose, please. Or Mum, if you prefer."

"Rose," I settled on, unable to voice the other option.

"Thank you for that. And for what you've done for my Kit."

"I haven't—"

"Nonsense," she interrupted. "I've been so worried over him, in town all alone. And the earldom... Every time someone uses the title, he's reminded his father is gone. But today... Well, he looks at you the way Teddy looked at me."

The onions were troubling me again, tears welling unbidden. The knowledge that this kind woman would be devastated when she learned the truth, or whatever story we landed on, had no effect on me at all. Even though I knew she would fret over Kit even more, and she would be right to do so. It was that sentiment that brought the next question out of me. "Can you teach me to make the stew?"

She astonished me by pressing up onto her toes to drop a kiss to my forehead, quick and soft. It was breezy and unconcerned, the kind of thing a mother does for a daughter. At least, I thought it might be.

"Of course I can. Finish up with those onions and come see me by the fire. Mind your fingers."

I brushed tears away with the back of my wrist, returning to the onions the way Kit taught me. Outside, he wrapped his sister into a familiar hug. It seemed this was an affectionate family.

Xander was a better brother than I deserved, but I couldn't recall the last time we'd hugged. The thought was foreign and I could practically see him tucking his head behind his neck like a little turtle were I to try it. The mental picture had me chuckling to myself as I finished up.

In the corner of the living area, Rory and Alfie, now scrubbed clean, were playing jacks with the older children. Mr. Earnshaw was trying to encourage the littlest one to eat small pieces of cut vegetables between worried glances at the door.

At last, I finished the onions and carried the bowl over to Rose. A massive pot hung over the fire, the smell of roasting beef slowly overtaking the corner. "Start with the beef and onions. You want the meat trimmed and cubed. Do you know how to do that?"

When I shook my head, she launched into an explanation with none of the derision I had come to expect. She continued in that manner, answering all of my questions without judgment.

I sensed Kit's return before I saw him, and I was able to school my reaction when his hand came to rest between my shoulder blades. "What are you two up to?"

"I'm learning to make your nan's stew," I explained, distractedly stirring the pot looking for the consistency his mother had described.

"You're... Well, it smells incredible."

"It was all Davina," Rose said. "Don't be modest," she added when I protested.

"She's a woman of many talents," Kit replied.

"That she is," Rose agreed. Something about the woman's concurrence left a knot forming in my chest.

"Do I add the peas now?" I asked, desperate for a reprieve from sentiments I wasn't fully comfortable with.

"Aye. You'll need to set the table, Christopher," she directed toward her son. "And get Sydney to help you pull up a couple end tables."

I didn't turn to see his response. But then I felt a quick press of lips against my crown. My heart gave a little jolt, but he was gone as quick as he'd arrived, murmuring to Mr. Earnshaw across the room.

When I glanced away from the stew to Rose, she was

examining me, something unfamiliar in her expression, her lips pressed tightly together and her eyes bright.

I felt Mrs. Earnshaw's gaze on my back, heavy and scrutinizing, and had to restrain my sigh. Surely I could not muck up the addition of peas under direct supervision.

A few moments later, she appeared with a stack of bowls.

"You go wash up, dear. We can serve it," Rose said.

I did as she bade and found my way to Kit's side just as he pulled over one last chair. He didn't say anything, instead pressing another kiss to my temple. He was certainly more demonstrative of his false affection with his family than I would have expected. But it was quickly becoming apparent that this family was nothing like what I knew. Particularly when Mr. Earnshaw caught his wife's arm, spinning her around to kiss her cheek, before spinning her back to return to the task of dishing up the stew.

I couldn't once recall father doing something similar with mother. Cee and Gabriel, perhaps, but they were not long at home before they moved to Rycliffe Place.

"Are you all right?" Kit asked under his breath as he tugged me to sit down next to him. There was none of the pomp and ceremony I was accustomed to in this house.

"Yes," I whispered back.

"Lizzie would like to speak with you after supper. Only if you'd like to."

I would rather not. In fact, I could think of few tasks I would like to perform less. But as I had told him earlier, I would not be the one to give insult here.

Bowls of stew appeared before us as the children scrambled up into chairs, save the littlest one who was perched on Rose's lap while she cooed endearments at him.

A spoonful confirmed that the stew was excellent and I felt a wave of pride wash over me. I may not have begun the day knowing how to cut an onion or brown meat, but I'd managed, with a bit of help, to do it justice.

Kit made an appreciative groan at my side. Across the table, Mrs. Earnshaw spoke up. "This is quite good," she directed to me.

"Thank you. But it was all Rose, I merely followed instructions."

"What did I tell you about being modest, girl?" Rose asked from a few seats down.

"She's right, Davina. It's exceptional," Kit added.

The children, Rory, and Alfie added their own nods. "Thank you," I said, turning back to the stew, my cheeks heating.

Mr. Earnshaw turned to me. "I'm given to understand your brother is in Scotland?" he asked. "Forgive me, I never would have guessed from your accent."

"Oh, Xander only moved last summer. My family is from Yorkshire, but my mother prefers town."

"How did your brother end up in Scotland?" he asked.

The truthful answer, which was that Gabriel won the property in an ill-advised wager and handed it off to his younger brother as a bit of a lark, would not impress these people. Before I could come up with some plausible falsehood, Kit replied, "I believe he wanted a change." It was as good an answer as any, not offering much room for further questions.

"And what does your brother do now?" Mr. Earnshaw asked.

"At present, I believe he has sheep." It wasn't entirely a lie. I'd received more than one letter complaining about the sheep on the estate, and, on occasion, in the house.

"Sheep?"

"Well, one sheep. I'm given to understand she's rather recalcitrant."

Silence echoed for a few seconds and beside me, Kit's

shoulders shook with barely restrained laughter. I gave his shin a sharp tap with the side of my foot.

"Sheep will do that," Mr. Earnshaw finally settled on saying.

"How is Katie?" Rose asked the tight-lipped man beside me.

"Hoping to see me wed—" He broke off with a cough when I gave him another kick but recovered quickly. "Well settled into the earldom."

"And little Henry?"

"She's determined he shall be called Harry among the family. But she's the only one who does so."

"Why is that?" Mr. Earnshaw asked.

"Well, he hasn't got much. Hair, I mean. It seems cruel to use the nickname."

I caught my lower lip between my teeth to keep from laughing.

"You should be forewarned, Lady Leighton," Mrs. Earnshaw said. My gaze shot to Kit, but he didn't react outwardly to the title. "We Summers folk have particularly unattractive infants."

"Oi," called the eldest boy, finally pulling away from where his head was buried in the stew. He was the only one close enough to monitor our end of the table. The rest of the children were absorbed in what were surely inappropriate stories from Rory and Alfie.

"You grew into the nose, darling," his mother replied, laughter in her tone.

The boy grumbled good-naturedly, returning to his supper and whatever thrilling tale Rory was entertaining them with that involved wide gestures that seemed particularly sword-like in nature.

"That's you and Kate, Lizzie. There's no indication that

unfortunate infants are a part of the male line," Kit volleyed back.

"No, but tragically the brow is a part of my line," I added quietly.

Kit turned to face me, gaze flitting across my face as one corner of his lip tilted into his familiar not-quite-a-smile. Without warning, he traced a finger along the aforementioned brow. "I quite like yours."

"I had to grow into it. Ask Cee, there was a year or two when she despaired of me ever being fit to be seen. Mama as well. She still finds them to be unseemly."

"Rubbish, you're perfect," he said, turning back to his soup. Kit said it so simply, so easily. As if it were an absolute fact, just a truth of life. The sky was blue, the year was 1817, and Kit believed I was perfect.

No one had ever considered me perfection before. Striking, with my pale skin and dark hair and brows—yes. Noteworthy, with my bright fashions in the latest styles—absolutely. But perfect? Celine was perfect. I was interesting.

I was vain enough to appreciate the compliment. Or I was until the moment I remembered he was merely playing the part of doting newlywed.

"And how is that partner of yours, Mr. Hart?" Rose asked her son.

"Disgustingly happy and still occupying half of my office."

"I'm sure he would say the same of you," she retorted.

"He cannot lay claim to half of my office. The rest of that I will not dignify with a response."

"Time for the lot of you to clean up," Mrs. Earnshaw announced. I rose with my bowl. "Not you, Lady Leighton. The cook doesn't clean."

I blinked, settling into both titles, wife and cook. I was suited to neither. "Davina, if you please." It would be better than Kit hearing the title that upset him.

"Davina," she accepted. "Would it be a great imposition to ask you to join me outside?"

"That would be fine," I agreed.

"Thank you," Kit added, lower.

"I'll be right out. Do you drink?" she asked.

"Like a fish," Kit muttered. Not quietly enough, if his sister's laugh was any indication. Mrs. Earnshaw stepped into the kitchen while I made my way out to the porch.

Night was falling and the air was crisp. There was a comfortable-looking little bench by the door and I plopped down, wrapping my arms around my rib cage.

It was a nice enough night, clear with no rain on the air. The big tree in the front yard stood firm but the smaller branches danced in the breeze. A rope swing swayed back and forth. I could still hear the gentle murmur of conversation and the clank and splash of dishes in the wash water through the open window. Beside me, the door opened and closed.

"Kit said you don't mind a nice whiskey?" Mrs. Earnshaw said, setting a bottle and two glasses between us. A familiar bottle. "Have you had this one? Kit brought it with him when he last visited and I quite like it."

"It's my favorite," I said, rubbing a finger across the label, *The Bonnie Barrel,* written in familiar script.

"Perfect." She poured a finger in each glass and handed one to me. I took a sip, savoring the sweet burn, hoping it would fortify me for another battle. Instead, Mrs. Earnshaw shocked me by adding, "I owe you an apology."

"I beg your pardon?"

"I've been unaccountably rude. And I owe you an apology for it."

"No, no. We've imposed. Truly, it was unintentional."

"My brother is always welcome here, not only on the best days, but the worst as well. And as his wife, you're welcome too."

Her offer rang hollow, particularly given my experience here today. But I replied with a polite, "I appreciate that."

"You aren't what I expected for my brother."

I swallowed the instinctive indignation, forcing a steadiness I didn't feel into my voice when I asked, "What did you expect for him?"

"Kit is a practical man. He's not a dreamer. He sets realistic goals and works hard to achieve them. You're the sort of girl he would've looked at and set aside as not for him."

"Why do you say that?"

"You're a lady. In your own right, not because of Kit's title."

I hadn't lied about it. I just hadn't offered that information. But it wasn't a difficult guess. "I am."

"Kit wouldn't even have thought of you, would've considered it improper. Except, he has a title now. I hadn't thought it had changed him at all. He spent months researching, trying to find a way to pass the title to the next in line. Hell, trying to find the next in line. I didn't know he ever stopped. But then he arrives with you. And suddenly, my brother is not quite the man I thought he was."

She was so hard to read. I wasn't certain whether that was an insult directed to myself, Kit, or a mere statement of fact.

"He hasn't changed much from where I'm sitting," I began my defense of him. "Title or no, he is the hardest working man I know. He is still kind and practical. He has never met a problem he cannot solve. I haven't found a single concern I cannot trust him with." The words poured from me. I'd never given voice to my thoughts. But they were the truth. Practical, sullen Mr. Summers was, perhaps, the single most reliable person in my life. Kit may have grumbled, but he'd never once faltered.

She wore an astonished look, probably matching my own.

But then it faded into something harsher, shrewd. "But you were not willing to wed him when he was a mere solicitor?"

"I was not willing to marry anyone. Ever. I didn't marry him for a title. I didn't marry him for wealth. I've no need for either. I married him because of him and in spite of myself." My breath was harsh in the dark, ragged. Because for a second, just a moment, I had forgotten myself.

I wasn't Kit's wife. He wasn't my husband. And this was all a lie.

She knocked back the rest of her drink, and the idea was so appealing I followed suit. "It seems that I've underestimated you once again. My apologies Lady Leighton."

"Davina, please. I prefer Davina. The title still makes Kit uncomfortable."

"All right, Davina. My siblings call me Lizzie." At my slow, confused blink, she added with a smile, "For better or worse, we're sisters. You'll not be rid of me now."

I brushed aside the turning in my gut at that thought. "Does this mean I now have nieces and nephews?"

"More than you can stand, to be sure."

"Oh, this is delightful! I've always wanted children in my family to spoil."

Eighteen

EARNSHAW RESIDENCE—APRIL 11, 1817

KIT

After the fourth time my gaze turned to the door, Mother called me over with an irritated, "Let them talk it out."

"But what if it's going poorly?" I asked as I found my way to her side at the table.

"Lizzie is in a snit because she thinks Davina doesn't love you the way you deserve. When she finally sees that she's wrong, she'll be nice as pie."

My chest tightened at the reminder that this was all a lie. Lizzie was wrong about many things today, but Davina's feelings for me were not one of those things.

"Chin up, dear."

I fixed a smile onto my face. It felt a little forced but Mother must have attributed it to nerves.

"I noticed something else today, ducks."

"What is that, Mum?"

"That girl's finger is bare."

I looked down at my hands against the worn table, feeling the flush creep over my cheeks and down my chest.

Suddenly, my mother's fingers, still elegant even though they now bore the creases and lines of age and life, dropped a delicate gold band into my hand. In the center of the fine-spun, oval-shaped gold filigree was a pearl.

"Mum..." Something about her closed-mouth smile read as proud to me. The expression ripped open my chest, guilt and love fighting for prominence.

"It was always supposed to be yours, my boy."

"But Lizzie or Katie?"

"Have jewels that welcome them into their husbands' families. This is to welcome Davina into ours."

I'd always known that my mother's ring was destined for my future wife. But now, seeing the graceful band, I could picture it sliding onto Davina's lithe finger. And I knew it would never suit another.

"Thank you," I breathed through the knot in my throat, hoping Mother would attribute the strangled tone to sentiment instead of what it was. I wasn't even sure what it was, to be truthful. Desire, desperation, shame, loss, affection, fear—there was no word for that swirling combination and any of the hundred other emotions I couldn't separate enough to name.

I slipped the ring onto my littlest finger for safekeeping where it hovered over my knuckle.

Just then, the door slipped open, and the two women stepped inside deep into a fit of giggles. My gaze met Sydney's whose expression mirrored my astonishment. My sister set the considerably lighter bottle of whiskey on the table before tugging Davina into the kitchen.

"Is the fire still hot?" Lizzie asked Mum.

"Yes. Why dearest?"

"We're making fairy cakes!" she announced proudly.

Davina's brow reflected her own confusion and bemusement when she glanced questioningly at me.

"You're making fairy cakes?" I asked.

"Dav wants to learn to make them," Lizzie said.

"Dav?"

"She gave me permission. Says all her siblings call her Dav. She makes you call her by her full name, so clearly she likes me best," my sister said with a smugness that only drink could provide.

Davina had clearly imbibed less. She was only a little bubblier than usual, not delivering drunken proclamations.

"Have someone help you with the fire? You've had too much to drink to be mucking about over there," I cautioned.

"Spoilsport," Lizzie called back, digging through her pantry with Davina at her side. An arm creeped out from behind the door and plopped a flour cannister into Davina's arms. She was startled but held on. Sugar followed. Then a few other things I couldn't identify. Slowly, Davina was nearly obstructed from view by ingredients.

Eventually, my sister stepped away from the pantry and dragged my wife to the counter. "Set those down, we need bowls." Davina seemed slightly overwhelmed by Lizzie's enthusiasm but washed up before taking Lizzie's proffered apron.

I made my way to her side. "What kind of fairy cakes are we making?"

Davina opened her mouth to reply, but Lizzie beat her to it. "None of your business. Go help my husband rearrange some of the children so you and your friends have a place to sleep tonight."

"Lizzie..."

"Christopher..." she retorted in that way that only my sisters had. Davina must have noted the trend because she caught her lower lip between her teeth.

I shook away Lizzie's scolding and caught Davina's hand in mine. "Are you well? You must be tired."

"No, I want to learn to make those little cake things you like so much," she teased.

"I've been reliably informed that they're called fairy cakes. But send me a signal if you wish for a rescue."

"What sort of signal?"

Unthinkingly, I pressed another kiss to her temple. That was thrice now that my lips acted without permission. It was also the third time she leaned in to my touch and that realization left me warmer than any whiskey. "You'll think of something. I have faith."

"Begone you." Lizzie shooed me out of the kitchen.

I spared a desperate glance at my mother who nodded her willingness to watch them around the fire before I went to help Sydney with the children.

We returned downstairs nearly an hour later after many bedtime stories to the sight of my mother, my sister, and my not-a-wife laughing around the whiskey bottle in the moonlight. It was clear that most of it had gone to Lizzie, but given how infrequently my sister enjoyed a few minutes for herself, I couldn't blame her. On a plate in the center of them were seven ramekins filled with what were presumably fairy cakes.

In between giggles, Davina caught sight of us and shot up from her seat. She quickly caught my arm and tugged me to sit beside her. I was beginning to adore the way she did that, dragging me about without a hint of concern that I may not follow.

She shoved me down in the seat, then plucked a ramekin off the plate. She dropped it in front of me, fingers dancing away the residual warmth. I caught her hand in mine and blew across the scorched digits. A few owlish blinks later, she settled beside me, not pulling her hand away. Pushing my luck, I kissed the tips of her fingers before releasing them.

"You have to try the cake thing."

I felt the smile inching across my face. "I told you,

someone much smarter than me informed me that they are called fairy cakes."

"Oh, just eat the damn cake thing." She pressed a fork into my hand. Her gaze was eager.

On closer inspection, these were not precisely the same as Mrs. Ainsley's fairy cakes. The lack of frosting was the least of my concerns, but I took a tentative bite. As expected, the center was more or less uncooked. But strangely, the outside had a sharp burnt flavor and texture to it. Worse still, were the lumps of unmixed flour sprinkled throughout.

"It's good," I warbled through a mouthful, questioning the wisdom of swallowing.

"You're a shit liar, Summers," Sydney retorted. Lizzie's repressed laughter escaped an in indelicate snort.

"I know there's no icing, but we got distracted," Davina confessed.

"Darling, I know you're soused, but don't make him eat that," Sydney added, this time to his cackling wife.

"Are they that wrong?" Davina asked, concern shifting over her brow. "I know they don't look like Mrs. Ainsley's, but I thought they might be all right."

Finally, I swallowed, regretting the choice almost immediately. "I should have warned you. Lizzie is a terrible baker on her best day. After five-eighths of a bottle of whiskey, it was always a risky endeavor."

In spite of my assurances, her face fell a little. I caught her hand again and laced her fingers through mine. I could feel the cool band of Mum's ring against my finger, waiting for Davina's. I tamped down the urge to slide it on without permission, resisted the urge to make her mine. "Don't be sad. If you really wish to learn, we can ask Mrs. Ainsley if she might teach us a simple recipe."

"You think she'll agree to it?"

"Will and I are her best customers. I suspect she might be willing to do us a favor."

"Ugh, you both ruined my fun," Lizzie said. "I wanted to see if he'd eat the entire thing just to keep from hurting your feelings."

"Go to bed, Lizzie. You're in the wind," I suggested.

"Can't."

"Why not?"

"'Cause I like your wife now. And that means I can't use my first plan anymore. I was going to have you sleep with the boys and her with the girls."

"Oh, I don't mind—" Davina began.

"No, you do. Sarah kicks and Maddie sleeps sideways."

"And where do we sleep now that you like her?" I asked.

"You're gettin' our room. But only for tonight. If you stay any longer, it's flying feet and head smacks all night long."

Sydney merely sighed, wearing a look of affection for his wife. "You heard the lady. Best hurry before she changes her mind."

Abandoning the children to their games, Alfie chose that moment to sit down and snag a fairy cake. He dug a nearby spoon into the ramekin and took a bite, seemingly oblivious to the eyes watching him with weary anticipation. And then he took another bite. And another. Until the ramekin was empty but for crumbs.

"This is great. Do ye mind if I have another one?"

We all shook our heads, watching with astonishment as he made quick work of a second before starting on the third. In the end, they were all cleared and stacked on the table beside him. He tipped the chair back on two legs, rubbing his belly in a pleased manner.

"And on that note, we'll be heading upstairs now," I said, tugging Davina along behind me for once, nerves and anticipation fluttering in my chest.

Nineteen

EARNSHAW RESIDENCE—APRIL 11, 1817

DAVINA

THE WHISKEY DID nothing to steady my nerves when I realized where Kit was leading me, though, truly, Lizzie had consumed the majority of the bottle.

But I knew what lay behind the door he was opening. And it was one very moderately sized bed. There was no settee, no lounge, not even a fluffy rug. Only a bed, a vanity, a wardrobe, and a tub behind a screen. And just one of those was conducive to sleep.

I knew how the conversation would go as well. Kit would insist on taking the floor, and, in ordinary circumstances, I might let him. But he'd hit his head earlier, and to be quite honest, I rather thought it might have been the explanation for his free affection today. So I would demand to take the floor, which Kit, even half-concussed, would never allow. We would both threaten to sleep on the ground before determining that the best course of action would be to share the bed.

And I was just so tired in the midnight hours. I couldn't bear the thought of the song and dance only to end up precisely where we were now, two unwed people about to share a marriage bed.

I wasn't certain why the thought was so much more intimate than the night before. Why was awakening beside him in a bed a more visceral prospect than doing so in the carriage?

But it was. And he knew it, too, if the way he looked at me was any indication.

"I have a suggestion," I began, exhaustion creeping into my voice.

"That's good, because I have none to speak of."

"What if we skip it? What if we merely skip to the end where we agree to share the bed and keep to our own sides?"

"Truly?" he asked, relief washing over his countenance. "Consider this a token protest. But, Lord, I am asleep on my feet."

"Protest noted and appreciated. Which side do you prefer?"

"Door, I suppose. I've never really considered it," he murmured, his fingers working the buttons of his waistcoat.

"The door is yours," I said, then turned my back to him once he shrugged out of the garment. "Buttons, please?"

He was less careful this time, either due to fatigue setting in or familiarity with the task. His fingers brushed along my back. Then, without prompting, he set to work on my hairpins, plucking them out one after another. I hadn't noticed the tension in my severe coiffure until he freed the last and I groaned with relief.

My hair fell in a dark curtain, shielding me from his gaze. Instead of a reprieve from the intensity of his touch, an emptiness lurked, my skin bereft of the heat that lingered from his fingers.

Kit urged the cotton down my back before loosening the silk corset ties with the same efficiency before he stepped back. The garments hit the floor in a heap of contradictory fabrics.

I considered my trunk, still in the corner by the door. I had a nightdress, but unlike the relatively plain chemise I wore now, it was decidedly French. No, the chemise was the safer choice.

Kit had settled at the edge of the bed, tugging at the loosened hem of his shirt and tangling his braces in his other hand. It was obvious from the way he fussed that Kit was unaccustomed to nightshirts and didn't sleep in trousers.

It wasn't such a strange thing. Gabriel had always complained when Mother purchased him a sleep shirt, saying he never wore the damned things. And as far as I knew, no men slept in such restrictive breeches. But I'd never followed that thought to its conclusion. No, I was nearly certain Kit made a habit of sleeping in nothing at all. The very idea had heat pooling on my cheeks. Kit would never, I knew he would never—not in my presence. But now, I suspected that he generally did.

Shaking the image away, I settled on the end of the bed and removed my shoes and stockings.

"What happened there?" His voice interrupted the tentative quiet that had fallen over us. I turned to him, confused, and he tipped his head to the hole in my stockings. I'd almost forgotten my fit of pique earlier that day.

"Just a snag."

"That's disappointing, they're very fine."

"It happens to all stockings one day. I may be able to do something with it. Embroider it. Add a ribbon. I'm not certain."

"Clever. Do you— The basin?"

I didn't respond with words, instead gathering my items and taking my turn. When I finished, I made a half-hearted effort at a braid at Lizzie's vanity. By the time I found myself perched at the edge of the bed again—facing the window—he was on the other side, mirroring me.

He pulled up the coverings, easing my passage underneath before joining me. Kit still wore his shirt and breeches when he let the blankets fall over us. Then he leaned over and blew out the candle, casting us into darkness.

It wasn't the same black veil of the carriage. There was a fire behind the screen, warming the room and casting shadows in that corner. But our positions... That was a closeness I wouldn't have been able to name.

Our breaths were loud as we stared, stiff, at the ceiling for long minutes. It was so quiet, I could almost believe he had fallen asleep. But his breath was too shallow and too unsteady, and he held himself like a statue.

"Kit," I whispered into the darkness, not turning.

"Yes?" he replied, no delay to indicate I had awoken him.

"If I tell you something you don't like, you won't tell anyone?"

"What could you possibly tell me that I wouldn't like? Unless—you haven't informed my sister you're with child or some such nonsense—right?"

"No, nothing like that. This is... it's about Xander."

"Oh," he said quietly. "The reason we're here."

"Yes," I breathed.

"No, I won't tell anyone."

"Even if it's... illegal?"

He sighed and rolled over to face me, but I couldn't bear it. Not for this. I may have been convinced that he wouldn't betray my confidence. But I wasn't so certain that I would risk watching an expression I couldn't unsee cross his face.

"Xander needs our help—your help—really. He's... he has a child that he is raising. And the boy will need to inherit."

"And the boy is not his?" Kit asked.

"He is. In every way that matters he is."

"I don't suppose your brother has wed in his absence?"

"No... Well, sort of." Lord, this was difficult to explain.

"Sort of?"

"There's no wife. And two husbands. More of a living arrangement, in truth."

For an infinite moment, there was only the sound of his breathing. My breath was trapped in my chest, tightening everything there to the point of pain. And then he said, "Oh."

"Oh? That's all you have to say? Oh?" I asked, incredulous and shrill.

"Well, it does explain a few things."

"Like what?" I demanded.

"A single, wealthy duke with two failed courtships isn't overly common. And his willingness to abandon town—and the accompanying marital prospects—for a property in Scotland. Is the babe's mother in the picture?"

"She is alive, if that is what you are asking."

"And the father?"

"He's not involved," I murmured.

"Is the babe's mother opposed to wedding your brother?"

"We have reason to believe she is Gabriel's natural-born daughter. So I expect there may be some objections on all sides, yes."

"It is a conundrum. Let me sleep on it. There has to be a solution, somewhere," he said, then rolled back over to face the ceiling again.

"That's it?"

His head rolled back to face me, but his body remained unmoving. "Well, you've not given me very much time to consider the problem. One so significant you felt the need to abduct me and take me to Scotland, I might add. If you give me a few hours, I might think of something."

"That is not what I meant," I insisted and flipped on my side to face him.

"What did you mean?" he whispered.

"You don't... You're not..."

His tired gaze sharpened, and he turned onto his side again. There was, perhaps half a foot between us, our bent knees brushed against one another. It wasn't a particularly spacious bed, after all. He caught my hand with his, his fingers tracing mine, lashes flicking down to watch them interlace.

Kit's tongue darted between his lips, the only sign that he intended to answer my inarticulate grumblings. "Your brother is a good man. He deserves to be happy, however that looks."

"You're not going to…"

"Have him arrested? No. It would be bad form as a solicitor to have my client arrested. And it would be unforgivable as a husband to have my wife's brother arrested."

"I'm not— We're not—"

"Actually wed? I am aware. I think I would remember that. But until we sort out *that* mess, you're as good as." His thumb and forefinger found the base of my ring finger, charting it. "Speaking of…"

Without finishing that thought, he brought his other hand up and plucked an elegant—feminine—gold and pearl ring from his littlest finger. "May I?"

"Kit… I cannot possibly— That is intended for your wife."

"Tonight, that is you."

"But—"

"Davina, please?"

"I don't— Why are you pressing this?"

"I do not know. I just— Would you just put it on? Just until we reach your brother? It will offer you a small measure of protection, at least."

"Fine," I pouted, unable to argue with his last assessment. He worked the delicate band onto my third finger, his thumb gliding along it as it slid home.

The ring should have felt foreign, awkward. Instead, it was a perfect fit, the metal disappearing into the crease where my finger met my palm.

"Kit?"

"Yes?"

"What are we doing?" I whispered, afraid to give the question too much body.

"I don't know that either."

"This doesn't feel like a lie."

His dark gaze finally abandoned my finger and tripped over my lips before finding my eyes. "We should go to sleep."

"We should."

"Everything will be clearer in the morning."

"It will," I agreed again.

He huffed in what I thought might be a laugh before pressing his lips to my forehead, lingering there for a moment, soft and warm.

"Go to sleep, little menace."

His back found the mattress again, but his fingers still curled around mine. And I was overcome with the desire to drop my own kiss on his fingertips. Instead I whispered, "Good night."

Twenty

EARNSHAW RESIDENCE—APRIL 12, 1817

KIT

BY ALL ACCOUNTS, it should have been a miserable night. My sister's bed was too soft, the fire too close, and I was trapped in too restrictive clothing. But something about the combination of exhaustion, a head wound, and Davina negated the annoyances.

While I had a tendency to overheat in my sleep, it seemed that Davina had no such qualms. She had pressed herself against my side, her head tucked into the space between my arm and chest. A tiny hand was curled near her face—one with an equally dainty ring on it.

I should have been bothered by the sight. Mere days ago, I would have been. But proximity and Davina's charms had ground my will down to a fine dust. And the morning light displayed those charms to the best possible effect.

Long, dark lashes rested lightly against cheeks softer and more pristine than the stockings she had shucked the night before. Sleep left her skin with a delicate flush. And a glance lower revealed—well, nothing I could contemplate and still name myself a gentleman.

No, any absurd dreams I'd had last night vanished startlingly quickly in the harsh light of day. The impropriety of our situation wasn't any less improper. The attraction that curled hot in my chest wasn't cooled. And the tender affection lapped over me in increasingly high swells.

There wasn't the slightest chance that we might arrive in Scotland with my heart intact. In fact, I was beginning to wonder if we would make it out of this bed without an unwanted profession of adoration spilling from me unbidden. Davina had been quite clear—she had no interest in a husband.

The beast in my breeches had no such qualms. He was making a nuisance of himself, taking the caress of Davina's even breaths against my chest as an invitation. Desperate for a reprieve, I considered how many of my nieces and nephews had been conceived in this very bed—that thought was enough to dampen his enthusiasm. Or it was until Davina nuzzled into my side in her sleep.

I abandoned my efforts as fruitless, instead allowing myself the luxury of dragging my fingers through her cool curls. Her ribbon had abandoned the silken strands of her plait in the night, leaving the ink-black waves to fall around her like a veil, free for my touch.

The stamps of young feet on the landing outside our door and trampling downstairs was enough of a distraction to cease my fondling. The sounds did not wake her though.

While I should, perhaps, rouse her, I was reluctant to lose her warmth. And once she woke, she would expect a solution to her brother's situation, and the only one sleep brought me involved the perpetuation of fraud. Hardly ideal.

Another set of feet tripped down the stairs, smaller and less coordinated. The sound caused Davina to stir, pressing into me before pulling back a second later. Her already flushed cheeks deepened with her awareness.

The tension returned next, as each and every one of her muscles tightened.

"Would it be easier if I feigned sleep?" I asked.

"Honestly? Yes, please."

"All right," I agreed, slackening my limbs for her and closing my eyes.

"Thank you," she replied, then pressed herself up with one palm. I caught the inside of my cheek between my teeth, restraining a smile.

"Please, do let me know when it is safe to awaken."

"After I've left, if you please," she retorted in the overly prim tone she sometimes used. The bed dipped as she pushed to stand somewhere near the end.

"I am happy to oblige. Except, I wonder, how is it that you plan to dress without my assistance?"

I caught the edge of a muttered curse before she sighed. "Fine. You may rise now."

Still at the foot of the bed and clad only in her nearly transparent chemise, hair wild and unbound, she was a vision. And a punch to the gut.

Eventually, I managed the torturous task of rising from the bed and helping her into her frock.

"What are we to do about the carriage?" she asked as I worked the line of buttons up her spine.

"The carriage is your mess. Why do you suppose I have a solution for it?" I teased.

"Because you are Kit."

"As it so happens, I do have a solution. Though not one I'm particularly pleased about."

She hummed, as I apparently affirmed her earlier assertion. "And what is this solution?"

I finished the last of her buttons, tugged her hair off her

shoulder, and brushed it with my fingers. "How do you feel about surveying your new estate... Countess?"

"I beg your pardon?" she asked, turning to face me.

"My *estate*. It's about a half day's ride north from here. Near Saxilby. A carriage should be no problem for an earl."

"But... You don't want it." Her voice was small.

"No, but it's what you need from me."

"I cannot ask that of you."

"You are not asking. I'm offering. And truly, unless you have an idea of your own... I've no other way to procure a carriage without substantial difficulty. And I don't think a mail coach will do for this."

"But..."

"It's a carriage. One that is technically mine. It is only a conveyance, not an agreement to forsake everything I am. Now come, we should break our fast and be on our way before Sydney puts the wagon to better use." I stuffed my arms through yesterday's waistcoat and dragged a hand through my own hair in lieu of any sort of styling. A quick scrub of my chin revealed a shameful amount of growth on my face, but I couldn't bring myself to ask Sydney for a blade.

Meanwhile, Davina tucked into the same stockings from yesterday, hole caressing her knee once again. When she stood, she tucked herself into my side and allowed me to lead her downstairs into the fray once more.

The breakfast table was entirely as chaotic as could be expected with so many children and more than one adult with the disposition of a child. Davina wore her expression of overwhelm delicately as food was snatched from plates in the middle of the table and crammed into mouths before ever touching a place serving.

I gathered more meat, toast, and preserves than I would usually consume, set it on my own plate, and slid it between us. She looked up at me gratefully.

"Anything else?"

"No, this is plenty."

I nodded, then turned to Sydney. "Can you spare the wagon for a day?"

He schooled his expression well, but I knew it was an inconvenience. "I suppose. Are you going to Leighton then?"

"It seems the best option."

"Take Jacob? So he can bring the wagon back with him," he suggested.

"I thought to send it back with a servant from the estate."

"I can manage without him for the day. Then you won't have to arrange transport back for the servants."

"If you're certain," I hedged.

Sarah squealed when Simon flicked a bit of toast at her. My sister groaned from her place at the table, her head clearly giving her some trouble.

"Rory, Alfie? Will you be ready to travel in an hour?"

"Aye," Rory replied.

I turned back to Davina, who was seemingly growing bolder as she snagged the last piece of toast. I pressed a kiss to her temple. "I'll go get our trunks."

Twenty-One

LEIGHTON HALL—APRIL 12, 1817

DAVINA

A FEW HOURS trundling along in the back of an uncovered wagon left me grateful for the discomfort of our late carriage. Kit had offered me nothing but a closed-lipped headshake when I tried to press him about Xander after we set off—following many hugs and kind words from his family. Instead, he merely nodded toward the front where Jacob and Alfie sat.

Rory lay sprawled in back with us, hat plopped over her face to shade it from the sun. Kit and I were bundled to one side, our trunks on the other as we bumped along across the countryside.

I sensed the precise moment we set upon his land. The way the shoulder I was resting against stiffened incrementally was a dead giveaway.

"We're almost there?" I asked, tightening my fingers where they were tangled in his.

"Yes. I'm not sure if my late uncle's wife, Tansy, is in residence. She had been visiting her sister during her mourning period, but she may have returned. She will be... difficult."

"She hasn't found other lodgings?"

"Not that I've been made privy to."

"It is kind of you to allow her to stay. Especially if you're not close."

"Allow her? It's her home." I sensed his curious gaze but was too comfortable to move to meet it.

"Well, technically it's not. It's your home now. You would be well within your rights to ask her to find other accommodations. Or at the very least move her into the dower house if there is one."

"The gentry likes to play at being civilized. But is it a common practice to throw a widow out of her home? And with a daughter?" Incredulity spilled from his tone.

"Once you're certain she's not with child—a male child—yes. Xander managed to buy Cee a few months before our father insisted. But Father wasn't happy about it." I could feel the clench of his jaw against my temple. "I wasn't trying to make you angry."

"I know. I'm not angry with you. But among other things, it is going to be so much more difficult to abide Tansy if I know I *could* have her removed."

I chuckled, tucking closer against his chest. He tugged our fingers free and slid an arm along my shoulders. "How do you still smell so good?" he murmured, half to himself.

Kit's blatant affection surprised me. I expected some of the ease we shared to wash away with the distance from his family and the necessary ruse. Still, it was a pleasant familiarity that left my chest warm. "I don't?"

"You do. There's vanilla, but something floral and something citrus. You always smell that way."

"My *parfum*, but I did not pack it. It's probably just lingering on my clothes. It's irises and bergamot. You've a good nose."

"It's nice." The words were simple, his tone anything but. It was thick with something I was afraid to name.

"Is this your first time back? Since—"

"Yes. I've managed everything through the steward. I don't mean— That's not how I prefer to do things. It's just that..."

"You don't want to see this place?"

"Among other things. I know men who are not born to the task inherit titles. Your brother, for example, manages his responsibilities with great care. And I know that some men who are born to it do not find that the task comes naturally— Hugh is proof enough of that. But... I am good at things. I know what is expected of me, and I exceed those expectations. I take pride in my work. But I studied and trained for it. I practiced under Will for nearly five years before he made me partner—rightfully so."

"But you've never prepared for this."

"Precisely. And, well, I like the life I built for myself. It's not perfect, but it's mine. I like being near Katie and her children—even if she drives me barmy. I like being able to help people—being able to help you."

"And you cannot help people in Lincolnshire?"

"I can, but not the same people."

I felt a smile pull at the corner of my lips. "Christopher Summers, are you saying you would miss me and my adventures?" That was a tempting enough thought to drag myself away from the comfort of his shoulder to study his response.

"Aye. My life is dreadfully predictable when you're not in it." A smile creeped into his eyes first, crinkling at the corners, before finding his lips. They were still closed, not a complete smile. It was perhaps seven-eighths of one. And it was entirely charming.

I couldn't have stopped myself from tracing one of the lines curving from his lower cheek under his several days of growth for the world.

"You look fascinated," he whispered.

"Your smile— It's— I like it." It was one of the greatest understatements of my life. Kit's smiles were rare and precious things, given only in partial measures. And without conscious thought, I'd been collecting them, hoarding them, for years. I numbered them and named them and felt a well-deserved sense of pride when I reached even the halfway mark. If I ever earned a real, true, complete smile, it would stop my heart.

"I'll take that under advisement," he replied, then dipped his forehead to press against mine.

"If the two of ye are finished with yer flirtin', we're here," Rory interjected. We broke apart in time to watch her haul herself over the side of the wagon with one hand.

Kit shifted, awkwardly, then helped me down from the back. We were just outside of the stables as Kit had instructed, suggesting that he preferred to arrive on foot rather than in the back of a wagon.

Once on solid ground, he brushed imaginary dust and hay from his person, smoothing ineffectual fingers through his wild mass of curls. Then he dragged a frustrated hand across the growth covering his jaw. And I couldn't have that.

I popped up on my toes, bracing one hand against his chest. His arm banded about my waist, seemingly on instinct if his astonished expression was anything to go by. And I whispered, "Don't. I like it," into his ear.

He blinked, slow and wide, before dipping his head to face the ground, a flush covering his cheeks up to the ear I'd just claimed.

Alfie dropped his portmanteau and my reticule by our feet with a pointed *clank*, and Kit's arm fell away. He leaned down, pulled out a coat—less fine than the one he had sacrificed to the muck—and shrugged it on.

It seemed his nervous tension was catching because I

found myself fussing with the sleeves of my dress and smoothing my coiffure.

"You're perfect." My gaze shot to Kit's and found nothing but earnestness. He held out an elbow, offering it to me. "Let's go."

The hall was an imposing brick structure in the distance. Smaller than Rose Hall, my family's country estate, but more austere, with two wings set out front of the entry. The landscaping was well maintained but sparse, though winter had just left this area so it may have been the season's doing. The corners of the three-story building were set in slate brick, contrasting against the red and matching the window framings.

"Lord, it's just as stern as I remember."

"Did you visit often?"

"More often than I'd have liked. We weren't allowed to touch anything inside. Or sit on anything. Or play anywhere outside where we might get dirty and bring it inside."

With a sigh and a last wipe of his palms against the leg of his trousers, he rang the bell.

A stout, balding man of no notable height answered the door almost immediately. His dull grey eyes found me first, surveying me up and down before turning to Kit where they promptly widened into something more impressed.

"My Lord, please come inside out of this dreadful damp."

Kit and I shared a look that conveyed our confusion at the man's assessment of the rather arid weather. He shrugged and followed the man into a sitting room. "Thank you. Gibbs, was it?"

"Yes, quite, sire. So good of you to remember. You must forgive me. I had no idea you were arriving. Your letter must have been waylaid in the rain the other night. I assure you, the staff would have been prepared to greet you outside."

"It's quite all right, Gibbs. We were waylaid ourselves by

the very same storm. I was not actually intending to visit but we had some difficulties with our carriage.

"Oh dear, it was something terrible. One of the girls at the market was visiting family in Grantham. She told me she came upon the most appalling scrap of an abandoned carriage—properly stuck it was."

Kit's jaw worked to hold back what I suspected was laughter. "Right, I'm sure more than one carriage suffered for the road conditions. I don't suppose Lady Leighton is available for visitors?"

"Oh dear, I'm afraid Lady Leighton and Lady Cordelia have left for the season."

Some of the tension in Kit's form loosened.

"Shall I have tea prepared for you and your... companion?" he asked, glancing to me with no small amount of curiosity.

"Yes, and we'll need rooms readied, please."

If Kit wasn't going to tell the man I was his wife, I wouldn't either. Eventually, sensing no answer to my identity forthcoming, he tottered out of the room.

Beside me on an ugly mustard-yellow settee, Kit dragged a tired hand down his face. When he reached his jaw, he paused, running his hand along the growth there with a one-third smile that had me catching my lip to hide a smile of my own.

Seeking a distraction, I peered around the room. It was papered in the French style but several seasons out of date, and, paired with the ugly furnishings, any beauty found in the half-circle windows lining the opposite wall was negated.

Kit shifted uncomfortably against the rough velvet, more threadbare on his side than mine. He wouldn't accept my hand, not here, not now, not when he would see it as improper. But the hem of my skirt was long enough that if I settled it right I could cover his muddy boots. And that allowed me the excuse to press the side of my shoe against his.

He turned, studying me for a moment before ducking his

head back to the floor. For a moment, I thought I may have overstepped. But then the side of his foot pressed back against mine.

~

KIT

Something about the hideousness of the room left Davina even more lovely by comparison. Or perhaps it was her. The simple fact that Davina was breathtaking in every room, day or night, cotton dress or glittering gown, awake or asleep. It was merely a fact of this life.

What I was not prepared for was the feeling of longing, itching beneath my skin, to introduce her as my wife once more. It was almost a compulsion, this desire to have her paraded around this estate—that I didn't want—as mine.

But it was becoming more and more clear that I didn't just want to *call* her mine. I wanted her to *be* mine. I had slipped into the role of her husband more naturally than any I'd tried before. Somehow, I knew that stepping out of the guise wouldn't be nearly so easy.

A middle-aged maid I recognized from my youth backed into the room with a tray of tea things—not the good china, I noted. She wore a housekeeper's cap so she must have received a promotion since my last visit.

"My lord," she said with a curtsy and a pinched expression. It certainly wasn't a warm welcome from the staff.

"Thank you, Mrs..."

"Reed."

"Thank you, Mrs. Reed."

"Indeed. We're seeing to the earl's chambers, my lord. Is there anything else?"

"Any chambers will do, one for each of us. And would it

be too much trouble for another two rooms? We have companions who are just seeing to the horses."

She *humphed* ambiguously, not even raising a brow at the direction for the extra set of rooms. "They'll be wanting supper, too, I expect?"

"Five of us, for supper, if you don't mind. We borrowed my brother-in-law's wagon and his hand needs to return."

She offered nothing more than a noncommittal hum before sweeping out of the room.

"Well, that was odd," Davina muttered.

"What was?"

"*That* was not the appropriate greeting for a lord returning to his estate after an extended absence. Let alone greeting him for the first time after the title." She reached forward to the tea tray and poured two cups.

"Well, they were not expecting us."

"Of course. You couldn't expect a receiving line. But you should expect something more than blatant hostility." She added a splash of milk to one cup and to the other, she dropped in three spoons of sugar. Without so much as a comment, she passed me the second.

"How do you know how I take my tea?"

"You've the sweetest sweet tooth I've ever seen. I'm sure you'd prefer more, just as you'd prefer coffee. But you would see any more than three spoons as excessive."

"Can you do this with everyone? Guess their tea preferences?"

"Oh yes. It's something they teach all accomplished ladies."

"Really?" I sipped with interest. The sugar was perfect. The tea itself, however, was bitter and astringent underneath the saccharine top note.

"No," she replied, absolutely stone-faced. After a delicate sip, she set her cup back on the table, with a nose crinkle. Mrs.

Reed had provided no accompaniment to the over-steeped brew, which was a disappointment. I could've used a biscuit. "This tea is a personal insult, Kit."

"It just sat a bit too long is all."

"Something is amiss."

"They're probably just busy readying the rooms. We were unexpected," I repeated.

"The earl's rooms should always be ready, Kit. Always. And another two guest rooms? That is nothing."

"But..."

"Kit, please. Believe me in this?" Her doe eyes pricked at my heart.

"I believe you," I assured her. "I just cannot countenance it."

Without warning, she rose and held her hand out for me to take. "Come, we're exploring."

"What? But we need to wait for..."

"Wait for what? It's your house, for better or worse. Everything is yours. And no one is coming to meet us."

"But surely Mrs. Reed will give us a tour."

"Kit," she said, snapping the *t*. "Come on an adventure with me." The fingers hovering in front of me wiggled in invitation.

And that was all that I needed. I clasped her hand and let her haul me off the settee.

"Really?" Davina grinned at me, her smile reaching the corners of her eyes.

"Yes, but you'll have to get *me* out of trouble if we find any."

"I can do that." With a gentle tug, she made for the door. At the threshold, she peered both directions before towing me along after her.

The hall was dim with the sconces unlit. I vaguely recalled the first room we peered into serving as a music room. There were sheets drawn over the furnishings and cobwebs in the corners.

"How many spiders do you suppose it takes to make that many cobwebs?" I whispered into her ear from my place crowding her against the doorframe.

She whirled around, brow furrowed. "Ugh, Kit! Why would you say something like that?"

"Curiosity," I said with false nonchalance. "Dozens? Or perhaps hundreds, do you think?"

She let out what could only be termed a grunt of frustration and stomped on my shoe. It was safe to assume she was holding back. I had no doubt she could make me wince if she really wanted to, but her effort was barely a pressure. I bit the inside of my lip, desperately trying to hold back a smile.

"Be careful there, little menace. I could lose a toe and then where would you be?"

"You would be perfectly fine without a toe. You're lucky that is all I've done for that suggestion. I have to *sleep* here tonight, Christopher."

I brushed aside the implied threat to my manhood. Her tone was breezy, surely she wasn't serious. "Ah, but I'm not overly inclined to help those who cause amputation to my person, even minor ones. So you would be stuck here. In Lincolnshire. In this house inhabited entirely by spiders."

With an impertinent little pirouette, accompanied by a less delicate huff, she continued down the hall to the next room and peered inside.

The billiards room was in a similar state to the music room and I watched, leaning against the doorframe, as she eyed the cobwebs warily.

I tucked a loose curl behind her ear. "Don't worry, I'll protect you from wayward arachnids."

Her lips parted on a breath as she turned to face me. I couldn't bring myself to pull my improper hand from her cheek. A pink tongue darted between her heart-shaped lips to wet them. I put forth a formidable fight against the groan the sight induced, but if her breathy gasp was any indication, I wasn't successful.

She pulled away from my hand and trailed deeper along the hall. "Just remember this moment when I wake you tonight with my night terrors. You've no one to blame but yourself."

"I have no regrets," I retorted, following at a more sedate pace. Her skirts swished in irritation.

"You say that now."

I stepped forward and caught her hand on the backswing of a flustered step, tugging her back to face me. "I'll mean it tonight too."

In the dim of the hall, her eyes were darker. Or perhaps it wasn't the light. Perhaps her eyes darkened with the same longing I was sure mine showed. And what on earth did that mean? And what should I do about it if I was right?

"Kit..." I could only begin to guess where she intended to take the thought. Regardless, it was interrupted when that curl escaped from behind her ear. And I couldn't very well allow it to go untucked again, could I? "You have to stop that," she whispered, low and silken.

I would've found the speech more convincing if she hadn't chosen that moment to lean into my touch, if her hand hadn't come up, clutching my own as I tried to heed her.

"We're on a mission," she added, lacing her fingers atop mine. My thumb was free to trace the bone of her cheek. "Important investigation to do..."

"All right," I graveled, but made no move to separate.

"We shouldn't be able to... do this—here. There should be people—footmen, maids. We should be scandalizing someone like this..." she trailed off when I slipped my hand lower, moving to thumb her jaw.

"'M just a man, touching his wife. Nothing scandalous to see here."

Her throat bobbed under my fingers. "We should—we need—focus. Adventures go best when you're focused."

"Am I finally to learn the secrets of Lady Davina's adventures?" I threw the name—her title—out in a desperate attempt to remind my body just how inappropriate our positions were.

It was entirely ineffectual. Instead, my feet, entirely without permission, took a step closer.

We were in the middle of the hall, she could have stepped back, maintained the distance easily. But she stayed precisely where she was, letting me crowd her.

"Not all of them. If you learned all of them you would too easily prevent future adventures."

"I wouldn't dream of it. My days would be dreadfully dull without them. And you wouldn't be Davina without your adventures."

A single finger of her free hand caught the edge of my waistcoat and clung there.

"You hate my adventures." Her retort wasn't sharp, but it was less breathy.

"I hate when you put yourself in danger. The rest—do you remember that day? With the pirate whiskey?" At her nod, I continued. "It was barely a fortnight after my father passed. It was a struggle to dress every morning. And that night... I went home and laughed for nearly a quarter of an hour. Your adventures—the ones without threat to life or limb—are my favorite part of any day."

"You did?"

"Davina... these last days have been, without a doubt, the most ridiculous hours of my life. I haven't the foggiest idea how I'm going to get you out of this with your reputation unscathed. I've lied to my family. I've been nauseated nearly the entire way. And on occasion, you would test the patience of a saint. But—and I may owe this to the head injury—there's a part of me that doesn't want to reach Scotland. I don't want to hand you over to your brother. Do you know how ordinary the rest of my life will seem by comparison? You're extraordinary, Davina."

For an unending minute, she said nothing. Her amber gaze sought something on my face, in my expression. Finally, her lips parted to speak at the same time that footsteps echoed around the bend we hadn't yet reached down the hall.

It was instinct that moved me. I caught her upper arm and pulled her into the nearest room and around the corner. That same instinct drove me to press her against the wall behind the open door, to cage her there.

I heard the precise moment the intruder's feet found the carpet lining the hall on the other side of the door. Through the crack between the door and the frame, the dull skirts of Mrs. Reed swished passed.

And then my eyes found Davina's. Burning embers in the light of whatever room we'd found ourselves in, they were wide and soft. Her breath fell in sharp pants against my neck, tantalizing. Her scent, earthy, spicy, citrus wrapped around us.

When her perfect plump lips formed the sounds of my name, something inside me broke. My hand found her jaw at the same moment my lips found hers.

Our lips met and the world split in two.

Before. And after.

The Kit before was good and noble and would never kiss a lady. This Kit, the new Kit, was going to ravish Davina against this wall until she was as mad as she made me.

Honor be damned.

Twenty-Two

LEIGHTON HALL—APRIL 12, 1817

DAVINA

K<small>IT</small>'<small>S</small> <small>KISS</small> was entirely unexpected, and entirely inevitable. In some ways, I had been waiting, my breath bated, since we woke that morning, since I proclaimed myself his wife, since I abducted him. Now that he was finally claiming me as his own, I could breathe again.

But I never would have anticipated he would kiss like *this*. That it should feel...

This wasn't the delicate pressing of lips I would have expected from him. A gentle tasting of one lip, then the other.

Nor was it the wild claiming of a man broken—though I sensed I may have broken him just a little.

This kiss was a systematic, methodical, sensual destruction of every last one of my defenses—the very thoughts in my head.

His impossibly full lips were even smoother against mine than I could believe. The brush of his overgrown stubble against my hand that made its way to his jaw was a sharp, erotic contrast. I guided that jaw, pulling him even closer.

And Kit responded by catching both my hands in his own, and pressing them back against the wall, slotting his leg between mine and erasing every whisper of space between us.

A whimper escaped from somewhere in my chest but he swallowed it as his own. Kit took it as a sign of permission to set about weakening my knees with the movement of his tongue. Was this what everyone felt? This ache? This fire? This dizzying desire?

Kit slipped his fingers between mine and tightened his grip when he dipped from my lips to torture my jaw. And something about it was so perfectly *Kit* that my heart tripped in swirls of lust fogging my head.

"Kit..."

"If you want me to stop..." His words ghosted against the skin of my neck. "I need you to tell me."

My response was instinctive, guttural, desperate. "Don't stop." I fought to free a hand that he released easily, sensing my intent. Once untangled from his fingers, it sought curls. Dark, messy curls that should have been coarse but were cloud soft.

"Davina," he groaned. The whiskey-soaked curse echoing through my mind only to be cast aside for sensation when his newly freed hand traced the edge of my ribcage. Up, up, up, it settled just below my breast, waiting for permission once again.

Kit, my Kit, grumpy, honorable Kit... The hand in his hair tightened to a fist, and apparently his hair had a direct connection to his hips because they thrust forward before he pulled back. Laudanum-heavy eyes found mine.

"Yes." I told him, nodding.

He swallowed roughly, the thumb hovering beneath my breast brushing upward. "Yes?"

"Yes," I affirmed.

"Fuck," he muttered as he released the hand still pinned to

the wall in favor of my neck, crashing our lips together at the precise moment his other hand found the swell of my breast.

Kit was careful with me. He didn't push or grab. He caressed. He teased. He drove me out of my mind in the most perfectly restrained way.

But the tightness in his shoulders, the sure sweep of his tongue, the grind of his hips... He was hanging by a thread. The devious part of me wanted to snip it, wanted to know, to see, to feel what Kit could do when he was untethered.

I rather thought he might ruin me, and not in the way everyone whispered about when they spoke of garden walks and empty alcoves. No, in a way that was specific to me. Because I never wanted to stop. And that way led to ruin. Ruin and something I'd never considered before.

Something more.

And then his tongue swept away even that thought. He was relentless, my Kit. I'd always known that. He was determined and focused in his work. And apparently in his single-minded destruction of every one of my defenses.

With one last press of his lips against mine, they trailed back down my jaw. His breath blowing my loose waves, brushing them against my neck. And when he tilted just right, his own curls joined in the dance against my flesh.

Then his lips darted lower still, dangerously low. His tongue traced the neckline of my bodice right over where his hand continued working my breast.

He would pause, he would pull away, wait for my affirmation, and I couldn't bear to have his lips from me that long. "Yes," I demanded, pinning his head in place. I felt more than heard his breathy chuckle.

Think me a wanton all you want, Christopher Summers. You made me so.

The hand over my bodice pulled away only so far as to tug

it down. It didn't matter that it was purposeful and temporary, my whimper was entirely involuntary.

"Davina... I'd never dreamed..."

One more yank, and my breasts popped free from beneath my corset. Before I had the chance to feel the chill, he slid to his knees. There he wrapped his lips around one and his hand across the other. My hands dug into the mess of his curls, pinning him in place.

He did something with his tongue at the same time he did something else with his hand and my head fell back to the wall with a *thunk*.

His lips abandoned my breast against the pull of my hands. "Are you all right?"

I forced my head back down to meet his gaze. "You won't be if you don't get back to it."

The smile started in the outer corner of his eyes. It bloomed down his cheeks, before it finally found a home on his lips. Finally, a full, complete, entire smile.

My heart skidded to a stop before starting again in a rush. One of my hands abandoned the bird's nest I'd made of his hair, to brush my thumb across his lower lip, tracing the new expression, memorizing it. I needed to keep this one safe, cherished forever.

He pressed a kiss to my palm, the smile returning as soon as his lips left my skin. There was something different about it this time, though. This one was more tender, softer, more full of...

Oh.

My breath caught as I waited for the instinctive panic, for the sheer horror that my realization was sure to bring forth. Before it could, he leaned forward once again and captured the other nipple between his quirked lips.

My head fell back again, but this time Kit's free hand was there waiting, slipping between my crown and the wall. He cradled the nape of my neck as he set about removing every other thought from my head with his lips and tongue and delightfully inquisitive fingers.

But even as he brought me to the edge of sanity, even as my fingers tangled in his curls, refusing to allow him a breath, his hand was a steady, sure presence.

Kit was quite thoroughly demonstrating that there was more to him than I had ever thought. But he was still *Kit*. And I was always safe with him.

"Davina..." The word was barely audible, probably not even intended for me to hear, but my body reacted instinctively to my graveled name. The sensitive cleft of my legs longing for his thigh once again.

I yanked inelegantly on his hair, pulling him to his feet with a demanding, "Up."

He allowed me to drag him about as he always did, offering little more than a chuckle, edged with self-satisfaction.

With his thumb—on the hand protecting me from self-injury—he brushed my temple. He gazed at me with the same adoration from earlier, and now that I saw the expression closer, I realized it was entirely familiar. He wore it often around me. This feeling—the one I wasn't willing to name, even in my head—wasn't new for him.

Those thoughts... They were too much for me. "You're supposed to be kissing me."

His smile came back, full and bright, and he pressed it to my lips. This kiss was inelegant but filled with something like joy. And over far too quickly, in spite of my efforts to keep him where he belonged.

"We should stop, Davina. We need to talk. And we shouldn't do this here."

"I don't want to talk." Even I heard the petulant whine in my tone, but it seemed that once the dam had broken Kit was rather free with his smiles. This wasn't a full one, it was more indulgent than the bright grin I'd received earlier.

"It's a shame that you cannot abduct me into ravishing you, then."

"You want me, I can feel it." And I could, pressing against my hip. Intriguing in all its mysteries.

"Where did..." He shook his head. "Never mind, I don't want to know. Of course I want you, I've spent two-thirds of this damned trip trying to ensure you *didn't* notice how much I want you. That doesn't change the fact that we need to talk. And I'm not going to tup a lady against the wall of this ridiculous house."

"Even if the lady wishes it?"

"Christ... Not the first time, Davina. And not at all until after we've talked. Rationally. With space between us." His gaze flicked down and a groan broke free. He set about righting my corset and dress with a reluctant little whine when he traced the—now proper—cut of my bodice. "And many more layers on you. Do you have a pelisse? Can you wear it with a spencer underneath?"

"Absolutely not. If you insist on putting a stop to our fun, I insist on making it as difficult for you as possible."

"Little menace," he grumbled as his forehead fell against my neck. His breath brushed against my chest reminding me of precisely where his lips had been mere moments ago. I very much regretted interrupting him now that he had seen sense.

Always responsible Mr. Summers... Though he certainly hadn't been responsible with his tongue trailing devilish delights along my breasts, now tightening at the ghost of a memory. "I have a reputation to uphold, you know."

"I've worked hard to ensure you have no such reputation," he murmured, his lips brushing along my neck with the whisper. With a thick swallow, he pulled back, his lidded gaze sweeping up and down my form. "Devastating," he breathed, shaking his head.

"A devastating mess," I added, patting the tangles atop my head. It was likely that my hair fared better than his, but only by virtue of having a more manageable natural state. His curls tumbled around his jaw in fuzzy, ill-defined ringlets, a chestnut lion's mane. *He is the devastating one.*

"You're breathtaking and you know it." Kit tucked a loose strand of hair behind my ear before pulling back. His hand trailed down my neck, shoulder, arm, to twirl his fingers in mine. With a feigned grunt, he pulled me off the wall and turned to examine the room we'd found.

It was the first time I recalled the world outside of Kit in some time—minutes, hours, days, eons—who cared? We had found a study. And if the massive mahogany desk was any indication, a study belonging to someone who believed the size of the desk indicated the import of the man behind it.

It was cleared of paperwork, nothing like Kit's usual cluttered piles in his offices. Behind it were neat shelves with aesthetically pleasing books. Unlike the other room we had explored, there were no cobwebs lining the corners. Someone was using this room—even if they hadn't enough work to cover the desk's surface.

There was a single window beside the desk, fortunately without a direct line of sight to the space beside the door. The walls had been papered a deep hunter-green stripe and the curtains were a heavy velvet. Even they bore no hint of dust.

"Why is this room so much cleaner than the others?" I mused.

"I was wondering that myself." Kit dropped my hand to sidle behind the desk and tug on a drawer. It didn't budge. He tried another to the same effect. "All locked."

I studied the bookshelf with vague disinterest. Not a single tome had a spine cracked. They were here to be seen, not read.

I let my fingernail tap as I dragged it along the spines, *click, click, click.*

And then my nail caught, just a bit, barely noticeable, really. It had tripped on the barely bent spine of *The Mysteries of Udolpho*. I slid it from the shelf. It was suspiciously light for the thickness, and I knew.

When I flipped it open, my suspicions were confirmed—hollowed.

Inside there was only a small silver key. I turned, key in hand, to give it to Kit. I was met with an open-mouthed gape.

"How did you... Menace." He plucked the key from my hand, sheathed it in the desk, and turned it with a creak before the familiar *snikt* of the lock falling open echoed through the room. "Absolute menace..."

~

KIT

It wasn't the first time I had been grateful Davina was on my side. But it was a pleasant reminder. She may have run off with half-baked ideas at times, but in the midst of those ideas, her instincts were absolutely brilliant—brilliant, beautiful, and just the tiniest bit terrifying.

And really, why had I thought to stop kissing her? *That* had been a wretched idea. I was a dolt, obviously. Which was why I plucked the key from her hand and slid it into the lock instead of ravishing her on the desk.

The drawer raked along the desk as I slid it free. The top was filled with nothing but blank parchment, spare quills, and inkwells. The next, though, was where my skill set came in.

Davina, determined to ruin me, pressed herself up to sit on the edge of the desk. She peered over when I pulled the drawer out farther and hauled a few of the files out. I set them beside her as I settled into the green leather chair behind the desk.

"What are we looking for?" she chirped.

"I'll know it when I find it. But something is wrong here. And we never should have been left alone as long as we have without notice."

"Oh, I cannot lament *that*."

My eyelids slipped shut against that mental image until I was able to will it away. Determined to distract myself from her temptation, I flipped through the file. The familiar cramped scrawl of my own handwriting stared back at me. Letter after letter, newest on top, were all there. A flick through them confirmed they were the entirety of that file. The next was a more detailed accounting of the expenditures and finances. I suspected any answers I would find would be there. I also suspected I'd require blood flow to my head to comprehend it. Alas, most of mine had settled in the vicinity of my breeches.

With a sigh, I flipped the file closed and made to put it back. Davina shook her head, holding her hand out. "What?"

"Trust me?"

I could only nod as she took the file from me, then pushed off the desk and headed to the wall of books. She plucked a few off the shelf, placed the file flat on the shelf where they once lived, and settling them atop it once again. It was entirely invisible unless one knew where to look.

"Lock the desk?"

I did as she bid, then handed her the key and watched as she put it back where she'd found it.

"Why are we hiding this?" I whispered, catching her around the waist and pulling her in between the desk and my chair.

"First rule of snooping: Don't let them know you've snooped. If they do, whoever has something to hide will move whatever you want to find." Her fingers found my hair again and raked through it. The resulting shivers down my spine were delicious. "I learned that when I was seven with Xander's journals."

When she dragged her nails along my scalp, I couldn't resist leaning into the motion. "Poor Xander."

She scoffed. "Poor me, they were dreadfully dull."

"Speaking of Xander and his predicament. I have something of an idea, but I'm afraid it's terribly illegal."

"Really?" she asked, straightening up with interest.

The sound of voices came from the hall. Without warning, Davina's mouth crashed onto mine, her fingers—still tangled in my hair—kept me tugged against her. It was instinct, born of recent experience, that had my lips slotting against hers, my tongue darting to taste hers.

For a moment, I forgot the indistinct words from the hall. I forgot that this was a distraction. I forgot that there was a world outside of her. It was so easy, too easy, to forget there was anything more important than kissing Davina Hasket. I wasn't sure there was anything more important, truth be told.

Even though I'd been expecting it, it took a few seconds for the shocked gasp to penetrate my skull. The general pinched expression of disgust mixed with scandalized shock on Mrs. Reed's face. It was an interesting combination.

I couldn't help but feel a little proud. I'd never scandalized anyone before—perhaps I was falling into the role of earl at last.

"Apologies, Mrs. Reed." I rose, standing beside Davina with a hand on the small of her back. The curve fit my palm so nicely.

"My Lord, I... This is most irregular."

Davina cut in. "You must forgive us, newlyweds and all." She did something with her hips while she said it, swirling her hem around her ankles in a way that had a smile pulling at the corner of my lips.

"My Lord?"

I forced my gaze off my *wife* to the housekeeper. "Yes, Lady Leighton has recently honored me with the privilege of calling her my wife." I could feel the dopey grin taking over. The title didn't sound quite as wrong when it was Davina's.

"Oh, good Lord... Gibbs! Gibbs!" she shrieked, turned, and fled from the room calling the man's name at a pitch I wasn't sure was entirely audible to humans.

No sooner had her skirts slipped around the corner than Davina's restrained laughter escaped in a near snort. Her face found my chest as her shoulders shook with laughter. Mine came out in an occasional huff into her hair.

"What have you done to me? I was respectable once and now look at me."

"Respectable and grumpy. Now you're a happy menace like me," she retorted, peering up at me with her chin on my chest. I caught the back of her head and pulled her frame against mine before dropping a kiss on her hair.

Mrs. Reed returned, panting and breathless, with a bewildered Gibbs dragged along behind her. She was still panting his name between every breath even though he was in her possession.

The man dug his heels in at the sight of Davina and me wrapped up in each other. "My Lord?"

Oh, good. This conversation again.

Before I could reply, Mrs. Reed wheezed out the word, "Wife."

Gibbs straightened, his eyes widening, darting between Mrs. Reed and us.

Who had they assumed she was? "Yes, I'm pleased to introduce Lady Leighton."

"Lady... My lady, I am all apologies. If we had known we would have had everyone available to greet you. I assure you!"

There was no discernible movement, no straightening of the spine, or shifting of the shoulders. But the expression Davina served them completely belied her kiss-reddened lips, mussed hair, and wrinkled gown. Not to mention the position we had just been caught in. She was every bit the duchess she had spent her life training to be.

"But not Lord Leighton?" She leaned back against my palm in apology for the title, but it didn't twinge in quite the same way when I heard it in connection to its match.

"We— That is— My lady..." Mrs. Reed stammered.

"Hmm." Davina managed to convey a great deal in that single note—disapproval, disbelief, disinterest, and a disinclination to hear more. "I trust preparations have begun for supper," she added pointedly. If the gulp Mrs. Reed gave was any indication, it wasn't a very impressive supper if they had.

"Of course, my lady. But if you had any requests, we would be delighted to accommodate them."

"I have none. But perhaps Lord Leighton does."

Three sets of eyes shot to me, though Davina's were filled with mirth. "None at all," I added with a gentle flick to her back. It would be a wonder if she felt it through the corset, but it made me feel better to reprimand her mischief.

"My lady, we could—a tour, perhaps—would be appropriate?" Mrs. Reed bumbled through the offer.

"Oh no, Lord Leighton and I were exploring perfectly well on our own." I couldn't disagree with her on that point. I'd enjoyed my earlier exploration of her person quite thoroughly.

Both looked like they wanted to protest, but Davina's unflinchingly innocent yet commanding countenance left them no room to argue. Her brow lifted a quarter of an inch and they both backed out of the room slowly.

"How did you manage that?"

"What do you mean?" She turned in my arms, straightening my cravat.

"Since I was a child—those two stalked me around this place like a wildcat with prey, convinced I was going to break something or go somewhere I wasn't supposed to."

"It's your house. Break anything you'd like." Her hand slid down to find mine, lacing our fingers together before leading me out of the room.

"Your world is strange."

"It's your world too," she replied, distractedly pulling me along after her to the ostentatious staircase at the front of the house.

"Perhaps." Something about my tone made her pause and turn to me. She understood—Davina always understood—the implications. I wasn't ready for more discussion on that subject, at least not at the foot of the stairs, so I tipped my head toward the steps. She took the encouragement and we started up together.

Once at the top, she pulled me down the hall to—if the open door was any indication—one of the newly aired rooms. It was, of course, the moment I realized the terrible mistake I'd just made.

I was about to be *alone*. With Davina. Near a bed. And a locking door.

I wasn't fool enough to think my honor and will would be any stronger there than they had been in the study. If she noticed the thickening of my steps, she didn't acknowledge it in any way.

"Davina…"

When she turned to face me at the threshold, I was certain she'd decided to ignore my efforts. The innocence of her smile was entirely too feigned.

And then she destroyed me with a single sentence.

"Come to bed, Kit."

Twenty-Three

LEIGHTON HALL—APRIL 12, 1817

DAVINA

His head hinged back on his neck to look askance at the ceiling. Or possibly a deity he couldn't see. I wasn't *trying* to torture him precisely. But now that I'd discovered I was capable of it... Well, I wouldn't make the effort to abstain either.

Under his breath I caught the word *menace* between irritated, indistinguishable mutterings and had to catch my lower lip between my teeth, lest my grin give me away entirely.

In spite of his grumblings, he followed me when I dipped inside and held the door for him. That was the extent of his acquiescence though. His gaze cast about the dark navy fabrics and rich cherry wood of the furnishings. With a mumbled curse, he pointed at the bed. "You, sit there."

He found a wooden chair near the washstand and dumped the towel unceremoniously on the floor. He spun the chair around so the back faced me and then straddled it. *All the way across the room.*

"Is this necessary?"

"Absolutely it is. If we could converse privately with a wall between us, that would be necessary. Ideally, there would be a small country between us but that seems impractical."

"You really think that little of your restraint?"

"Yes, and I think yours is nonexistent."

I let the smile slip across my face. "You're not wrong. But where is the fun in restraint?"

He shot me a familiar disapproving look. They were becoming less frequent and much less severe. "We could have fun with restraints. But first, we have two very serious conversations to have. Which would you like first?"

I wasn't entirely certain what he meant by the first comment, but I set it aside. I rather hoped one of the conversations would end with little in the way of conversation. Best to get practical matters out of the way first. "You mentioned you had a plan for how to help Xander."

"*Plan* is maybe too strong a word. And it's considered fraud in at least"—he lifted fingers as though counting—"seven countries."

"Do tell."

"The good news is he's in Scotland—no need for the bans, only two witnesses. We could find a willing woman to claim the babe and wed your brother. We would only need a few easily bribed witnesses to swear the wedding took place months ago." My disappointment must have shown on my face because he asked, "What?"

"I just... He and Tom shouldn't have to live a lie."

Kit's brows hit his hairline. "Tom? Tom Grayson? My brother-in-law, Tom?"

Damn, I'd forgotten I'd left that part out. "Yes?" It wasn't intended as a question, but it sounded that way.

Kit considered for a moment, head tilting like an adorable spaniel's before he released an ambiguous, "Hmm," paired with a shrug.

"I don't know what that means."

"Oh, just that Katie will be quite disappointed. She had grand romantic plans for him."

"That's all?" Incredulity dripped from my voice.

"I suppose he aims quite high, doesn't he? Duke and all... Though I cannot fault him for his choice. There is a certain appeal to a Hasket sibling..." He gave me one of his quarter smiles, an edge to his tone that I quite liked.

I indulged him with a put-upon sigh and crossed my legs at the knee in a way my governess would have screeched about. "Any other ideas?"

"A more blatant fraud. We would find a recently deceased, unmarried woman of marriageable age. Then we swear she and your brother were wed before the babe was born and she died in childbirth. Or we create a woman entirely—that would probably be best. She could be just unsuitable enough that society will assume he ran to Scotland because she wasn't an appropriate choice. Then we simply explain to the clergyman that the mother passed when we have the lad baptized. We'll need to find a way to forge the mother's burial records, of course. But it shouldn't be too difficult."

"You were not in jest when you mentioned fraud."

"I wasn't," he agreed, shaking his head simultaneously.

"Devious..." she teased, brow arched in appreciation. "Well, it's better than the nothing I had thought up."

"That is why your brother pays me so well."

"Does he?"

He chuckled. "Oh yes, I get a bonus every time I rescue you from whatever mess you've gotten yourself into. I expect I'll be able to live on what he gives me for this adventure until I die. Assuming, of course, that he doesn't have me arrested instead."

"I wouldn't let him have you arrested."

"That's very kind of you." His gaze flicked to my lips and I knew his thoughts were not far from my own. "We had another topic to cover—"

"We were covering it quite well before you decided to be sensible." His eyes slid shut on a single huff of laughter.

"Davina..." he growled, low and warning. "I cannot ravish you against a wall."

"I think we just proved that you can. Quite well, in fact."

A flush settled across his cheeks and rose up to his ears as he cleared his throat uncomfortably. "As gratifying as that is to hear... it won't happen again."

"Do you not wish to ravish me on this bed?"

His closed as he shook his head with a tiny smile pulling at the corners of his lips. "Very much, but I won't."

"Why not? Do you want me to do the ravishing?"

"Lord no." My surprise must have been apparent because he continued. "It might actually kill me."

"Well, I don't understand what the problem is."

"It was inappropriate. We're not actually married."

Ah, the honor was back, and the frown. Truly, Kit was much happier when he forgot the rules. I uncrossed my legs and pressed myself off the bed. "In the eyes of absolutely everyone here... we are married."

At my first step toward him, he scrambled off the chair and backed away. "That's not the point."

"There's absolutely no difference between our declaration and what Xander will do when we arrive."

His back met a wall and he winced as I continued to advance, closing the gap in a few short steps. I caged him to the wall with my hands on each side of him in precisely the same way he had me.

"There is one fundamental fact. And it is that you have no wish to be married to me." There was a strained desperation in his tone that had me stilling my pursuit.

"No one need know. Gentlemen have dalliances all the time."

"One, you are a lady, not a gentleman. A lady whose family has placed their trust in me time and time again. And two, gentlemen may have dalliances, but I'm not a gentleman."

The last sentence tripped around in my head as I struggled to interpret it. "What does that mean?" His gaze lowered, likely aiming for the ground but they were distracted by my bosom on the way.

"It means we shouldn't have done that earlier. It was wrong."

"Kit, tell me."

His voice dipped low. "Gentlemen may have dalliances. I do not," he repeated. Something warm and possessive curled in my belly as understanding took hold. My smile turned predatory. He groaned, his forehead falling to my shoulder. "That wasn't an invitation."

Even as his response pleased me, I knew it made my efforts less likely to succeed. Any other man of six and twenty who had never laid with a woman would be an easy mark. But Kit... It would only make him more determined. "How?"

He pulled back from my shoulder, gaze catching mine. "When would I have time? I spend all my time chasing after you."

"I'm not going to succeed in seducing you, am I?"

With a gentle hand, he tucked a still-loose curl behind my ear. "Not for lack of desire. But if you hope to succeed, you'll have to marry me first."

Instinctive incredulity thrust the word from my lips. "What?"

His fingertips settled against my neck, warm and soft, while his thumb traced my lower lip. He held me in place and leaned in with a delicate kiss. Lips still brushing mine, he whispered, "Marry me. Marry me and you can do whatever you want with me. Marry me and I'm yours."

"What?" I repeated dimly, as he pulled back just enough to meet my befuddled gaze.

"I know you've no wish to marry anyone. I don't understand it, but I don't need to. But I cannot lie with you unless we're wed. I cannot have only a part of you. I won't be able to give you up. It will be nearly impossible as it is. Davina, I want it all."

My heart was in my throat, a throbbing knot trapped there by his earnest gaze. "Kit, I..."

"Don't say no. Don't say anything yet. Give me the rest of our journey. Think about it. I don't want you to give up your adventures. I want to go on a new one with you, together."

"I infuriate you."

It was his smile—a quarter one—that screamed predation this time. "Aye, you do. In the best possible way. I want to spend the rest of my life being infuriated by you."

"We could not be more different."

His gaze dropped down, his hand caught mine. He brought it up between us as he slid our palms together. One by one his fingers slid between mine and his other hand came up and settled atop mine, pushing my finger to clasp his. "We fit. You and me, we bring out the best in each other."

"Kit..." I tried again. The hand that wasn't clutching mine caught my jaw again. How could so new a sensation feel so comfortable, so right, after a handful of occurrences?

"Don't... Remember? You don't have to say anything." He sealed that promise with another kiss, not the sensual dance of tongues and teeth from earlier. Instead a mere, desperate, pressing of lips. A pressing that left me dizzy and weak-kneed.

I didn't want to be married—I didn't. I knew that. But for some strange reason, I was struggling to remember a single reason why. I was struggling to remember anything but the feel of Kit's lips on mine and his woody, inky scent around me.

When he pulled away, it was abrupt and my lips chased his instinctively, only to be met with empty air and a self-satisfied chuckle.

"Why are you being so difficult?" I whined.

"You get your way far too often. It's good for you to be denied on occasion." He was pleased with himself, far too pleased. Men who proposed and received no response really ought not wear such a smug expression.

"When did you become so patronizing?"

Something about the insult had him gifting me a full smile. This one was quick, easy. His eyes and lips were in perfect sync, his cheeks rising with the grin. "You're so beautiful," he replied, completely ignoring my very valid criticism.

Unfortunately, his compliment combined with the deadly smile had the effect of dampening my frustration.

His hand slid down from my neck to span the width of my shoulder.

"You're truly not going to kiss me properly again unless I agree to wed you?"

That easy smile turned wicked in a flash, his eyes darkening. And oh, I felt that expression in delicate areas that ladies weren't supposed to know anything about. Whatever he said next, it was about to wreck me.

"I never said *that*. I said I wouldn't lie with you until we were wed. But I suspect I'll need every tool at my disposal to convince you to say yes."

"What?" I repeated for a third time, decidedly annoyed but unable to form another word.

"I have no intention of making it easy for you to say no. We could be good—great—together."

"And you intend to do this by seducing me?"

His lips found mine again. "Just a little," he whispered before claiming them once again.

Twenty-Four

LEIGHTON HALL—APRIL 12, 1817

KIT

Kissing her like this—it was the most exquisite torture known to man or beast. Excitement, lust, something dangerously like love thrummed through my veins. Most of my head was entirely focused on drawing more of the enticing little whimpers from her throat, appreciating the salty, musky taste of said throat, and tracing the curve of her spine. It was a heady, powerful feeling, one that was tempered by a sense of desperation, of preemptive heartache.

She didn't want to marry *anyone*. And I thought to convince her to marry *me*? The girl who had everything, and I had nothing more to offer her than inexperienced fumblings and my heart. A smarter man would have taken what she offered and treasured the memory when it was over. A better man wouldn't be pulling her hips tighter against the hardness in his trousers. Why couldn't I be smarter or better?

But then I wouldn't know the delicious misery of her hands in my hair and on my chest. I wouldn't know the curve of her breasts or the taste of her lips. All tinged with the bittersweet knowledge that this was all I would have.

Even as I clutched her tighter, I vowed not to give up. It certainly wasn't the worst plan I'd ever been involved in. Davina was impulsive. She'd been denied nothing for her entire life. She might fold with the first denial. I rather doubted it, but I could dream.

The hand on my chest trailed surreptitiously downward. Oh, my little menace was playing dirty. That was fair, if I could try to seduce her into a marriage, she was well within her rights to test my will.

I caught the hand as it neared my lower abdomen and laced our fingers together. She gave an irritated little "Humph" against my lips.

It was followed immediately by a pointed cough, and not from her lips. When recognition finally dawned, it was a bucket of icy water over my head. Dragging my lips from hers was nearly painful. When I met the bemused gaze of Rory over her head, I couldn't hold back my groan.

"Milord," she drawled with a smirk, leaning against the door.

My head fell back with a *thunk* against the wall and I dragged a calming hand across my lower face. My lips were tender from Davina's attentions.

"Rory."

Davina glanced behind her before burying her face in my chest coquettishly. I wouldn't have expected it of her and the gesture left me feeling protective. I squeezed her hand in mine, dragging my other hand down her back.

"Supper is ready if ye two *newlyweds* are finished."

"Thank you, Rory," I said, dismissing her.

She responded by crossing her arms, a single brow tipping skyward.

"Your disapproval is noted," I added.

"Good, release the debutante."

"I want it added for the record that *she* is the one who seduced *me*."

"Hey!" Davina's head popped up from my shoulder with a glare.

Rory chuckled. "I well believe it. I was sure yer ballocks would shrivel and fall off before ye touched her. But I should remind ye that yer not actually wed."

"I was working on that," I retorted over Davina's indignant noises of protest.

Rory blinked slowly before shaking her head derisively. "Dafty, the pair of ye. Come on, supper is getting cold."

Davina pulled away and turned to the door. That was the precise moment I recognized the problem associated with leaving this room.

"You two go ahead, I'll catch up."

"'M sure ye will," Rory retorted, a knowing amusement in her tone. She caught Davina about the waist when she reached the door and dragged her into the hall.

I was left alone with overly tight trousers to consider obscure taxation laws until they loosened.

～

Supper began as a stilted affair, with Mrs. Reed and Gibbs casting curious gazes at Rory and Alfie between courses.

Alfie, as usual, was blissfully unaware of any subtext occurring around him and had a roasted chicken leg in each hand. Why one was any different from the other was anyone's guess.

Originally the housekeeper had set Davina and me at opposite ends of the long table. I wasn't interested in that at all and moved my seat beside her when I arrived a few minutes after everyone else.

When both Mrs. Reed and the butler had left the room for a moment, Davina whispered, "Where are the footmen?"

"There's hardly anyone in the stables," Alfie added, moving to the potatoes, fortunately with a fork. "Just a groom."

I had a rising suspicion of what was happening here, but I didn't want to believe it. Not until I reviewed the documents anyway. My gut twisted uncomfortably at the thought. Truth be told, I'd studiously avoided it since we had arrived. Because it would mean that I was no better than Hugh. And I prided myself in being a better man than my sister's husband in all things.

Gibbs returned with a new bottle of wine, gifting me with a more natural excuse for a change of subject. "How long do you suppose until we reach our destination?" I asked Rory. Alfie was too distracted snatching at his new glass of wine.

Rory plucked the glass right out of his hand and swapped it with her water goblet. "With the carriage in the stables? And fresh horses? It'll depend on whether ye want to stop for the night. Can manage in a bit over two days, if we dinnae stop. Three's more reasonable though."

Three days... three days to convince Davina to abandon her lifetime determination to never wed and marry me in spite of herself. It wasn't enough time, not nearly enough.

If I were being honest with myself, I knew I'd be unlikely to succeed if I had a hundred years. Davina's gaze caught mine, something unreadable in her chestnut eyes. I wanted to believe she was sharing my sentiments. But that was the delusion of a man half in love with a woman he had no business touching.

Gibbs still lingered, not particularly surreptitiously, beside the door. His expression shifted seamlessly between derision at Alfie's table manners and intrigue as he searched Davina and me for evidence of... I didn't know what. If I were being generous, both were more than fair. If Davina were my wife, if we were to take up the earldom and settle into a life here, our relationship would set the tone of the house. But since we were not and would not, the interest mostly chafed. And Alfie's table manners were truly appalling. I'd missed it when we were at Lizzie's house, distracted by her brood.

Rory, apparently also having had enough, slammed her fork to her plate. "For fuck's sake, lad. Chew yer damned food."

At the curse, Gibbs dropped the serving spoons he was pretending to study, jaw hanging low on his face.

I could do little more than drag an exhausted hand across my face. My life was a farce, a beautiful, ridiculous farce.

At my side, Davina let out an unladylike snort into her plate and I felt a chuckle brewing in my chest.

When she recovered, Davina called out to the scandalized butler, "That will be all for now, Gibbs. Thank you."

The man started to reply a few times, never getting further than a syllable before he finally left.

"So," Alfie mumbled between bites. "I hear you're wed again. Why did you not invite me to the wedding?"

"We're not actually wed, Alfie," I said.

"Oh, then why were ye kissing her in the study?"

I gestured over to Davina to handle that one. "It was a ruse."

"Was it a ruse in the bedroom too?" Rory looked positively tickled by the situation, speared a potato, and bit into it with an amused grin.

"No," Davina replied. "That was Kit refusing to blow the grounsils."

I choked on the bite of chicken I'd managed to scrounge from Alfie's gaping maw while Rory cackled in delight.

Alfie's brow furrowed in confusion. "Of course he would. The bed's right there. It's much more comfortable. They dinnae call it a feather-bed jig for nothing."

"Alfie…" Rory sighed. "We dinnae need a list of euphemisms."

"What's a euphemism?"

"A more… delicate alternative to what ye mean."

"Oh. I thought I cannae say *fucking* in front of a lady. But then ye did. So I can?"

"You may use any euphemisms you like, Alfie. You needn't censor yourself on my account," Davina insisted.

Rory was not interested in that outcome. "No, ye'll not, lad. Yer ma will have my hide if she hears ye talking like that."

"Rory…" he whined.

"No."

The bickering continued for several moments while I very much regretted the choice to attend supper instead of requesting a tray for the feather bed. I wasn't fond of dancing, but for Davina, I could have mustered a jig.

Twenty-Five

LEIGHTON HALL—APRIL 12, 1817

DAVINA

By unspoken agreement, Kit and I refrained from more pleasurable activities after supper as we waited for Mrs. Reed and Gibbs to retire. Fortunately, it seemed that the hubbub of actual residents in the house left them both exhausted and they retired shortly after we did.

We padded barefoot through the hall, past the cacophony of snores from Alfie's room, down the stairs, and into the study by candlelight. Kit had shucked both his overcoat and waistcoat and tossed his cravat on the bed before we left the chambers. The sight of his forearms in the flickering light was so distracting I nearly tripped down the stairs. Kit's hand found my waist at the same time mine found the railing, an impressive reaction truly.

My innate love of an adventure warred with my newfound lust, and it was genuinely difficult to decide whether to kiss him senseless or continue to the study.

Kit's response to what was surely a wanton expression on my face was a half growl, half groan as he turned and guided me down the rest of the steps. It was heady, the understanding of what I did to him, even if I was studiously not considering his requirement.

He closed the heavy wooden door behind us, dropped my hand, and pulled my candle from the other. A flush rose up my neck at the sight of *the wall*. My lips were still swollen from his attentions there and I wanted nothing more than to worsen them.

A few years ago, Celine finally gave in to my whining and we had a *little talk*. It was mostly her desperate attempt to prevent conception or disease as she didn't trust me to refrain from liaisons. Cee was a practical woman. She didn't object to discreet, safe arrangements. She had been rather graphic when she described all the ways a man and a woman might find pleasure. Most of her explanations hadn't seemed overly pleasant at the time, but they were suddenly very intriguing. One in particular... Well, I couldn't help but wonder if my skin would tingle everywhere the way it had when Kit's beard met the skin of my jaw.

"Absolutely not," he grumbled behind me. He spun me around to face him, hands fastened on my shoulders. "No walls. No floors. Not for the first time. And not until after you've promised to be mine."

"But—"

"I'm a determined man, Davina. Once I decide something, I'm not easily swayed. And I've had years of practice denying my attraction to you."

"What?" He'd reduced me to an imbecile who only knew a single word once again. It was an irritating talent.

"Oh, didn't you know? I've been besotted forever." He offered a cheeky grin. If I hadn't already seen his true smile, I might have counted it as a whole one. "Since the pirate whiskey, at least. Before, really, but I didn't realize it until that day."

"No, you weren't," I insisted.

"I was. You wore that peach dress. Speaking of— I will be absolutely devastated if the mud has rendered it unwearable." His hands slid from my shoulders and traced, featherlight, down to catch my hands.

"Usually you were all covered with lace and ribbons and finery, and it wasn't hard to remember that you were so far above me. No point in falling in love with a goddess, after all. But that day you were a just... a woman. That was when I knew."

"A peach dress? That's it?"

"I told you, it was just that peach dress. But like I said, you were always lovely and lively. You made me laugh, even when I shouldn't. My heart always nearly fell out of my chest when you'd done something absurdly dangerous. But I think I knew there was no point to those thoughts, so I never followed them to their conclusion. You opened the box that day, though, and I've never been able to stuff it all back in."

"Kit, that was more than a year ago."

"Aye, it's been a long year. But you should know what you're up against. I'm in the practice of self-denial."

How did this man keep doing this to me? At every opportunity he spun me around and around until I didn't know which way was up and the only thing I could manage was to cling to him. How had I ever thought him dull?

"Come," he whispered. "We've a mystery to solve. I need the expert." I tripped after him, my feet at first stuck somewhere near the door with my head.

He found the book where we'd left it and handed me the key. I knelt before the desk drawer and popped it open with ease, seemingly undisturbed from this afternoon. I hauled out the files and plopped them on the desk before feeling around the bottom edges of the drawer.

"What on earth are you doing?"

"Looking for false bottoms," I replied, distracted when I found a notch in the back corner. After a bit of fumbling, I determined it was a natural imperfection in the wood.

"Why?"

"Gabriel kept some of his things in the false bottom of a drawer. We might have solved his murder years earlier if we'd found it. A person who hides a key in a hollowed-out book seems like the kind of person who might employ a false bottom."

"Carry on then." He settled in the chair beside me and flipped open a folder.

I knocked on the bottom, but the *thunk* was solid. I tried the top drawer next but was met with the same disappointment.

I grumbled, finally glancing up at Kit. And that was the precise moment we both recognized my position. His throat bobbed in a way that left absolutely no question about the direction of his thoughts—the same as mine. For a moment I froze, our gazes locked.

Then a mischievous thought overtook me. I was just as capable of torturing him. I settled my hands on his knees, then slid them up his thighs before using them to press myself up.

"Menace," he muttered as I stood, then turned back to the desk to flip through pages at a rate that almost certainly indicated he wasn't reading them.

Pleased with myself, I hopped onto the desk, letting my feet swing. Though he tried to hide it, a smile graced his lips. I couldn't rate it from the angle, but it delighted me nonetheless.

"It seems this mystery is one best solved by a solicitor," I said.

"I know," he grumbled. "It's what I was worried about."

"What do you mean?"

"I'm nearly certain I know what is happening here. And I

rather suspect it's my fault." He stopped flipping, snatched the file with his letters, and flipped through them.

I watched as he checked the dates, unsure what he was searching for. Eventually he found whatever it was and skimmed the contents. "Damn. Damn, damn, damn." He spoke under his breath and mostly to himself.

"Damn," I added and thumped my fist on the desk. It earned me a half-hearted smirk—not even a quarter smile. He didn't even look up from the pages. "What is it?"

"I asked the steward to cut costs with no one in residence. I meant food expenses, firewood, candles, that sort of thing."

"And he terminated some of the staff." I'd had my suspicions as well. But this was extreme.

"I thought I was being prudent. The future earl—the *real* earl—would thank me for being respectful of his funds." His voice was tight.

"It was a mistake, Kit."

"This isn't who I am. I don't ignore problems, I solve them. I just... People lost their employment—their livelihood —because I was avoiding life. Lord only knows what else I'll find in here." He still hadn't turned to me. Instead his head hung low above the desk, curls spilling over his brow.

"It's not your fault. You didn't know."

"No, but I should have. I should have reviewed the ledgers in detail instead of just matching totals. I should have done better."

Unable to take the tight anger straining his voice, I dragged a hand through his hair before sliding onto his lap, my legs across his.

"Davina..."

"Don't dismiss me. I have something to say." One hand curled around his neck, tangled in the short curls there. The other found his chin and lifted it so his gaze meet mine. He was reluctant but eventually obeyed and I continued.

"Men train their entire lives to manage the responsibilities of an estate. And more than a few who train are rubbish at it. You lost your father. You gained responsibilities you never prepared for or wanted with no warning. You did not intentionally dismiss staff. Your steward should have clarified before taking such drastic measures."

"It's my responsibility. That I was unprepared for it is of little help to the people who lost their income. No wonder Gibbs and Mrs. Reed are ready to string me up."

His muscles were coiled tight and a frown was etched into his face, deeper than I'd seen in days. I pressed a kiss to the divots above his brow. His arm unfurled before sliding around my waist, but the tension remained.

"You cannot go back, only forward. You might inquire about rehiring anyone who is still without work. Can you afford backpay?" He nodded and turned his attention back to the documents, even while his hand tightened on my waist. "Start there. You know, though, that you have to make a choice."

"A choice about what?"

"Are you going to accept the earldom?" My question was barely audible.

His eyes slipped shut on a deep inhale and his forehead found my neck. The whisper of his breath against my skin sent my heart pattering.

"'S not a choice.'"

"What do you mean?"

"There is no choice. Not accepting it is only hurting other people. And I'd already made my decision."

"You had?"

One by one the muscles of his back uncoiled.

"When?" I pressed.

Cold settled over the skin of my neck, abrupt and unpleasant, when he pulled away to meet my gaze. "You know, Davina. You know."

I had known, he wasn't wrong about that. But the irrefutable certainty... I hated it. I couldn't be the reason he abandoned everything he'd worked for. Especially when I couldn't—*wouldn't*—be what he wanted.

"Kit—"

"Don't. It's my choice."

"Not for me—"

"It's for a hundred reasons. Obviously, pretending it will go away if I ignore it isn't working. You're only one of the reasons. Admittedly my favorite reason but still only one. I know you don't want to marry, I haven't forgotten. But I wouldn't have proposed if I didn't understand what it means to be your husband."

"What does it mean?" The question escaped in a breathy whisper. I'd never, not once, needed an answer more desperately.

He took a moment, his gaze searching my face. "You're not an ordinary woman. An ordinary marriage would never satisfy you. No, I imagine I would spend the rest of my life chasing you all across the globe to keep you from being killed. Or from taking over a small principality. It's even odds, I expect."

Words from more than a decade ago came back to me with a barely concealed gasp. Gabriel, in the throes of denying his attraction to Celine, once told me that I should find a man who knew the things I was capable of and adored me *for* them, rather than in spite of them. He may have been a terrible man, but he was a good brother to me.

"And you would be all right with that?"

Kit shrugged. "I'd prefer finer conveyance—I don't fancy another head wound. And I suspect I wouldn't do well atop an elephant or in one of those air balloon things, or whatever fantastical idea you're considering now."

My heart clenched pitifully. "It would be a large principality," I retorted, refusing to consider the way my blood rushed. "It would not do to underestimate me."

"Never," he said, his forehead finding mine. "Perhaps a continent?"

"A large one," I said and broke away to cover an indelicate yawn.

"Only the largest," he vowed, then slipped a hand under my knees and tightened his hold around my ribs.

He stood without warning, leaving me to cling to his neck. "Kit!"

"Davina!" he squeaked, mocking the high pitch of my cry as he stepped around the desk and made for the door.

"We need to put everything away," I protested.

"The benefit of accepting fate? Those are my things, I do not need to put them away."

"But—"

"Come, we need to leave early tomorrow if we're to reach Scotland before winter. You need to rest." He swooped me down to grab one of the candles while he blew out the other.

"It's April."

"Precisely. At the rate we're traveling, it could be months."

I *humphed* at his jest and opened the door for him. He carried me all the way back to the earl's chambers, his arms never once faltering. His breath never deepening. But his efforts did allow me the opportunity to feel his muscles against the skin of my back and thighs.

And the demonstration of strength was really quite lovely.

Twenty-Six

LEIGHTON HALL—APRIL 12, 1817

KIT

When I set her down in our chambers—*ours*—it was with great reluctance. Though she hadn't really shown it, she had to be exhausted. I was.

But I wouldn't find sleep tonight. Not after what I'd discovered in that study. And not after what I'd decided. I was Lord Leighton now. For better or worse, I was an earl with all that entailed—most of which I had no notion of.

Undressing Davina would never become a tiresome task, but I was becoming more skilled at it. I didn't knot up her corset once.

By the time I settled her beneath the covers, she was halfway to sleep. Still, she grumbled quietly when I pulled away. The sound was enough to leave me hesitating.

"Stay," she mumbled.

I crawled into the impossibly soft bed. I'd never slept in anything so luxurious and a part of me cringed to crawl into the fine linens in the same breeches that had spent the morning in a dusty wagon.

No sooner had I stopped moving than Davina pressed herself into my side. The way she fit against me when I settled my arm around her shoulder was exquisite perfection. Or it was right until the moment her icy feet tangled with mine. The yelp that escaped me was manly and impressive, in spite of her sleepy giggle that might have suggested the contrary.

"Did you rest them on a block of ice first?"

"'S just the way they are."

"We should call a physician when we reach Scotland. Surely that cannot be healthful."

"So many big words. Shh, it's time for sleep."

"Go to sleep, little menace," I whispered against her forehead, then pulled away after a kiss.

Eventually she calmed, her breath evening out. Even her toes warmed to a temperature that could be described as tepid. When I was sure she wouldn't wake, I slipped from her arms, regretting the choice instantly.

She curled a little tighter into herself, and I tucked the blankets around her. I grabbed the still-lit candle and padded back down the stairs and into the study. I braced myself for a long night, lit another candle, and pulled a quill and a few pieces of parchment from the unlocked drawer.

A clock somewhere in the hall chimed hourly. I stopped hearing it entirely sometime after three.

When I woke, it was to the strangest possible juxtaposition. My lower back ached in a way that suggested I may never be pain-free again. My neck, likewise, protested my position. I'd fallen asleep in front of my work on more than one occasion, so it was a familiar pain. New, however, was the scent of coffee. And equally new and more pleasant were delicate fingers combing my hair.

"Kit..." Davina whispered, fingers moving to my shoulders. "My feet are cold."

"Told you," I grumbled, finally rising and twisting my

neck from side to side with a truly absurd amount of pain. The punishments that resulted from falling asleep at one's desk never fit the crime. "We're seeing a physician about it. It's clearly a condition."

Davina pressed deft fingers into the place where my neck and shoulders met. The groan that escaped me was truly obscene but I couldn't bring myself to care.

"How did I know I would find you down here this morning?" she whispered into my ear. It probably wasn't intended to be seductive, but there was a sensual note to her voice and the way her breath ghosted along my skin had me swallowing another groan.

One clever hand slid down the front of my chest. Her palm pressed along the divot between muscles. That hand was headed in a truly interesting direction before it veered off course and wrapped around my ribcage. The effect was a sort of hug from behind with the back of the chair between us. It was awkward and unsatisfying and had my heart swelling with affection all the same.

I turned my stiff neck and kissed the flush of her cheek. It was then that I noticed her frock. "You're dressed," I stated, definitely not in a tone that could be described as whining.

"Yes, that happens when you fall asleep at your desk. I had to have Mrs. Reed assist me."

"But I like doing that part."

"I like it too. If only you hadn't fallen—"

"Asleep at my desk. Yes, yes. What time is it?"

She slid onto my lap once again, an arm wrapped around my neck, teasing the tense muscle there half-heartedly. "Half seven. Rory and Alfie are readying the carriage, and Mrs. Reed has packed us some breakfast and snacks. I let Gibbs know that you may wish to speak with him before we left. But I thought you would rather dress first. I left some things out of your portmanteau for you."

Her forehead was infinitely kissable and I chose not to resist. "Thank you."

"Oh, no need to thank me. Your packing choices were absolutely fascinating…"

I struggled to recall what I had tossed into my bag in the few rushed moments I had before we set off. "What was so interesting?"

"Oh, many things. Your soap, it smells almost like you, but not quite."

"I smell?" The defensive nature of my tone was clear and open. At least it was until she dipped her head, burying her nose against my neck with a heavy sniff. It should have been ridiculous, and it was, but for some absurd reason it was also a little arousing.

"Something woody, cedar I think—that's the soap. Then there's the parchment and ink."

"Obviously." I gestured to the mess of a desk before me.

"No, you always smell like ink and new parchment. I think you spend so much time around it that it's a part of you. Sometimes there's a bit of leather but not always. Mostly it's just Kit."

"Just Kit?"

"It's a good smell," she assured me.

"You smell citrusy, spicy citrus, and something floral. Even when you're covered in mud. And sometimes like whiskey."

A quick kiss was all she allowed before she pulled herself off me, even against my resistant fingers. "You need to dress. Otherwise you will meet with Gibbs like this…"

"Ugh, fine." I rose from the desk, finding new places that were stiff in the process.

"You're starting to sound like me," she said. The smile was clear in her voice and when I turned, it was etched across her face. "Go, dress yourself. Before you scandalize the entirety of your staff."

"I'll scandalize *you*," I muttered while stretching out my legs.

"I'd love to see you try," she called after me as I strode from the room. "I'm not jesting—please, do try!"

∽

A FEW HOURS LATER, I woke to delicate fingers carding through my hair for a second time. My head rested in Davina's lap where I'd been lulled to sleep by the gentle rocking of a well-sprung carriage.

Pulled by four horses instead of two, the Leighton carriage was the opposite of our first conveyance in every way. The navy velvet seats were plush and comfortable, the walls were solid and present, and absolutely nothing was strapped on.

Despite my protests, Davina had pulled me down to rest against her as soon as we set off. I intended only to rest my eyes for a few minutes, perhaps half an hour, but I knew by the angle of the sunlight pouring through the—glass-covered—window that it was much later.

"What time is it?" I pushed myself off her lap with no small amount of reluctance. As I stretched, a groan broke free.

"A bit after noon, I think."

"We didn't stop to change horses?"

"We did. Twice." There was a teasing note to her response.

"You didn't wake me?"

"You needed the rest. I would have woken you at the next stop though, I was losing feeling in my leg."

I apologized, scratching the back of my neck. Her pink skirts were wrinkled where my head had lay, though I couldn't bring myself to feel too badly about it. At least there was no damp spot from drool.

"Do you have any notion of where we are?"

"Not even a little," she chirped. "How did you sleep?"

I tipped my neck from side to side, testing the muscles. There was none of the bone-deep soreness I would have expected. "Well."

"Good, then you can explain what you were doing falling asleep at your desk, leaving me all alone with the potential spiders." Her tone had shifted to something scolding.

"Potential spiders?"

"I don't know if there were actual spiders because you weren't there to be certain they didn't crawl in my ears and lay eggs."

"Your ears?"

"Or nose! The location hardly matters."

"Right." I bit back a smile but the effort was almost certainly unsuccessful. "Do you need me to check? For the spiders?"

She rolled her eyes. "Obviously not, I've already done that."

"How, may I ask?"

"It involved a candle and a series of mirr— That is not the point. The point is that you are now tired and sore, and I was left to defend myself against the hideous beasts. All because of your poor choices."

"Terribly sorry." I tried to inflect some sincerity in my tone, but if the glare I received was any indication, I hadn't managed it.

"I read what you were writing," she added, quieter this time. "It was a very generous offer. And it was good of you to make it."

"It's what they were due in the first place. I shouldn't have to offer the former staff missed wages because there never should have been missed wages."

"I think that almost made sense." Her shoulder knocked against mine, teasingly.

"I needed to fix at least a few things before we left. I

couldn't leave it as it was. And I'll need to return to London—finish things up with Will—before I return."

"You're determined then?" Davina's hand found mine and offered a reassuring squeeze.

"Yes. Now, I just need to stop twitching every time someone uses the title."

"Oh, I don't know. It might set you apart from the other earls."

"I hadn't thought of it that way. I can be the only gentleman who has a fit every time someone addresses him."

"Eccentric..."

"Yes, and perhaps I shall take up some peculiar hobby. I must solidify my position in society as the most absurd gentleman to live."

"Do you suppose you will insist on performing all the duties of a gentleman?" On the surface, there was nothing noteworthy about her question. But in her tone... I was missing something about it.

"What are those duties?"

"Oh, you know, estate management, parliament, heirs, that sort of thing."

My mind caught on the third item, the one I rather expected she had feelings about. "Parliament, that sounds a dreadful endeavor. I daresay I shall have to, won't I?"

She nodded, unlaced our fingers, and stole her hand from mine. "And the rest?"

"Are you asking if I am now in desperate pursuit of heirs?"

"I suppose I am."

I tucked a loose curl behind her ear and tipped her chin to face me. "I wouldn't object to the begetting... With the right woman, of course. But, if I were to die without an heir, well, I won't be available to care very much about it."

"So you would be fine, without children I mean?"

"I like children. I'd like to have them—with you specifically—in case that wasn't clear. But if that isn't something that happens, or if you don't want... If that is why you don't wish to marry— I want you more, is what I'm trying to explain, rather inelegantly."

"Kit... I still don—"

"Not to worry then. I have two days at least to leave you half as flustered as you leave me. Then you will have no choice but to agree to be mine."

Twenty-Seven

NORTH ROAD—APRIL 13, 1817

DAVINA

His refusal to accept my denial should have irked me. Were he any other man, it would have left me furious.

But Kit wasn't any of the other men I'd known. He wouldn't try to buy my affection with shiny gifts. He wouldn't circumvent my wishes by going to Xander. No, he simply impressed me, continually, in ever more surprising ways.

The instructions he'd left for his steward—the offers he was making to former employees—were more than generous.

Much as I had scolded him for abandoning me to my arachnid-infested fate, I'd never once thought he would end the night anywhere else. Kit was a good man, on the surface, underneath it all, and every bit of him in between.

But I didn't want a marriage. I didn't want to be a man's property. So why did it sound so right when Kit called me his?

Before his hopeful gaze overtook me, I felt the subtle shift between dirt and cobblestones indicating a new coaching inn.

I pulled back the curtain—such a novelty—and the Bull and Mouth greeted us, the courtyard looking very much like every other courtyard we'd seen thus far. Kit hopped through the door, his pleasure at no longer having to wait for Alfie or Rory to unbuckle us evident. He handed me out properly, then guided me to talk with our drivers, a hand on my lower back.

"We'll have a quick meal. Do the two of you need a longer break?"

"Nah, it's much nicer up here. Can you bring some sandwiches though?" Alfie asked.

Kit nodded, then escorted me into the inn. We ate quickly before returning to the carriage and slipping inside.

"Next time you abduct me, I require a finer carriage," he murmured, a lazy grumbling sound of a satisfied man, and I couldn't help but wonder what he would sound like when he was truly *satisfied*.

I settled beside him and smoothed my wrinkled skirts for something to do. Kit was travel-worn and unbearably handsome. And the beard... The man should never, ever be without at least three days of growth again.

"I suspect my abduction days are at an end."

He caught my hand and dropped a kiss on the palm before knotting our fingers together and resting them on his knee. "Don't say that."

"I think my brother would have liked you." The sentiment broke free and the tilt of his brow gave away his befuddlement.

"Does he not already?"

"Gabriel, not Xander."

He gave me a single huff of laughter. "I very much doubt that. And I'm not entirely certain it's a compliment."

"I didn't mean it like that. You wouldn't have been friends."

"What did you mean?"

"He once told me I wasn't allowed to marry a man who

underestimated me. I'd nearly forgotten he made me promise."

"But you've remembered?" There was an eager lilt to his whispered question.

"Yes..." I breathed, unable to stop myself. "It's not— I don't—"

"No, I know," he rushed to assure me. "It's not an acceptance. I wouldn't accept anything so reluctant anyway."

"I just... If I were to— It wouldn't... *not* be you."

"Wouldn't not?" His brow hit the curls tangled across his forehead.

"That is what I said."

"It wouldn't not be me..." he repeated, a full, warm smile crossing his face. My lips twitched at the sight.

"It's not a yes."

"I'd gathered that. Solicitor, you know. I'm very skilled at interpreting vague, tricky language. But it wasn't a no either."

"Kit..."

He straightened, facing me fully. "Do you know what I've just realized?"

"What?"

With both hands, he grabbed my hips and hauled me overtop him. He settled each of my knees against his hips, ignoring my astonished squeak entirely. "I'm wasting valuable time."

He cupped my jaw and tugged my lips down to his. A sigh escaped me when we touched, and I felt him sink into the cushions below.

The first press was soft, adoring. His fingers traced my chin, my jaw, my neck, settled against my shoulders, and pulled me closer at the same moment his tongue swept the seam of my lips.

I thought kissing merely involved the mouth, but the man kissed with his entire body. He sank into it, he surged forward, he wrapped me in his arms, he was everywhere, all at once, moving against me.

I was trapped in tangled layers of skirts and underthings, unable to close the distance the way we both wanted.

For the first time, I felt his smile against my skin. It was quick, bright, and replaced quickly when I opened my mouth to him.

While his tongue worked every last thought away, his hand traced from my knee, down, down, down to my ankle. There he found the hem of my skirts.

Kit proceeded to rip an astonished grasp from my chest when he grabbed the hem of the skirts, petticoats, and chemise, and yanked the lot up to my waist in a swift movement.

"Kit!"

"No?" he asked, finding that precise spot on my jaw he'd identified yesterday and then set about stripping every last thought from my head. I clutched his shoulders and neck, desperately trying to regain an equilibrium. "Davina, yes or no?"

I couldn't remember the question, not in the wake of the smooth whiskey of his voice. But I knew the answer. "*Yes.*"

"Good." He pulled away and tipped my chin to meet his gaze. His free hand found my ankle again, his heat burning through threadbare stockings. "Davina, I've had months to try and fail to avoid thinking about what I might like to do to you—with you—" He broke off, distracted with the hinge where my neck and jaw met. A mewling noise came from somewhere in my throat when he pulled away. "In every one of those fantasies, you're an enthusiastic participant."

"Kit..." It seemed to be the only word I was capable of at the moment.

"You're my brave, brazen, beautiful menace. You'll tell me

if I do something that isn't to your liking, won't you? I only want to please you."

Who was this man? Where was my buttoned-up solicitor? Where did he learn to say things like that? Why were they affecting me so?

"Kit," I whimpered as he found my clavicle with his tongue.

"Say no, Davina," he whispered against my skin.

"No?"

"Good, remember that word." He pulled back from the skin of my throat, his lidded gaze meeting mine. "Now, just as important, you must promise to tell me whenever I do something that *is* to your liking. You're free to use whatever words—or sounds—you wish." His hand slid up my calf, his fingers catching in the notch behind my knee before continuing doggedly forward.

"Kit…"

"Good choice, I especially like that one."

I swallowed the lust he'd managed to create. "I thought you wouldn't—not until I agreed to marry you."

"I won't risk getting you with child. Any other concerns? We would be good together, so good."

The hand that wasn't inching up to the edge of my stockings was occupied with the buttons lining my back. He caught my lips again, distracting me as he worked on the row of buttons.

"Who *are* you?"

"'M Kit. You know the word—didn't seem to know any others a few moments ago." His lips traced the bodice of my gown, loosening with every freed button.

He tugged it down with a finger. The molten chocolate of his gaze sought my eyes. "Yes," I agreed, too eagerly.

And then he set about stripping me of not only my gown but every last thought in my head.

Twenty-Eight

NORTH ROAD—APRIL 13, 1817

KIT

I WAS BEGINNING to suspect it was possible to die from lust.

Lust and love.

That's what it was, the feeling I'd been hesitant to name before now. Before the moment she hinted that *I* didn't underestimate her. That acknowledgment filled me with a heady confidence that astonished both of us. The realization that followed also left me petrified.

It would destroy me if I couldn't convince her to say yes. My chest would crack into a thousand tiny pieces if I had to leave her behind in Scotland.

I couldn't—wouldn't—let her. I just needed to prove to her that it would be worth it—I would be worth it.

Another "yes" broke from Davina's lips when I managed to free one of her breathtaking breasts.

I worshiped the silken globe with my tongue, feeling her nipple pebble between my lips. "Do you like this?" I asked, fairly confident in her response. The physical evidence of her arousal was helpful.

Her breathy grunt and fingers clutching my head tighter seemed to be an affirmative.

Much as I wanted to strip Davina bare and leave her a boneless, desperate mess, I had nothing in the way of practical experience. I'd kissed a girl once or twice, but nothing more. What I did have was a single, drunken conversation with Celine while Will worked late one night and we worked on a bottle of scotch.

My hand under Davina's skirts inched ever closer to that secret space I'd only dreamed about. "Davina?"

"Wha?"

Her deft fingers made quick work of my waistcoat, moving to shove it off my shoulders. The problem came when that effort required me to remove my hands from their home on any patch of her skin I could find.

She seemed to realize the issue and abandoned the waistcoat in favor of the cravat.

"Davina," I tried again, dragging my hand ever closer to the junction of her thighs. Heat radiated off her. I knew when I finally closed the distance it would be a burn, a brand of her that I would never be able to see, and never be able to forget—not that I could envision a world in which I would want to forget. "May I touch you?"

"You are touching me," she replied, distracted before she released a pleased little cry when she unwrapped the fabric from my neck.

I palmed the enticing flesh of her thighs pointedly. "I want to give you pleasure." I wanted to do more than give her pleasure. I wanted to extract every last drop of indulgent, sensual bliss her body was capable of giving her. I wanted to leave her a wrung-out husk whose only thoughts were *yes* and *more*. I wanted her to be as obsessed with me as I was her, until the mere thought of denying me, of refusing to wed me, hurt her as much as it did me. I more than wanted it, I needed it.

I wasn't entirely certain what I would do if she said no in this moment. Stop, of course, but possibly die as well. Fortunately, I didn't have to find out because she nodded, a becoming flush spreading across her cheeks and chest.

"Yes? You want me to spread these soft, velvety thighs and slip my fingers inside you? It would be easy, I can feel your sweetness running down as we speak."

"Kit! Solicitors don't speak like that!"

"This solicitor does when he's speaking to you. Answer the question, love."

If she caught the slip, she made no sign of it. "Yes," she whispered. I yanked her lips back to mine at the same moment my fingers found the soft petals of her sex. I had never been so aroused, nor so full of love. The combination left me dizzy and weak.

I had to make her love me. I had to.

Guided by instinct and little else, I slipped my fingers along the wet heat. There was something heady about the knowledge that I'd done at least this right. She wouldn't be dripping on my fingers if I hadn't.

Her breath caught when my finger rubbed her pearl. I doubled back, gently tracing it. "Yes?" I asked, keeping the distance between our lips as small as possible. I hoped the desperation wasn't as clear in my tone as it sounded to my ears.

"There." One of her hands lowered to clasp my wrist, holding me in place.

"Like this?" I drew a delicate circle with my thumb over the precious spot that was giving her pleasure.

"'S perfect." Her hips helped me along, swirling and pressing in ways that offered hints about pressure and direction.

Her hair was a tangled halo around her, the pins she began the trip with scattered to who knew where. Sweat glistened on her temples. The skin of her neck and chest were reddened from my attentions. I should have—if only for her comfort—stopped, but the sight didn't induce the guilt it ought to have. No, it was evidence that I was here, that *I* had Lady Davina writhing against my lips. Kit Summers, solicitor, was here. It was a possessive kind of pride that I would never admit to aloud.

By all objective measures, she was a mess. She was also so beautiful, taking her pleasure in me—from me—that my heart actually ached.

"Davina," I breathed, catching her hooded gaze. I switched my fingers for my thumb seamlessly. I curled my fingers up, just glancing against her entrance. "Yes?"

"Yes. More..." And that was all the permission I required. Davina's surprised cry overtook my gasp as her eyes fell shut.

"God, look at you. Never seen anything so exquisite. You should always look like this. Always."

She reached out, grabbing me into a filthy kiss as my hand worked between us. Davina was generous with me, rocking against my hand in a way that pleased her until I found the right combination of fingers and thumb.

"There!" Her lips ripped off mine on a panting breath. I would do *anything* for her to hear that again. I worked against her—with her—to give her what she needed. We could do this forever, until the sun ceased to rise, and it wouldn't be enough.

Her motion faltered and a frustrated cry broke from her chest. I caught her hip in my free hand, returning her to the pace that worked for her.

My lips found her throat, licking the beads of sweat glistening there. Anything to keep from proposing again, the words desperate to spill from my lips. But who could blame me? Who could see Davina like this—feel her like this—and want anything short of forever?

"Are you going to peak for me? I want to see you fall apart in my arms." I needed it more than air. Even if she refused to wed me, she would think of this moment, dream of it, always. I would dream of nothing else.

"Kit, I—"

"What do you need? Tell me and I'll do it."

"Harder?"

I shifted the angle of my thumb and the force of my fingers. "Like this?"

She nodded, pulling my mouth toward hers. Halfway there, she was seemingly distracted by a spark of pleasure because she gasped and threw her head back.

"So sweet, telling me what you need," I muttered, then found the peak of her breast with my tongue. A hand fisted in my hair, the tug just shy of painful and somehow leaving me even more aroused than I was a breath before.

I was going to marry this woman. I had to. One taste of her pleasure and I was addicted. My chest ached with the possibility that this might be the only moment I had.

Desperation to please her, to show her how incredible we could be together, warred with the need to draw this out, to extend every last second of this moment because I might never have another.

"Davina, God, Davina. I... Please," I begged, more desperate than she was. "Please." I pleaded into the skin of her throat.

Instinct had me quirking my fingers, sheathed inside her, just so. Davina's cry was wordless and full of agonized pleasure, her walls fluttering around my fingers as she shuddered against me. Or perhaps they was my shudders.

Her face was buried in my shoulder, her breath warm and damp against the thin fabric of my shirt.

Slowly, gently, reluctantly, I pulled my hand away from her

channel. Whether the resulting whimper was hers or mine would remain a mystery.

I shifted her malleable form, pulling her to lay across me. Though it was a futile effort, I straightened her skirts and bodice, leaving them respectable but for the very scandalous wrinkles. Her head found my shoulder with a soft sigh. Davina allowed me to set her to rights, as much as possible. Her hair was certainly beyond my pitiful skills, but I plucked the loose pins free and combed the silky strands with my fingers.

A little hand tangled on my waistcoat again, fingers inching toward my swollen member. I caught her fingers, laced them with mine, and raised them up to drop a kiss on them. "That's not what this was about."

"But..."

"Not right now, little menace." She made an indistinct sound but allowed me to set her fingers over my still-pounding heart. "How are you feeling?"

She was quiet for so long, I began to wonder if she had fallen asleep, when her fingertips brushed the edge of my shirt away. Her hand returned to my heart, this time with nothing between us. "Different."

"Different?" My breath caught.

"Cee, she gave me a little talk—after a great deal of cajoling, of course. I knew there was pleasure to be found... But it wasn't what I expected."

"How?" I fought to keep the panic from my tone and my muscles from tensing.

"Usually, my thoughts move too fast for my body. I can't stop or slow them. But when you kissed me yesterday, they slowed, they were sluggish. And just now... I don't think I've ever felt like that."

My tongue darted out to wet chapped lips. "Like what?"

"Everything was clear. It was too many sensations but not

the way it always is, where I want them all to stop. It was overwhelming in a good way. I didn't have to try to shut it all out. You did it for me. There was only you."

"Is that... good?"

"Yes, Kit, it was good." I felt her smile against my shoulder. "You need not continue fishing. It was—you were—are... It was incredible. My head has never been so singular like that before."

"Before?"

I couldn't see her face, but I knew she had rolled her eyes at me. "There's never been anyone else. I just meant... alone."

That single word broke something in my head. I was flooded with images of how and when she might have tried what we'd just done, alone. And then the need to watch those moments in person, desperately.

I swallowed the depravity that threatened to escape my mouth. Instead I asked the very reasonable question, "Are you feeling anything else?"

"You were perfect."

No force on this earth could've held back that smile. "Thank you. I did actually need to hear that. But it's not what I meant. I don't want you to regret anything about this—us. And I want to make sure I didn't hurt you."

"I'm well. I have no regrets, except that you are being stubborn and refuse to allow me to touch you. I regret that very much."

"You're a menace, have I mentioned that?"

"Once or twice. I'm still cross with you."

"You'll be even more cross with me when you see what I've done to your hair. I suspect there will be no recovering it." Instead of the scowl I'd expected, there was something coy and mischievous about her smile when she shifted from my chest to meet my gaze. "What?"

A hand snuck up to the mop on my head. Her fingers

carded through only to become stuck half an inch from my scalp. With teasing eyes, she caught her lip between her teeth.

"What've you done to me?"

"It's not my fault! If I wasn't supposed to touch it, you should've told me. And possibly restrained me."

And wasn't that thought intriguing... I filed it away for a later date, for use if she ever accepted me. Meanwhile, I sighed in feigned irritation, patting down the fluffy mess. I wouldn't have given up the feeling of her fingers clutching me to her for the world.

"It's a lucky thing you're a man and you don't need to attempt to find some sort of order with those curls. You can just swan about saving the day and look the part of a disheveled rogue."

"Disheveled rogue? 'M a solicitor."

"A disheveled solicitor who swans in and saves the day with his cleverness and roguish good looks."

"I suspect the beard is doing a great deal of the lifting in that descriptor." I dragged blunt fingernails across the growth on my cheek. Davina pressed her lips together in a way I wasn't certain how to interpret. "What?"

"Don't shave it," she blurted, the words escaping nearly on top of each other.

The chuckles that broke free surprised me. They arrived before I had finished parsing her meaning, entirely instinctive delight. "I promise, if you marry me, I'll never be without a beard for as long as it pleases you."

"And if I do not marry you?"

"Then the beard is gone. I'll not be ostracized by society without the proper incentive."

"Like you care a fig about society," she chirped.

"You're not wrong. But I won't brave another of Mother's lectures about how I look unkempt and sloppy without the reward of a breathtaking wife to return to."

"I cannot believe you're holding the beard hostage. That's cruel."

"A man does what he must."

Twenty-Nine

NORTH ROAD—APRIL 13, 1817

DAVINA

He traced the lines of my spine with a warm, oversized hand as the gentle rocking of the carriage lulled me, not to sleep but to a quiet, contemplative state.

Draped across Kit with my face buried in his shoulder might have been the safest I'd ever felt.

If pressed, I wouldn't have been able to recall a time I felt particularly unsafe, but here, in the cocoon of our—now functional—carriage, sated and warm, I was protected, cherished.

He seemed to have no particular inclination to speak after teasing me into submission. I had no need to fill the silence either. Especially not if the chatter required me to pull away from the swirls of cedar, ink, and parchment that called his skin home.

Here, I could trace the surprisingly muscular planes of his chest where his shirt hung loose. I'd probably stretched it permanently in my distracted tugging but I doubted he'd find it in him to complain when he noticed. The skin here wasn't any lighter than his face, which meant his skin tone was naturally a shade darker than mine, with a burnished golden undertone. It wasn't a surprise given how much time he spent in the offices.

The light dusting of hair was every bit as soft, dark, and curly as the riot atop his head. I hadn't managed to work up a shred of guilt over the disaster I'd left his overgrown curls.

I closed my eyes, breathing in the familiar scent of Kit. The carriage was so smooth over the terrain, I could almost forget that every mile carried us closer to the end.

Kit was going to accept the earldom—not that he'd ever had a real choice. That decision would be the end of his rescues if any of my adventures went awry. He'd be days away in his estate.

I would be alone.

I hadn't particularly liked it when Xander left for Scotland or when Cee had remarried, but those changes hadn't impacted me terribly much. I still caused mischief. Kit was still there to sort it out if everything went sideways.

I rather thought Kit's choice would change everything. That understanding sat in the depths of my stomach, churned around like a ship at sea in a storm.

It was selfish, the question on the tip of my tongue, and I bit it back. He wasn't abandoning me. And even if he were, it wasn't as though he wanted to, he'd made that clear. I couldn't ask him to stay, to be my solicitor—no matter how much I wanted to.

To be quite honest, I'd love for him to give up that position as well. He would have no need of other clients. He could spend all day pleasuring me. When we required a break, he would accompany me on all of my adventures. We had an understanding, and I was certain he would only intervene when it was necessary. We could live quite happily like that.

Except that Kit wouldn't be happy. Or he would be, but his honor would never allow it. But this Kit—my Kit—would have to forsake that fundamental aspect of his being. And then he would cease to be Kit.

"You're thinking too hard. I thought I put a stop to that." His chest rumbled against my cheek when he spoke, low and deep.

"You should be proud. I do not think my thoughts have ever been silent as long as they were earlier."

"Deep thoughts?"

I hummed, considering whether I wanted to share. "You're an honorable man. It's quite annoying, really."

"I know. It irritates me as well."

"You should consider being less honorable."

"I would say I was at least a little dishonorable no more than an hour ago."

"You were. You should do it more often."

"I'll take that under advisement."

Before I could scold him for the blatant lie, the carriage rocked as we turned to the inn. I leaned across him to peer out the window. To my astonishment, the smoky blue of dusk greeted me.

The Crimson Lily glowed with light from the hearth. "When did the sun set?"

Kit was frozen for a moment before silent laughter racked his chest, jostling me. My smile formed in response.

"I have absolutely no idea," he said.

"Hour or two ago," came the response when the door opened. Rory's bemused face peered in. Struggling to right myself, I slid off Kit's lap in slow motion and sank toward the floor. He caught me awkwardly around the shoulders just before I plopped on my bottom. "All dressed in here?" she asked, repressed chuckles wavering in her tone.

"Rory..." Kit warned, still hauling me back up and settling me beside him.

"What? It sounded like ye may've had a wild beastie in

here. Thought ye might've had to sacrifice yer delicates to satiate it."

"Be nice, Rory. I just got him to stop trying to sit across from me. We don't want to scare the little turtle back into his shell."

Kit groaned. "Oh Christ, you're not going to start calling me a turtle like you call Tom a cricket, are you?"

"One, Thomas is a little cricket. His legs and arms are too long for his body and it's adorable. Two, I hadn't intended to but now, absolutely, I will be doing that."

Something bordering on a growl escaped his chest, and he stomped out of the carriage, not pausing to hand me out.

"Wait, *mon petite tortue*," I called after him as I snatched my reticule from the opposite seat. I turned to Rory. "How long do you suppose I can continue to call him that before he abandons me by the side of the road?"

"We're driving, lass. He cannae abandon ye. And if the sounds I heard out there were any indication, he'll let ye do a lot worse than that."

I watched as Kit turned back briefly to be certain I was still behind him, then continued on, albeit at a more sedate pace.

"Do you really think?"

"Aye. Go get him."

When I entered the inn after righting myself just the tiniest bit, it boasted a raucous crowd of men several drinks into their evening and seemingly a few rounds of hazard as well.

Kit shifted uncomfortably at the table he'd procured when I entered, then rose to guide me over. There was a tall, fair one, who was passably handsome. He directed the others in that slow, loud, overly enunciated way drunken men had. There was a smaller, greasy looking man with unnaturally yellowed skin. And a portly one with ruddy cheeks and a loose smile.

I noted that Kit placed me so my back was to the group as

well, while he faced them. I hardly thought it a necessary gesture, but the effort made me smile at the table.

With his obvious discomfiture, it seemed needlessly cruel to tease him as I had planned.

He forced his gaze from the group and turned to me. "I, uh, I asked them to bring out the roast. Is that— Does that suit?"

"Yes, thank you." A cry rang out from the men and Kit's gaze shot that direction. "They're fine."

"They're groggified, and you're the only lady here—and the prettiest any of them have ever seen."

"How could you possibly know that?"

"Because you're the prettiest anywhere." He'd reverted to the grumpy tenor that had lessened over the last few days. I caught my lower lip between my teeth to hold back a laugh. Only Kit would be annoyed by the fact that other men thought a lady he was... courting?—wooing? regularly proposing to?—was pretty. "You know you're heart-stopping. It isn't usually a problem, but they know it as well."

"They haven't even looked over here."

"Oh, yes they have," he insisted, frown deepening, and the little divot above his brow reappearing.

"I am far less interesting than a game, Christopher."

He shot me a disbelieving look. "Do they not have mirrors in Hasket House?"

"Actually, we have quite a lot of them, some rather expensive. Mama loves nothing quite so much as her own reflection."

The tall, fair-haired man stumbled to his feet with a delighted cry and was met with groans and at least one shout of "Cad!" He called to the barman for another round of drinks. Across from me, Kit winced.

A maid ducked by with our plates, and Kit tucked in with

a speed born from a desire to be elsewhere more than enjoyment.

From behind me, one of the losing men slurred to another. I couldn't catch the entirety of it, "Turn up a flat," was clear enough to predict the next several minutes.

Unwilling to worry Kit, I turned to my supper, but I had no sooner taken a bite of the roast than the winner of the previous round noted our presence. "Oi, do you play?" he called to Kit. "These two were under the hatches before we began."

"I don't," Kit responded, forcing a disinterested tone.

"Come now, I need a decent opponent."

"Then you'll want someone else. As I said, I don't play."

"One game, and we'll leave you and the little lady to your meal. We'll even buy your supper."

"No, thank you."

The more he denied them, the more irritating they would become. They had plans to fleece Kit of every coin he had and weren't about to leave him be.

"You think you're too good to play with us?"

"I didn't say that," Kit insisted.

"I am," I interjected. Kit's wide, panicked gaze pinned me in place.

"I beg your pardon?" The man slurred once again.

"I am too good to play with you."

"Davina..." Kit growled, too low for the rest of them to hear.

"Well, darling, I don't suppose you have any pin money to put where your mouth is."

"Stake?" I asked and stood from the table while Kit looked on in horror.

"Five pounds," he said proudly, as if it were a profound sum of money. To him, it likely was. To me, it was actually pin money.

I nodded and sat down in an empty chair beside him. He finally returned to his seat while the other two scooted closer with jovial interest. Kit had followed and stood statue-still behind my chair, hands gripping the back of it. I leaned back, trapping him there, reassuring both of us of the other's presence.

"You need a drink, girl."

"Do they have Bonnie Barrel? Neat. For my companion as well. Of course, as a gentleman, I presume drinks are also included in your earlier offer."

"You have yourself a little spitfire there," he directed to Kit as if I wasn't there. Kit, who, when I turned to glance at him, looked as though he were fighting back a fit of apoplexy. He would survive, though I did worry he might grind his teeth to nothing in the interim. "She for rent?"

Kit's bit out, "Absolutely not!" was overshadowed by the raucous laughter from the men at the table.

I waited for the guffaws to die down before retorting, "I do not know whether to be more offended that you think me a doxy or that you suppose you could afford me if I were. Regardless, in a few moments, you're going to be in such low water that your great-grandchildren won't be able to afford a three-penny upright."

The men I hadn't insulted burst into jovial laughter. Kit and the blond one to my side remained silent. I'd annoyed that one. Good, angry men were reckless men.

The maid brought the whiskey over and glanced between me and the men with wide eyes. I offered her a subtle nod that not a one of the others caught or would have understood if they had.

"You have the coin to back up that mouth?"

No sooner had I pulled the drawstring of my reticule than Kit squeezed my shoulder. He dropped a five-pound note on the table beside me. While I understood the wisdom of not allowing these men to know I was carrying coin, I was annoyed at missing the opportunity to humiliate the man by pulling out one of the notes from my bag.

"I don't suppose you gentlemen would like to join us?" I asked, offering the other men an enticing smile. The greasy one agreed easily, while the portly one patted his pocket a moment before nodding. "And you generous soles, you wouldn't mind if I was the caster first, would you?"

The instigator grumbled but handed over the dice. The same ones I conveniently dropped to the floor. I scoffed as the greasy one leaned to grab them. "Allow me," I insisted.

A five and three faced up. I nudged them with my foot and watched as my suspicion was confirmed. Five and three again. I scooped them up before sneakily switching them for Gabriel's old pair in the bottom of my reticule.

"We haven't been properly introduced, gentlemen. I'm Davina, and you are?"

The handsome-enough one was Ambrose, the greasy one was called Wickens, and the ruddy-cheeked, friendlier one was Oliver.

"Well then, now that we're all friends, shall we begin?" Confidently, I rolled for the main, with a close eye on Ambrose. I was certain when the dice landed on a four and a three and his eyes widened slightly. No one else reacted in any way that I caught.

Even a weighted die didn't *always* land the way they were expected, or it would be too easy to find them out. One roll wouldn't confirm his fear.

The next one did though. Two fours. Only Gabriel's rigorous teaching kept the smirk from my face as Ambrose reached for his glass and took a heavy swig.

He couldn't very well complain that I had switched the dice without admitting the originals were weighted. It was with clear reluctance that he put his stake down. The other two were quicker, already prepared with the possibility that they might be parted from it. Though, they certainly considered it a more remote possibility by my presence.

With a carefully crafted expression of innocence, I rolled again and hit two twos. The other men groaned. They hadn't lost, but neither had I. Wickens put another one pound on the table. Kit matched it from behind me without question. I was a little surprised he was familiar enough with the rules to go forward without clarification. Though, I supposed solicitors, often second and third sons, frequented gaming hells just like titled gentlemen.

Ambrose's complexion reddened.

Another roll, this time a five and six. I generously refrained from performing a little dance in my chair as both of my innocent victims groaned, fished out the necessary match for my stakes, and handed over theirs. Ambrose's skin darkened further, turning an unflattering aubergine shade. That couldn't possibly be healthful.

"Another round? Or have you had enough?" I directed my gaze to Ambrose over the edge of my glass as I sipped the buttery, smooth whiskey pointedly.

Finally, he could take it no more and the words I knew were coming burst from his chest. "You cheated! She's a cheat!"

Kit's hand grasped my shoulder as he moved to haul me out of the chair. I caught it with mine, trapping it there, willing him to wait for a moment. The tension in his grip didn't lesson, but I wasn't yanked from my seat either.

"Did I? Or did I perhaps uncover your weighted dice and switch them for my own, unweighted ones?"

"What?" Wickens cried.

He drowned out Oliver's, "Blaggard!"

Ambrose shot to his feet. "How dare you? How dare you accuse me of such a thing!"

Wordlessly, I pulled his dice out from the folds of my skirts and shook them in my palm above the table. "Eight, a five and a three." When I dropped them from nearly a foot above the table, they landed exactly as predicted. "Well, look at that." He grabbed for the dice but I snatched them before he got his hands on them and rolled again to the same result.

"You bastard! You owe me nearly twenty pounds," Wickens shouted, righteous sweat pouring off his brow in rivulets to land on the table.

"I think we'll leave you gentlemen to sort this out." I tipped my whiskey glass toward Ambrose, swallowed the last of it, and grabbed Gabriel's dice before they were lost to the ensuing scuffle. I allowed Kit to pull my chair out from the table and help me up just as the unwitting victims overturned it. "Oh, and, Ambrose, do not worry about covering our meal, I think you'll need the rest of your coin."

Kit's hand found my lower back as he grumbled at my side. "Bloody brilliant, beautiful menace."

Thirty

CRIMSON LILY, NEWCASTLE UPON TYNE—APRIL 13, 1817

KIT

The little menace I was in love with tucked into her roast with less smug fanfare than I would have anticipated while a small fistfight occurred at the nearby table. Yes, her cheeks were flushed with victory, but I'd expected at least a few words of excitement.

I was still wavering between absolute awe at her magnificence and the need to beg her to give a damn about her own safety.

We continued in silence, consuming but not enjoying our merely edible meal.

Davina's fork clattered to her plate, which caught the attention of no one but me, while another entire table's worth of dishes and glasses fell to the floor nearby. But her single utensil yanked my gaze from my plate.

"Oh, for the love of— Just have at it," she demanded.

"Have at what?"

"Whatever lecture you're working on. I know I shouldn't

have done it, but I couldn't resist. And they were intending to fleece you of every scrap of coin you had."

"I wasn't working on a lecture. And I know, that's why I said no."

"They weren't going to accept your no. And of course you are."

Ambrose groaned as his compatriots managed to down him, directly into what was probably once a bowl of soup but was now a puddle of soup and broken china.

I turned back to her. "If I were to stress to you how essential your safety is to me, explain precisely how many grey hairs I've found that are entirely your fault, press your hand to my chest so you can feel the way my heart still has not recovered, would it stop you from running headfirst into the next one?"

"Probably not," she replied. I thought I caught a bit of sheepishness in her tone, but that might have been wishful imagining.

"Then why would I bother? I'm merely glad I was there to step in if need be."

"That's it?"

"Oi! A little help here," the sweaty man called over to me as he clung to one foot and the fuchsia-faced one clung to the other.

"Put your back into it," I called over. To Davina, I added, "That's it. Do I wish you were more concerned with your own well-being? Absolutely. But we have one, perhaps two days left together. Why would I waste them on unpleasant, fruitless endeavors? I'd rather waste them on pleasant, fruitless endeavors." I added what I hoped was a rakish grin, but it was unfamiliar on my face and I rather worried it was a bit silly. Davina's giggle all but confirmed it.

Before she could respond, the maid stopped by the table. She tipped her head toward the three men writhing in the mess of supper. "Any chance you can assist in removing those three before they destroy the entire place? Ernie ain't what he used to be." She pointed a thumb at the ancient barman. "Dinner and as many drinks as you want will be on the house."

"Can I hit the blond one while I do it? Just once." Then I recalled the way he'd implied Davina was a whore. "Eh, maybe fifteen times."

"You'll hear no complaints from me."

I sighed and tossed my napkin on the table. Davina rose to follow. "Stay there, there's broken... everything."

For once in her life, she listened to reason and sat back down, then turned her chair to face the fray. She propped an elbow on the table and rested her chin on it, settling in to watch the show.

Ruddy and Sweaty were still clinging to the other man's thrashing legs while he smacked them about the ears. I rounded the top of him, my boots crunching in dishware. I bent down and wrapped both arms under his shoulders and heaved. I managed to get him partly upright before the weight of three—not particularly small—men became too much. "Would you louts let his legs go? We're taking this outside."

It took them a moment to obey, but then they released him at the same time and I nearly stumbled back at the lighter weight of my singular charge. When I regained equilibrium, I marched him outside, his arms flailing between us.

He was covered in bits of food and soaked with drink. There were stains I suspected were blood from broken glass and I struggled to ensure at least a few inches of space between us. The other two men followed, equally covered in food. I shoved him away and he stumbled to a knee. Glancing down, I saw that I hadn't escaped their mess. My waistcoat and shirt had bits of Lord only knew what all over. This trip hadn't been kind to my wardrobe.

Ambrose righted himself, turning on me. "You! You and your strumpet!"

As much as I joked, as much as I wanted to mill the man before, I *hadn't* intended to do so. It was something of a surprise when one moment he was glowering at me and the next he was on the ground.

It took a moment for the pain in my hand to register. I'd struck him. I'd never struck anyone. No matter how many times I fantasized about pommeling Hugh during settlement negotiations for Katie, I hadn't actually done it. I shook my hand out, waiting for the pain to worsen or subside.

Now that he was down, the other two had found a second wind and were smacking him pathetically.

I dragged my uninjured hand through my hair just as Davina appeared at my other side. She caught my hand in hers, examining it. A soft thumb traced my knuckles, before working my thumb back and forth.

"First time?" she asked, seemingly assured of my hand's ability to function again someday.

I nodded.

"Thrilling, isn't it?"

I ignored the implications of *that* question because my heart quite literally could not take it. "A bit, yes."

Just then, Alfie and Rory appeared from the stables wearing rather quizzical expressions.

"What's this?" Alfie drawled.

"Gambling misfortune."

"That's not what I meant when I told ye to go get him, lass," Rory added.

"You should have been more specific. Come on in, Kit has just earned us free drinks," Davina said, gesturing to the inn with her thumb. I rather thought the offer hadn't extended to our drivers, but I had no doubt Davina would work her magic.

The three of them made their way inside while I tried to

gain the attention of the—still slapping—Wickens. I kicked the bottom of his boot. "I'm going inside now. Don't let him back in."

The man nodded, or perhaps that was the way his head moved while he was wheezing. Regardless, I was sufficiently assured of having done my duty and joined my companions.

Davina was up against the bar, speaking to the frail, elderly barman. Rory and Alfie worked together to right the overturned tables. In but a few steps, I found myself at Davina's side.

"Mr. Matthews, I really do not think my husband is in want of a poultice for his hand. Particularly not one made of cow dung."

"Well, I've never heard of anyone refusing a dung-poultice works miracles. We've no ice anyway. We could do a vinegar bath. I'll even add a splash of brandy. It's not as good as the dung, but if he's a dandy, it'll do in a pinch."

"Thank you, Matthews was it?" I interjected.

"Yes, sir. I owe you a debt of thanks. Those three were fixing to destroy my establishment."

"You're most welcome. And I appreciate the effort to locate a cow-dung poultice, was it?"

"Aye."

"Thank you, truly. But my hand is not so injured as to require treatment."

"If you say so. I'll have Sally fetch the ingredients if you change your mind later."

"Oh, I'm certain that's not necessary," I insisted.

"It's no trouble."

"Oh really, I couldn't possibly. But do you know what would improve matters? My friends and I find ourselves quite in need of a drink."

"Of course, what'll it be?"

"Four whiskeys. Bonnie Barrel, please," Davina supplied.

"Anything else?"

"The roast? For our friends."

"Aye. I'll send Sally out with it."

I thanked the man and dragged Davina away before she could argue against the efficacy of bovine feces in healing. Alfie and Rory had made themselves comfortable at one of the larger tables and we settled in to join them.

I eyed our original plates of roast wearily. It hadn't been particularly appetizing before it had sat there for nearly an hour.

"I hear you hit a man, lad," Rory said. I neglected to point out that I hadn't been a lad in some time, and if anything she was perhaps younger than I was.

"He did!" Davina added. "I thought he was unflappable. But apparently, there is a limit to Kit Summers' seemingly unending self-control."

"You've seen me mad more often than most," I retorted. Alfie eyed our discarded plates with interest. "Help yourself, Alfie. Though I did order fresh for you." Unconcerned with quality, he snatched both plates and made himself comfortable.

"Oh, I know. I truly thought you might hit Mr. Decker—the milliner—that time you found me working in his shop. I was certain if a man was as furious as you were and didn't hit another man, there was nothing that could induce you."

The reminder of yet another man insulting my Davina had my fingers twitching for a nonexistent whiskey glass. And that one had hit her as well. "Should've killed that one," I muttered.

"What?" she asked, and Rory echoed the sentiments. Alfie was chiefly occupied with his supper.

"He hit you," I said, certain that was all the explanation required. It sufficed for Rory, and Alfie hadn't managed to work up a care. Davina still wore a puzzled expression.

"You didn't know me—hell, our singular meeting to that point was an utter disaster."

"Two meetings. We'd met once before Katie's wedding."

"We did?"

"It was a spring day, she and I were promenading—which is an absurd word for walking by the way—at my aunt's directive. Katie needed to be seen and no one had called on her after Hugh was an arse at her first ball. So I was the only available gentleman. You and Celine were walking together and stopped to speak with her. You were wearing what I now know to be one of your less ridiculous frocks, a stark-white thing with bits of green lace and embroidery. I remember thinking it was an absurd choice for a *walk* through a muddy park."

"I know the dress, but I don't even... How do you remember all that?"

We were interrupted by the arrival of the whiskey and I took a heavy sip.

"Yes, do tell us why you remember all that detail," Rory added, propping her chin on her hand and gazing with interest.

"I was one and twenty and she was a pretty girl. Of course I noticed her."

"I was standing next to Celine," Davina murmured, still wearing a confused frown.

"Yes..."

"What was *she* wearing?"

"I don't know, probably something purple." It was a safe guess, Celine seemed to like purple.

"You don't remember?" The words escaped slowly, a beat hanging between each.

I leaned toward Rory. "What have I done wrong?" I questioned, under my breath. I didn't make much of an effort to whisper, Davina would hear regardless.

"If ye dinnae know, I'll not be the one to tell ye."

"You don't remember," Davina repeated, smoother and without the questioning tone. Slowly a smile spread across her lips.

"What is happening?"

"Nothing, just... It's the effect Celine has on people. I didn't know anyone was immune."

"Oh, that. Yes, it's quite amusing when she arrives at the offices. Every one of our clerks stares at her until Will closes the door. And they spill things too. Higgins dropped an entire pot of ink weeks ago and we still cannot get the stain up. It was quite the lark when she and Will were— Can you call whatever they did courting? But it is becoming tiresome."

Davina's hand grabbed mine and brought it to her lips where she kissed my palm. I wasn't entirely certain what I'd done, but it seemed to be a good thing.

At last, the maid, Sally, brought the roast for Alfie and Rory. And a few odds and ends for us to munch on. The cheese seemed fresh and the bread was actually soft. Apparently minimizing property damage entitled one to the edible food.

The roast looked to be improved, too, as Rory took a calm bite. Alfie merely moved on to the next full plate. "Are we not feeding you enough?"

"He could eat this entire place down to the studs and still be hungry," Rory grumbled. "He'll eat precisely as much food is available."

I had a vague recollection of sharing that sentiment when I was his age. I shrugged and snagged a bit of bread before he ate that, plate and all.

Davina sipped her whiskey, continuing to examine me with bright eyes.

Rory picked hers up and tipped it toward me. "If I have any more than this, I ought not drive. And he'll be asleep as soon as he finishes stuffing his face. Are we staying the night?"

Yes, was the instinctive response, but the reasonable part of me knew Davina likely wanted to reach her brother before the babe turned seven.

But when I glanced at her, she was peering up at me with an eager sort of expression. She nodded and I rose to go talk to Matthews.

Thirty-One

CRIMSON LILY, NEWCASTLE UPON TYNE—APRIL
13, 1817

DAVINA

I WAS SOMEWHAT disappointed when Kit returned with four sets of keys and another round of whiskey. Two or three keys would have been preferable, but his determination to cling to his honor had not been shattered with Ambrose's nose.

After a brief cheers, or in the case of Rory, "*Slàinte mhath*," we settled in to enjoy the next hour. The broken glass had been cleaned up, for the most part. I still wouldn't be willing to risk wandering about barefoot.

"So, the fisticuffs, Christopher?" Rory asked.

He dragged an agitated hand across his beard in that way he seemed to favor. What he did when he was agitated and had no beard was a mystery to me, one I wanted an answer to. Though I also wanted the beard to stay, always.

"Ask the little menace, it's her fault."

My cry of "Slander!" was overshadowed by Rory's, "I never doubted that for a moment, but I asked you."

"He was crude," was the only explanation Kit offered.

I scoffed, shooting him a look over the rim of my glass.

Kit sighed before explaining the game with none of my due praise for my hazard prowess, wit, and brilliance.

"Well done, lass," Rory said with a smile, clearly recognizing my magnificence even in Kit's insufficient explanation.

"Where'd ye learn to play?" Alfie asked between bites of his third helping of roast.

"My brother taught me."

"Do ye think he'll teach me?"

"Oh, not Xander. Gabriel, my late brother."

Kit's hand found its way between my back and the chair, warming my lower spine.

"No, do not even ask. She cannae, lad. Yer mother will have my hide if ye take up gaming."

As soon as Rory turned back to her meal, I gave Alfie a quick nod. I wasn't looking at Kit but I could feel the smile in his gaze. Probably at least three-quarters of one.

When Sally stopped by the table to check in, Alfie requested another round. She was off before anyone could object. Usually, I would have appreciated his initiative. But I knew, without a doubt, that if I had another glass, Kit wouldn't touch me for two days. He had been very, very concerned with my acquiescence in the carriage. I sensed the flush rising in my cheeks at that memory—of the gravel in his voice when he pressed me to practice my yes and no.

That hadn't been part of Celine's little talk. Nor had the thrumming of my blood as Kit's thumb traced the line of my spine. It was a casual effort. I wasn't entirely certain he was aware he was doing it. But it reminded me of the way he'd used that thumb in other, more delicate places, to ecstatic effect.

When our drinks arrived, I made no move toward mine. Kit, too, left his untouched. But he did abandon my lower back, leaving it cold and lonely in his absence. Instead, he found my hand and laced our fingers together under the table.

His thumb continued its erotic dance, this time over the pulse on my wrist.

A glance under my lashes at him confirmed there was a smug quirk to his lip. Oh... He knew precisely what he was doing to me. And he was thrilled.

I slid a foot along the floor, to press against his ankle in punishment.

When Rory was once again distracted with her meal, I passed Alfie my drink, trading him for the empty glass.

Unlike my opponents earlier, Rory wasn't fooled by my sleight of hand. "Alfie, for Christ's sake. Three roasts and what is this, yer third drink? Are ye gonnae eat the table too?"

"With the right sauce," he retorted, drinking deeply.

"And ye, yer encouraging him," she accused.

"Sorry, Rory. I was only thinking it was time to ready for bed. It's been a long day, you know."

"Aye, with that boisterous game of traveling piquet ye two played, it's no wonder."

Kit coughed and withdrew his hand to scratch at the back of his neck. "I'll go gather our things. Alfie, a little help?" He didn't wait for the boy to object, instead yanking him away. Alfie still clutched the half-finished glass of whiskey in one hand, attempting to tip it back while stumbling forward.

Rory watched them leave before glancing around to ensure privacy. "All right, lass. We've only a few moments. Ye ken how to prevent conception?" she whispered.

"I don—that's not a concern."

"Dinnae play me for a fool. He may have gotten a room for each of ye, but ye have no intention of using it."

"I—he won't." I sighed, frustrated with fits and starts. "He says that he won't... risk getting me with child until we're wed. There won't be... penetration."

"He may say that, but men lie."

"Not Kit."

She rolled her eyes. "Well, regardless. That would be the best option to prevent conception. But assuming he's a man and ye're a foolhardy, reckless girl with more audacity than sense, ye best not allow him to finish in yer... you know."

"I do know. I've had this talk already. But—I cannot have you thinking so ill of Kit. He would never. He was very concerned about my consent."

"Oh, I ken. He is a chatty little thing. I wouldnae have expected it of him, if I'm honest. It's always the quiet ones though, I suppose."

"Rory!"

"What? Did ye think the carriage walls were impenetrable? It's better than the one we set out in, but it's not brick and mortar, lass."

"You cannot say anyth—Kit would die."

She offered me a crooked smile. "I'll not say anything to the lad. If he were anyone else, he'd be sitting up front with Alfie while I enjoyed a plush coach cushion. But it's clear he loves ye. And I think he's good for ye. Ye need someone practical. Someone to tell ye it's a terrible idea to kidnap a man ye barely know and drive him to Scotland in a great heap of a carriage. But someone that will go with ye anyway."

"He's not—"

"In love with ye? Oh, lass, that lad was desperately in love with ye long before I ever set eyes on him."

"He's just worried about my reputation. It's not—he would do the same for anyone."

"Ye're still wearing his mother's ring." She grabbed her glass, taking a pointed sip of the whiskey. Clearly she felt that she had made some kind of point. But it was truly for convenience's sake. I could give it back. I would.

Before I could offer my protests, Kit and Alfie returned with my trunk and Kit's bag. They clambered up the stairs just past the bar.

I hadn't consciously decided to move, only recognizing that I had when the drag of the chair against the wooden floor registered in my consciousness. "I think I'll retire for the night.

"I'm sure ye will. See if you can have yer solicitor bring in my bag before he beds ye."

"Rory!"

"Yes, ye're terribly scandalized. Ye should've thought about that before ye did whatever I had to listen to in that carriage. *I'm* scandalized."

Hands pressed to my flushed cheeks, I turned and made my way up the rickety stairs to where Kit and Alfie were leaving a room.

"Davina," Kit said, his voice honey smooth. "We've put your trunk in this one." He gestured toward the room second from the end of the worn but clean hall. He pressed the key into my hand.

"Where is everyone else?"

"I'm on the end there, and Rory is next to you, with Alfie beside her."

"Aye, I'm excited to not be kicked in the shin every time I snore," Alife added with a grin.

"Are you ready to retire? Do you need me to see if they have a lady's maid?" Kit asked.

"I think I will retire. But I don't need a maid."

If he knew why I had no need of a maid, the understanding didn't cross his expression. Instead, he offered a nod as he re-plucked the key he had just placed in my hand and turned it in the lock. His hand was distractingly large as he pressed the walnut door open, the knuckles barely reddened from his fisticuffs earlier. Those fingers, surprisingly long and elegant, had been inside me. They had driven me to ecstasy in a way I'd never known, in a way I was certain I would never be able to replicate. I was possessed with the sudden desperate desire to see those hands against my skin.

Feeling them beneath my skirts, it wasn't enough. I needed the sight.

As if he knew where my thoughts lay, he cleared his throat. His other hand caught my lower back, urging me into the room. The heat of him spanned the entire width of my back and his fingertips stretched from the divots at the base of my spine all the way beneath my rib cage. Had they always been so large? Or was my newfound appreciation for their talents changing my perception?

Behind me, Alfie muttered something about returning downstairs if we were going to flirt with each other until sunup.

"Good night, Davina," Kit murmured, warning in his tone, when I resisted his urging hand at the threshold.

"Christopher," I teased back.

"I'll send a maid up," he retorted. I spun to face him with an eye roll. "Menace." A smile spread across his lips as he said it.

Far from a reprimand, it had become his term of endearment. There was always a little gravel in the way he said it, and I felt that sound low in my belly. It was the sweetest—and most sensual—endearment I could imagine. And nearly daily, I listened to Will's drawl of "love" after every sentence he spoke to or about Celine.

I pressed up onto my toes, offering Kit a kiss intended to entice. It was a calculated thing, but immeasurably pleasurable. I worked his lips with mine and pulled back when his tongue brushed the swell of mine. His lips followed, catching mine once, twice, a third time before pulling away. There was fire in his burnt-umber eyes.

"I'll see you in the morning," he rumbled.

"I'm sure you will." I allowed the mischievous smile to bloom.

"Go to bed, Davina."

I slipped past him, peering around the edge of the door as I slid it shut. His gaze was heated as it clashed with mine. The latch echoed in the quiet room. Between the base of the door and the floorboard, a sliver of light spilled in, interrupted by the unmistakable form of two feet. I waited, wondering if he would truly leave.

"Lock the door," he added through the wood barrier.

I sighed, loudly so he wouldn't miss the effect, and turned the key. When the feet finally disappeared and I could no longer hear footsteps in the hall, I turned to survey the room.

It was small, and well worn, but clean. The fire burned warm in the hearth on one side. My truck was tucked neatly against the opposite wall. There was a large green rug covering the floor, and it had seen a few too many days but had been beaten recently. The bed looked large and comfortable enough, with two pillows and a grey quilt atop it.

Too bad it wouldn't be slept in.

I turned to my trunk, knowing what I was looking for.

I'd slept in my chemise for too many days, too exhausted or unable to change. But I'd packed precisely one nightgown. It wasn't anything fancy, not like the daring cut of the French silk and lace negligee I'd seen in Celine's wardrobe. But it was nicer than the practical, serviceable underthings I'd brought. And I'd always loved the way I felt in it, elegant and sensual.

I set it out on the bed, then moved to find my brush and a few other necessities.

Before Sally knocked, announcing herself, I had my hair undone and brushed, and had washed my face. She unbuttoned my dress and undid my corset with practiced efficiency. "Thank you, Sally. I can manage from here."

"You're welcome, ma'am. If it's not too bold to say... If I had a husband like yours, I wouldn't insist on separate bedrooms."

"A stickler for propriety, that one," I said by way of an

explanation. "Don't worry, we've only been married a short while. I'll have him stripped of those habits in short order."

"Oh good. It would be a travesty to have a man who looks like *that*, and so noble too, and not take full advantage."

"Thank you, Sally. That will be all," I bit out.

Sensing she had overstepped, she ducked out with nothing but a curtsy. I wasn't interested in discussing how attractive she found my husband—not-husband. I knew he was handsome, I knew he was kind and gallant. And more than her, I knew he was intelligent, witty, and dedicated. I knew why he smelled of parchment and ink. I knew what every one of his smiles looked like and I knew how precious they were. I didn't require another to tell me such things.

With those thoughts, I shrugged off my chemise and slipped my nightgown on. A quick glance in the mirror revealed an unbecoming flush and mussed hair. I was too irritated with maids who didn't have the sense not to ogle my husb—not-husband—to do anything about it.

Full of restless energy from my earlier win, the ensuing fight, the memory of Kit's fingers working along my sex, I paced the too-small room. Before I gathered enough speed to be satisfied, I reached a wall and had to turn again. It was almost worse than sitting at the edge of the bed, doing nothing. But I couldn't think that way.

The sound of feet on the weary stairs outside echoed down the hall. At least two pairs. I pressed my ear to the wall I would share with Kit. When I finally caught the click of the latch, I returned to my impotent pacing.

What was probably only a few minutes felt like an hour before I was convinced no one else would come up the steps.

I steeled my courage before finally slipping out into the hall to knock on Kit's door.

Thirty-Two

CRIMSON LILY, NEWCASTLE UPON TYNE—APRIL
13, 1817

KIT

I HADN'T TRULY EXPECTED to sleep alone, but propriety demanded a second room. I'd only stripped down to my braces when the expected knock came though, a tentative, nervous little rap.

I nearly ripped the door from its hinges in my rush to bring her into the safety of my room before someone else caught her about alone at night.

"You shouldn't have come. It's not safe. You could have been—" The sight of her finally registered and the mild lecture failed me. "Davina..."

She was sweetness personified, rosy-cheeked and full-lipped, her hair falling about her shoulders in tousled waves, with her big, beautiful eyes soft on me. Ignoring my failed scolding, she slipped inside and rounded to meet my gaze.

Her face might have been that of an angel, but her body, silhouetted against the fire in gossamer white silk was temptation from the devil himself. She was, of course, entirely unaware of the erotic figure she cut in the flickering light, long limbs and gentle curves outlined for my sinful gaze. With my last useful thought, I closed and locked the door.

"Get on the bed." Though the words were demanding, there was something soft, beseeching in her tone.

"What?"

"Get on the bed," she repeated, a little more forcefully.

"Davina..."

She rolled her shoulders back, her chin tipping forward. A lady in posture if not in behavior. "I'm not going to steal your virtue, Christopher. I merely wish to try something."

"On the bed?"

"I promise you'll still be able to call yourself a maid when I'm through with you."

"All right." Cautiously, I made my way around her to settle at the end of the bed. "What are you going to do with me?" My blood was already humming with anticipation.

"I— Celine told me about a—" her hands knotted together in front of her. "It's easier to just show you. Is that all right?"

"Yes, I... Yes." I caught her wrist and brought her palm to my pounding heart. Davina should know the effect she was having on me. She should know I was hers.

"You remember what we talked about in the carriage?" she asked, allowing me to pull her in closer by the waist, slotting her between my spread knees. Our positioning left me eye level with her breasts, wrapped in transparent silk just for me. I knew what I wanted to do with the loose neckline of her gown, but Davina was determined to... do something. I wasn't about to ruin her plans.

"I remember a lot of things about the carriage," I whispered, unable to resist an attempt to drag her lips down to mine.

She held back—just a little, merely the pressure of her palm overtop my heart. "Yes and no, Kit. It goes both ways."

No force on earth could have restrained the smile that curled across my lips. "Yes, Davina, and no, Davina. But I suspect that will be the last time you hear no from my lips for the foreseeable future."

She nodded but caught her lip between teeth, gnawing on it.

"Davina, talk to me." I wrapped her free hand in mine and laced our fingers together. "We don't have to do anything. I could just hold you. Or we could have a repeat of the carriage. I want nothing more."

"No, I know." Her gaze flitted toward the ceiling. "I want to try, I do. I'm just nervous."

"Do not talk yourself into anything—"

"I'm not! I want to, it's only that I haven't before and I want to do it properly."

"When have we ever done anything properly? Wrong doesn't exist here, Davina. Not between us."

She nodded and finally released her lip from between her teeth. And I had to capture it with my own. I simply had to. This time, she allowed it, let me worship her as I desired. She melted into the kiss, her arms finding their way around my neck, nerves abandoning her.

I was perfectly content to sip from her whiskey lips until judgment day, but Davina had other ideas. Her hand fisted in the folds of my shirt, tugging up.

This was dangerous territory for my control, but I had, only moments before, told her wrong didn't exist. And if I was honest, I couldn't have denied her anyway. It wasn't in me.

I shucked my braces and we broke apart only long enough for me to help her yank the offending linen over my head and away—somewhere. Our lips slipped back together as if there hadn't ever been an interruption, but her hands... eager fingers traced the planes of my chest.

I was fairly certain her exploratory touch wasn't intended

to arouse, more to find her bearing on a new landscape. But I was positive that her searching palms were more erotic than the most skilled courtesan's touch. Her little hands with the elegant fingers raked through the sparse hair before dipping to trace the lines of my abdomen.

I tried to tug her forward, to pull her over my lap the way she had been mere hours before. Instead she pulled away, dragging a groan from my chest.

"I have plans," she whispered.

She used the opportunity to study my form, watching her fingers repeat the same patterns they'd learned by touch. I swallowed the desire to beg—for what, I had no idea. Her hands moved to my arms, one finger teasing the line of my sternum, finding my collarbone, and dancing along whatever path took her fancy.

"Kit..." Her voice was soft, reverent. It was a heady thing, hearing her say my name like that. I would be happy to never hear another sound for the rest of my days. Or I was until a moment later when she spoke again. "Take off your breeches."

It took an embarrassingly long amount of time to discern that she had spoken aloud and that sentence wasn't a figment of my imagination.

I should have protested, a good man would protest. Instead my hands dropped to the fall of my breeches, working the buttons there with little grace but no complaint.

I rose to shuck them, forgetting I still wore boots, and nearly fell over in my attempt to free myself from all vestiges of clothing. Though I felt like a prize idiot, her giggle was lovely against the warm crackle of the fire. I fell back onto the bed and, before I could set to work on my boots, Davina decided to shred the last of my sanity. She kneeled at my feet.

My voice abandoned me when she yanked first one boot, then the other off my feet and set them aside.

"Davina," I croaked, reaching for her. She shook her head and nodded at my breeches again.

I was beginning to suspect the crux of her plan. It wasn't as though I hadn't heard of such a thing. But I never, not in my wildest fantasies, thought I would experience it. And with Davina Hasket? Never.

I released a great shuddering breath and stood again, then shucked the fabric more successfully. I dragged the stockings off along with the breeches, slightly more graceful, in spite of the fact that I'd lost sensation in my extremities. Every drop of blood in my body was rushing toward my cock with alarming speed.

I was a terrible man, headed straight for hell. Because I couldn't find a single word of protest for what I suspected was about to happen.

Davina sat back on her heels, examining me my person with a fascinated expression. Her brows were drawn and lips parted. And her eyes—they had darkened in the firelight, flickering amber. I was able to read enough of her countenance to know that whatever she was feeling, it wasn't revulsion.

I swallowed my heart back down in my chest where it belonged. Nothing could slow the pounding though.

"May I touch you?" *Nothing except that.* That stopped my heart entirely.

My response wasn't so much a word as it was the desperate sound of a wounded animal. She seemed to interpret it as permission—which it absolutely was.

The second her hand found my prick, I had to bite back desperate, pleading words of love. Whatever was left of my head knew this wasn't the time or place to confess my feelings beyond what I already had. I had to literally bite my tongue to manage it.

Never in my life had I been harder than when her fingers

wrapped around my shaft, testing an instinctively perfect stroke.

And then, without a single warning, her lips dropped to my cock and I died. Blood rushed through my ears, drowning out sound. My periphery darkened. There was nothing in the world outside of Davina Hasket's lips on my cock.

The combination of her intuition and my inexperience had my knees buckling. I fell back to the bed, which was fortunately still behind me, cursing as I slipped from her perfect mouth. Davina, my brilliant, beautiful menace, rectified that situation almost immediately.

I fisted the bed coverings as she took me in, desperately fighting the urge to thrust my hips.

She pulled away with an obscene *pop*. "Talk to me, Kit."

"I'm trying to keep from proposing again."

A wicked smile flashed across her face before she returned her lips to their task, working up and down my shaft in a way that might actually kill me.

"Christ, Davina!" I cried when she did something with her tongue I couldn't describe. "How are you real?"

A lock of hair fell across her face, distracting from the most erotic sight of my life. Carefully, I unclenched a hand from the bed coverings and brushed it behind her ear. Then she hummed her appreciation and shook my soul from my body—swallowing my cock in one quick motion.

"Fuck! Davina, darling... Please, don't stop."

I could see the smile in her eyes. She was pleased with herself as she stripped every moral from my body through my cock. Christ, I loved her.

"Davina..." *I love you.* "Please..." *I love you.* "Davina," I said again. Until her name was the only word I could confidently utter that wasn't *I love you.*

My climax built slowly. A match stoking a fire, she added fuel to it, swirling her tongue and humming in a way that had a wordless cry breaking from my chest. She built me up to an inferno, one that threatened to explode at any moment.

"Dav—" I choked out and tugged on her shoulder to warn her. She met my gaze with determination in her eyes. And the detonation was unstoppable.

When I came back to earth, limbs still numb and brain still hazy, she allowed me to pull her off her knees. I dragged her into the slot between my legs, my forehead finding her bosom as I drew in ragged breaths, hoping at least one of them could bring coherent thought back.

Gentle, magnificent hands carded through my hair, waiting for me to catch up.

But all I could think was *I love you. I love you. I love you. Please let me be yours.*

Please.

Thirty-Three

CRIMSON LILY, NEWCASTLE UPON TYNE—APRIL 13, 1817

DAVINA

I'D NEVER FELT QUITE like this before. Powerful, beautiful, sensual... loved. When Celine had described that particular act, it had seemed degrading, but somehow, with Kit, I knew it wouldn't be. And it hadn't been.

No, it was loving. Kit loved me. He didn't want to marry me because it was proper—though I was sure that wasn't an insignificant part of his proposal—he wanted to marry me because he loved me. It was in his eyes and his face. It had slipped from his lips the moment he lost his senses.

At present, I was taking great pleasure in mussing his already mussed hair. His hand spanned my waist as his head rested against my breasts. It seemed that, like my experience earlier, he needed a moment to come to grips with his new reality. I was content to allow it. I hadn't expected to enjoy the same sense of safety and serenity after giving him pleasure.

"Davina..." he grumbled and finally pulled his head up to catch my gaze. "Where did you learn that?"

"I pestered Celine into drawing a few diagrams a few years

ago. And Gabriel had some books that I liberated shortly after his death before father or Xander could get them."

He processed that information slowly. "I don't even want to know what was in those."

"Celine indicated that some of the acts weren't quite... *de rigueur*. Which made sense, some of the images required specialized equipment."

He gave me a disbelieving chuckle. "I had something in mind, no specialized equipment, of course. But with your vast, hard-earned knowledge, do you have something else you want to try?"

The hand already on my waist began to ruck up the folds of my chemise, slowly, gently.

I did actually have a thought. But I didn't quite know how to ask for it. And I was more than curious about what was in Kit's head. "Show me."

Something about that response had Kit groaning and dragging my lips down to his. He wasn't shy or tentative in the way he had been earlier. No, this was a kiss with intent. Kit had an agenda and I was the only item on it.

He kissed with everything he had, moving against me, pulling me toward him. Until there wasn't even space for breath to pass between us. Not that I was interested in breathing, not when the alternative was Kit.

His kiss was tinged with the bite of whiskey, and the taste —so familiar to me, brought the edge of a smile to my lips. He didn't taste like just any whiskey, he tasted like *my* whiskey.

His lips drifted away from mine to wreak havoc on the rest of my person. I could take in great heaving breaths of that distinct combination of ink and parchment that clung to him, while he found every place on my neck and chest that he'd already claimed. They were his now, the place beneath my ear, the divot at my throat, the dip in my collarbones, the crevice between my breasts. Never again could I touch them—see them—without thinking of soft lips and the tantalizing nip of his beard.

When his lips reached the edge of my nightgown, he traced the hem with his tongue. "Did you bring this with me in mind? Or are all of your night clothes this lovely? Lovely and flimsy..."

"For you. I didn't know it, but it was for you."

"Right answer, darling. Now, much as I will treasure the sight of you, wrapped up pretty as a picture all for me. This needs to be elsewhere. Yes?"

At my nod, he pulled the fabric up and over my head in one swift movement, then tossed it away. And then he froze.

His gaze should have been unnerving. But this was Kit, and there was fire in his eyes and awe in his open-mouthed gape. For a moment his chest didn't move at all, then his breath came more rapidly.

When his gaze dipped from my breasts to the curls below, it was my turn to forget how to breathe.

He stood, and I understood in that moment, just how perfectly we would fit together. He was made for me. Kit wouldn't have to stoop to kiss me, no contortions would be necessary for that hard, proud part of him to slide inside. He could live inside me, forever, and neither of us would need to move for discomfort.

He ripped a gasp from my lips when he bent, just the tiniest bit, and grabbed just under my thighs to pick me up. Kit chuckled as my arms and legs scrambled for purchase. "I've got you."

When he settled me on the bed a moment later, I clung to him, enjoying the way the muscles of his shoulders bunched and flexed.

He pulled too far away to continue to grasp, and I followed up onto my elbows. And then he settled onto his knees on the floor.

"Yes?" he asked, his hands rubbing the tops of my stockings.

"Yes, please."

Kit's smile was quick and blinding before he pressed a kiss to my knee and then dragging the silk down my leg, slowly, drawing out the caress of silk on skin. He turned his attentions to the other one, pulling it free with the same care.

He rubbed the tops of my thighs with both hands, not a sensuous touch, but a comforting one. "I want to taste you. Do you want that too?"

My cheeks heated even as I nodded.

"Remember the words?" he asked.

I sat all the way up, caught one soothing hand, and laced our fingers together. "I must say no if you do something I do not like."

"Good." He kissed my other knee, peering up at me with heat in his gaze. "And…"

"Yes, when you do something that pleases me."

"I'll also accept 'more, please,' 'Kit,' prayers to a deity of your choosing, and any groans or whimpers ripped from your body."

"Cocky."

"Mostly determined," he retorted, then squeezed my hand before settling and dragging my leg up to his lips. He rained kisses from ankle to thigh before resting my leg on his shoulder. "Breathe, Davina. It's just you and me on an adventure."

The words, the earnest tone, the adoration in his eyes, it was too much. I felt tears welling, and I blinked them back desperately. "We're quite good at those, aren't we?"

"The best." His smile was perfection, sweet, warm, and full of love.

And then, without warning, he grabbed my hip with one hand and yanked me to the edge of the bed. Without giving me a moment to be self-conscious about his face pressed to my center, he descended on me.

He licked a single stripe along my opening, top to bottom, groaning in appreciation, and I forgot the entire concept of self-consciousness.

Kit must have taken notes earlier in the carriage, for there was none of the exploratory hesitance. Instead he applied the movements he'd perfected with his fingers to his tongue. He worked my bud with the exact pressure and motion I liked.

When he slipped a finger inside my channel, he ripped a, "Kit!" from me.

I felt his smile against my flesh, at least three-quarters of one. Pushing myself back onto my elbows, I dug a hand into his hair. His eyes met mine down the length of my body and it was the most erotic sight of my life.

My breath was too ragged and I tried to swallow past the knot that was forming in my throat. At that precise moment, he did something with his fingers and sucked on my bud. Incapable of words, I nodded, encouraging him.

I couldn't speak, not when the only words trapped on the edge of my tongue were, *Yes, please, I'll marry you. I love you.* My chest ached at that realization, a sharp contrast to the mind-numbing pleasure his efforts wrought. It was everything I'd never wanted. All I could do was clutch his hand tighter, give him the words I couldn't say that way.

Too soon, I found myself at the edge of a cliff, much higher than the one I'd jumped from earlier. Kit beckoned me over with his lips, tongue, fingers, the scrape of his beard, and the gentle way his fingers tightened against mine, urging me to let go. It was all I needed to embrace the ecstasy of the fall into his arms.

Dimly, I was aware of being bundled into the bed and pressed along Kit's side, but it took several moments for my sluggish thoughts to catch up.

He twirled a curl around and around on his finger with a quiet smile on his face. Even though it wasn't the wide, broad thing from earlier, the entirety of it lived in his eyes.

He caught my gaze. "No, I thought I had a few more moments with languorous Davina."

"You do," I murmured, snuggling into the nook that had become mine in recent days.

"Good. You're always moving, and I adore that, but it's nice to study you like this too."

"I don't move in my sleep."

"The bruises on my shins suggest otherwise."

"I kicked you?" I pressed up on his chest to meet his teasing smirk.

"Worth it," he whispered and pressed me back down. I found his free hand and traced the long fingers with my sleepy ones. The hand that brought me to peaks of ecstasy was the very same one that defended my honor. I pulled them to my lips, kissing each one.

Beneath me, Kit shifted and leaned down in what was surely an uncomfortable way to meet my lips for too brief a moment.

"Kit?"

He hummed.

"You're a good man."

I felt his single huff of laughter more than heard it. "I try."

"It's annoying, of course. But you are."

"I know, imagine how annoying it is to *be* me." There was laughter in his voice.

"I'm not entirely certain how you live with yourself, day in and day out."

"It is most inconvenient. But I've learned to distract myself by rescuing beautiful menaces."

I pressed up on his chest, ignoring the *oomph* he made. "You're not allowed to rescue anyone but me."

He pulled me down for a lingering kiss. "I wouldn't dream of it. Besides, there are no menaces like you."

And there are no grumpy solicitors like you. "Good. See that you don't."

"Every time I begin to forget you're a lady, you say something like that in that haughty tone. I think you've ruined me."

"What do you mean?"

"I don't think it's entirely normal for one's member to harden when a woman orders one about."

I burst into giggles, and his joined mine. His face found my shoulder, hovering above him. "You should always harden when I order you about."

"Yes, my lady. That shouldn't be a problem," he whispered between grinning lips.

"Only me though, no one else," I insisted.

"I wouldn't dream of it, possessive little menace."

"Good," I said, tracing his still-grinning lips with my fingertips. He kissed them gently before I pulled away and settled back against him. I moved my fingers to his chest, where his heart beat steadily. There, I traced a large *D*.

Kit didn't say anything, but I felt his lips quirk against my forehead.

"Good night, Davina."

I nuzzled in closer. "Good night, Kit."

It was a long time before his breathing evened out, and longer still before I finally closed my eyes.

Thirty-Four

NORTH ROAD—APRIL 14, 1817

KIT

The closer we got to Scotland, the more pensive Davina became. Waking in her arms, likely for the last time, had been a beautiful torture.

But now, every mile brought us closer to goodbye, and the ache in my heart grew with every hoofbeat.

Our luncheon at the George and Boar had been unremarkable and we were hurtling toward the border as the sun began to set.

Davina was lovely as always in the evening light wearing a new-to-me purple frock that was at once plainer than what she usually wore and still more embellished than the other dresses she'd worn thus far on our journey.

A few miles ago, she grabbed my hand and dragged it to the lavender folds of her gown. She seemed content to trace my fingers with hers.

"We should probably drive through the night if Alfie and Rory can manage it," I said, breaking the heavy silence.

"All right," she agreed without argument. It was worrying.

Davina was nothing if not full of opinions. And usually ones well worth considering.

"Unless you object?"

"No, we should get to Xander. We've already been delayed."

"Davina... You've been quiet today. Is everything well? You're not... regretting last night?"

She turned her sharp gaze on me. "No! You're not? Are you?"

"No, no. I could never."

"Well, good."

"Are you nervous about managing things with Tom and your brother? Because I feel confident in our plan."

"I do too," she insisted. "I'm just... considering a few things."

"Like what? Perhaps I can be of assistance."

She turned on the bench to face me fully and tucked an ankle under her knee in an unladylike fashion. "I need to explain something to you. It doesn't change anything, but I just... You deserve to know."

"All right..."

"I'm not denying your proposal to be contrarian. It's not marriage that I don't want—or not just marriage. It's love."

"What?" I could hear my heart breaking along with my voice.

"You didn't know my father, and you don't know my mother well. My mother is... She's magnificent in her own way. But people don't— She's too much for a lot of people. She feels everything too deeply, and while those feelings are usually self-centered in nature, her responses can be—well, too much. My mother loved my father, as much as she was capable of. My father was one of the people who didn't understand her. He was cruel to her. He dismissed the things that were important to her. And he loathed her feelings, excessive and reasonable alike. The things he said to and about her in the weeks after Gabriel died... He's burning in hell for them, I'm certain of it. Sometimes I think he hated her. But she still loved him. She mourns him to this day, in her own eccentric way."

I tightened my fingers around hers, offering the little comfort she seemed willing to accept. She was so calm, so even through her speech. It was as though she had gone elsewhere and it was only her body delivering her explanation.

"That isn't the only reason. Celine, beautiful vivacious Celine... You would not recognize her today if you had seen her after Gabriel died. She sobbed herself to sleep in the muck above his grave. Not once, but day after day after day. Love destroyed her."

"We wouldn't be like that—"

"And Xander, poor Xander. If anyone were to find out about his love—he could be hanged. One mistake and I could lose my brother forever. To love."

"Davina... I—"

"So it's not that I won't marry you. I could marry, if I absolutely had to. But I cannot give you the kind of marriage you want, the kind you deserve. When I say no, it's not because I enjoy denying you or that I'm toying with you. I need you to know that. It's because I refuse to doom you to what a marriage with me would mean."

She could have cracked my chest open and left my organs free for the carrion birds. It would have hurt less. I had assumed—wrongfully, so wrongfully—that her aversion to marriage was due to the loss of the freedoms she enjoyed as a single lady of independent means.

I knew she didn't love me. But it had been so, so easy to pretend last night. And to have that shattered at my feet... It was devastating.

"Who gave you leave to decide what I can and cannot abide in a marriage? You do not love me, that much is clear.

Just say that. Do not suggest that you're denying me for my own well-being," I snapped, my fury taking even me by surprise. She ripped her hand from mine, brows raised in astonishment.

"Kit—"

"You've never been a martyr before, Davina. I cannot believe you've chosen now to begin. And to what purpose? Did you think refusing to wed me would keep my heart intact? I can promise you that it hasn't."

"I don't—"

"And your explanation, it's shite. You love so deeply. The way you speak about your mother? It screams of love. Cee? You love her better than I love my own sisters. And your brother? You've kidnapped me in order to help him. You've committed a literal felony."

"It's an abduction act—"

"Yes, thank you, that was the point of my speech, so good of you to catch it. Do you suppose denying the love you feel for your family will leave you any less broken should something happen to any of them?"

"No, but I cannot help..." I recognized the exact moment she realized the implication of that statement.

"Help it. You cannot help but love them. It's just me you can so easily resist."

"I didn't mean it that way," she protested.

"Well, I cannot help it, Davina. I cannot will it away. I cannot wish it away. Lord knows I've tried. I love you. I'm in love with you. It happened quite against my will. I cannot even name the moment it happened. But I suppose I am evidence of your point. Because this... this is devastating. And the truth is, I do not know what is worse, the searing ache in my chest or the understanding that you are determined to live without love."

"Kit..." her voice broke, eyes welling. And damn me to hell

and back. I thought my heart already broken but apparently, faced with tears I'd caused, it shattered full to pieces.

"Oh, Christ, don't cry." I yanked her into my side. A sob broke from her and she buried her face in my chest, clutching my shirt. And wasn't that enough to make me feel like a prize arse?

"Don't you see?" she cried into my shoulder. "We're not even wed and already you hate me." Shudders racked her frame.

"I don't hate you. That's the entire problem, you little menace."

"But you would. You would and I couldn't bear it."

My shaking hand found the back of her head, quite of its own volition. Would this be the last time I touched the silken strands? Would this be the last time I held her in my arms?

"I don't hate you. You're allowed to not love me. I cannot particularly blame you. I'm a stubborn grump who's about to spend the rest of his life floundering with an earldom I'm neither interested in nor prepared for. I'm hurt—it hurts to love someone who doesn't love you. But I've decided it's absolutely worse that you don't want love. Fortunately, in spite of your best efforts, you get absolutely no say in whether other people love you. And, Davina, you have so much love to give."

Her inhale was shaky, and her exhale even more so. It wasn't until a tear landed on her curls that I recognized I was crying as well. I flicked the traitorous drops away with my wrist.

"This has to stop, Davina. We cannot keep going on as we have. I need—we need—a bit of distance. I cannot keep loving you physically if you will not allow... You said you're doing this for my own good. You may be able to separate the physical and emotional acts of love making, but I cannot."

She pulled me tighter.

"If you're certain that this is what you want, I have to let you go now." My voice was thick, syrupy, and I hated it. If I had thought my speech would convince her to stay, but it certainly wouldn't after this masculine display of tears.

"One more minute?" She whispered into my chest.

"I'll give you two."

In the end, we had three. And it wasn't nearly enough.

Thirty-Five

NORTH ROAD—APRIL 14, 1817

DAVINA

It was better this way, in the long run. A little hurt now to prevent devastation later.

Kit was quiet as night fell, sober as he stared at the passing Scottish darkness. Not at me, never at me. It was quite clear that he couldn't bear to look at me. And I hadn't noticed, hadn't realized, quite how much time Kit spent looking at me.

He frowned at me when I did something I knew he would disapprove of. After every adventure, he surveyed me for injury with a worried brow. And most recently, he looked at me with joy, with love. The emotion was drawn his warm eyes and in the full, lovely smiles I'd earned.

And now... nothing. He glared steadfast out the window. In that moment, I couldn't help but worry about the smiles. Who would coax them from him now? Would they know how rare and precious they were? Would they recognize the false, quarter smile with the half-hearted lip tilt? Would they learn the blinding magnificence that began in the corners of his eyes and traveled along his cheek to the soft fullness of his lips? The thought made my heart ache, deep in my chest and all the way to my fingertips.

It seemed unlikely that Kit and I would meet again after we parted. Perhaps we might see each other in passing at a ball someday. But Kit was not my solicitor any longer, not my protector.

Suddenly, I recognized how utterly alone I was. Mother was my mother. There was never anyone first in her mind but herself. Cee had Will now, and while she made time for me, it was not the same. Xander had Tom, his son, and Scotland. I had nothing but my adventures. Adventures that would become a lot riskier without Kit's dependable rescue.

It was rather a lot of *little hurts* I was feeling. Between the knot in my throat and the ache in my chest, I was struggling to breathe between surreptitious glances at the back of Kit's head.

Tears threatened to escape again, but I'd managed to restrain them after he released me. Now they were a silent companion, unobtrusive to anyone but me. My head had begun to throb some hours ago, the way it so often did after a cry.

I'd almost broken again when we stopped to change horses and Rory looked at me, turned to Kit, and then turned back to me and wrapped her arms around me. But I'd managed to choke back more tears.

At some point, late into the night, I must have fallen asleep, because when I woke it was daylight. It was day and I still ached, my head, my throat, my heart, the very center of me. It was all agonizing.

Kit still studied the window. If he'd moved at all, I wasn't able to tell.

We changed horses again quickly at an inn somewhere north of the border. Kit made no move to get up, so I grabbed a loaf of bread and butter and returned just as Alfie and Rory were finishing the change.

"Oh, lass, we'll turn off to yer brother's estate about a mile ahead. Then it's only ten or so on."

I nodded, then slipped back inside the carriage. My throat was so tight, I couldn't actually verbalize my contribution, but Kit turned when I set my offering between us.

"Thank you," he replied, his voice gruff with disuse and sentiment. He made no move toward the food, instead turning back to the window.

Too soon, we turned off the main road onto a smaller path. Kit gave no indication that he noticed.

A glint caught my eye. Light spilled in from the window, catching the gold of the ring still on my finger.

The tightness in my chest left no room for air. And so, devastatingly breathless, I tugged Kit's ring off my finger. It clung to my knuckle, begging to remain where it belonged. But I worked it over the joint.

"Kit?"

He turned to me, his gaze catching on the same flash of light, this time from the palm of my hand. His eyes, the color of burnt charcoal, made no effort to hide his sadness. The canyons between his brows were so deep I couldn't imagine them ever filling again. His lips parted at the sight of the ring before he swallowed thickly. The nod was nearly imperceptible, and the subsequent exhale quiet.

Slowly, with the long, masculine fingers I had so admired, he caught the ring between the thumb and forefinger. Not even for a fraction of a second, did his finger touch my palm.

I watched as he pinched the gold band and worked it between his finger and thumb, studying the ring. After a moment, he slipped it on the littlest finger of his right hand. It got stuck somewhere before the knuckle, but he was apparently convinced of its security because he merely turned back to the window.

I turned back to my own hand, where the third finger sat empty. It should have felt strange when I put the ring on. Twenty years with that finger bare and now it longed for the impossibly familiar metal band.

This, these sensations, were precisely the reason I didn't wish to enter into a marriage in the first place. They were the reason I avoided attachments. But Kit refused to be placed into the appropriate box and now I had all of these feelings. It was entirely his fault.

No sooner had I resolved to channel my unwelcome hurt into anger than we turned off onto a gravel drive.

A house came into view in the distance, just beyond a copse of trees and beyond a small pond. The stone facade had once been a tan shade, I expected, but it was blackened with grit and dirt.

Every window on the second floor had panes missing and one lacked panes entirely, instead boarded up haphazardly. Vines had climbed all the way to the roof long ago, using the stones as footholds, and had since died.

And a solitary, formerly white sheep with a black face stood in front of the house eating the grass that had sprung up in areas of low gravel in the drive.

Underneath the arched front door, a stark form appeared and my heart leapt.

The carriage hadn't fully stopped before I stumbled out and into Xander's waiting arms.

"Thank God, you're all right, Davina. What the bleeding hell were you thinking?" he whisper-shouted into my hair, wrapping his arms tighter around me.

"Xander, please, I'm fine." And I was, of course, physically entirely unharmed. I rather thought my heart would be damaged for some time.

"And you!" he loud-shouted over my head. "I pay you to have sense. What were you thinking, allowing her to galivant across the entire bleeding country?"

"*Allow* is a strong word," Kit grumbled. I felt him skirt around us to stand on the drive. "When have you ever allowed your sister to do anything, Your Grace?"

"You should have put a stop to it!"

"I'm too tired for this," Kit grumbled. "Talk to your sister. If you want me hanged when you've finished, I'll be around somewhere."

"It's not his fault, truly," I added.

The gravel crunched behind Xander and I pulled away to see Mr. Grayson wearing a sheepish expression. His legs were still too long for the rest of him, but he'd filled out. The adorable little cricket.

"Lady Davina, Kit, good to see you both," he mumbled, with cheeks flushed.

"Tom," Kit added and pulled him into a half hug. It was so quiet, I wasn't entirely certain I hadn't dreamed it up, but I thought he whispered, "'M happy for you."

Tom wouldn't allow him to get a quick release and instead pulled Kit closer. "Thank you," he breathed, his voice thick with emotion. It was that moment when I realized Tom had no idea of his reception. He didn't know how easily Kit had accepted the news about him and Xander in the carriage days before. Kit was his family by marriage, so it made sense he was relieved. "Thank you."

It was a sincerity I wasn't used to from my brief interactions with Mr. Grayson. He was quick-witted and jovial, always eager to make light of a tense situation if Kate was to be believed.

"Let's get you both inside," Xander muttered, glaring at Kit, though his intensity had lessened after the display with Mr. Grayson.

A few unusual servants took his words as their cue to step into action and haul my trunk off the back of the carriage at Rory's behest and direct Alfie to the stables.

The sheep took objection to the movement around his—her?—luncheon choice and offered a disgruntled *maaaah* before charging at a passing servant who dodged him or her with a practiced sidestep.

"You were not jesting about the sheep," I said, feeling the corner of my lip turn up for the first time in nearly a day.

"No, we never jest about Fenella," Xander said.

"Fenella?" Kit asked.

"The name came with the sheep, and the sheep came with the house." Xander guided me inside. The foyer smelled of fresh-cut wood and recently laid lacquer. Everywhere I glanced, there was evidence of Xander and Mr. Grayson's efforts to restore the house. Dust and various tools I didn't know the names of were strewn about every available surface.

"There's, uh, there's really only a few rooms that are functional at the moment. We rushed to finish up an extra bedroom when we received word of your arrival," Mr. Grayson explained.

"What are the chances you can show me to a room, any room? His Grace and Lady Davina need to speak," Kit said.

"Of course. Are you hungry? I can have something sent up."

"Not particularly. But thank you." Kit studiously avoided turning his gaze in my direction and his shoulders relaxed a fraction when he followed Tom up the stairs.

"Best avoid this board." Tom pointed to one that had been painted a bright red. "It's rotted out and we haven't had a chance to fix it yet."

"Noted."

Xander took the opportunity to drag me down the hall and into a study. The decor was aged and there were the remnants of water damage underneath the window. But he'd clearly made progress with the space. The floor had been repaired and the wall was patched in a few places.

He all but shoved me into a seat beside the fire, then took the matching dark leather chair. "You're unharmed?"

"Yes." *Physically.* "I'm entirely unharmed."

"Because Mr. Summers looks quite worse for wear."

"I'm fine, Xander. Truly. So is he."

"Good. Then I have to ask again, what the bleeding hell were you thinking? Do you know how worried I've been? How worried Celine has been? The letter came by express two days ago. I've been positively sick!" Xander's hands twisted into frustrated knots in front of him.

"I'm sorry for worrying you. I just—I thought I could help. Ki—Mr. Summers solves all of our problems. You have a problem, and he was sure to have a solution."

"So you kidnapped him?" His tone had shifted to incredulous.

"It's abduction, actually, when it's an adult."

"Dav..."

"Well, I didn't want to tell him about you and Mr. Grayson until I was sure he wouldn't be wretched about it. And if I had told him I wanted to take him to Scotland without explanation or a chaperone, he wouldn't have agreed. And *abduction* is a strong term. He came more or less willingly."

"It's a felony."

"I let him pack before we left, Xand. It was hardly a crack job."

"Christ... And since you so helpfully pointed out that you were unchaperoned with the man for days, perhaps you'd like to explain to me why I shouldn't have him waiting for you at the end of an aisle."

"Nothing happened," I lied.

"I find that very difficult to believe." His overgrown brow was furrowed in an attempt at solemnity. It wasn't particularly ineffectual.

"It didn't! K—Mr. Summers was the perfect gentleman."

"Oh, I very much believe that. It's you I don't believe."

"There was one incident with a game of hazard in an inn. But I wasn't compromised." *Then*.

"Davina…"

"You know I have no interest in marriage."

"If you could be with child that's not really relevant—"

"I'm not," I rushed to assure him, briefly grateful for Kit's restraint.

"Fine, I will not drag you down the aisle. But if I discover that you are with child, I will force the issue."

"And you won't see Mr. Summers hanged?"

"No, I imagine several days in a carriage with you was more than enough punishment for the crime of not allowing you to get yourself killed. What did you do to him anyway? Why does he have stitches?"

A carriage accident was absolutely not the right answer. If Xander hadn't noticed the Leighton crest on the carriage, I wasn't about to point it out. "Well, there was also an incident with the weather…"

"The weather…" he repeated, wariness settling deep into his voice and frame.

"And the carriage…"

"If you are about to tell me there was a carriage accident, I may have a fit of apoplexy."

"I'm perfectly well!" I assured him in an overly cheery tone.

"And Mr. Summers?"

"He… You know, we're both well. So perhaps we don't need to discuss all the details."

"You know what, it's better that I do not know. I suppose you wouldn't be you without a bit of mischief."

"You suppose correctly. Now enough about this, where is my nephew?"

"He's resting. Do you want to meet him?"

"Do I want to cuddle my nephew?" I asked, incredulity spilling into the words. Without a shred of doubt, I knew that snuggling a babe was the only thing that would ease this ache.

"All right, ridiculous question. Come along."

Thirty-Six

KILMARNOCK ABBEY, EDINBURGH—APRIL
15, 1817

KIT

"How was your trip?" Tom asked as we stepped around the rotten board.

"Eventful."

"How so?"

"If it's all the same, I'd rather not talk about it." We navigated a hall with peeling paper and broken sconces before we came to a few closed doors at the end of the hall.

"Right, sorry. You said you were tired." Tom's tone was weary and I immediately felt guilty when faced with his wary expression.

"No, I apologize. I'm not fit for polite company at the moment. But I'd like to leave as soon as is practical. Do you think we can sit down at dinner and discuss our options?"

"Options?" He opened the third door from the end of the hall and ushered me inside. It wasn't much, but it was clean, which was more than I could say for the rest of the house. The blue bed coverings were recently laundered and there was a fresh basin of water and clean linens in the corner adjacent from the window. The window had a single pane that had been boarded up, but I doubted it would signify much.

"Da—Lady Davina brought me here to help with the legitimacy issue."

"Oh, I didn't—the letter didn't specify why you were coming."

"That's my fault. I wasn't informed of the reasoning or direction of my abduction until halfway to Lincolnshire."

"Right. Good. Uh, I don't know how much you know about... well, why I'm here. You said you're ha—"

"She told me," I interjected.

"Well then, I suppose that's that. You're—are you... Never mind." He spun on his heels, closing the distance to the door in one long stride.

"Tom, I truly am not at my best. I'm almost certain to make a muck of what I'm about to say. And it's absolutely not my place to say it." He paused his retreat but didn't turn. "But you should know... I'm proud of you. What you've done, the life you've built. It was a brave thing."

He turned then, his eyes wide and wondrous. "You mean that?"

"Realizing what you want, who you love, and choosing them, building a life together in spite of all obstacles? There's nothing braver. People with far fewer impediments make the easier choice every day."

"That might have been more words strung together at once than I've heard from you in the entirety of our acquaintance." Tom's voice was thick with sentiment.

"Really? I'm quite loquacious."

That shocked a laugh out of him, but it had a heavy, thick note. "Is there... You have... someone?"

"I thought so, but I was very wrong."

His blue-green gaze narrowed shrewdly. "Ah. Hasket siblings... They're infuriating, and impossible to forget."

"I didn't say that," I insisted. I wouldn't have Davina—not that way, not forced to wed me with dread in her eyes.

"I won't say anything," he assured me and shifted his weight to one hip.

"There's nothing to say."

"All right." His smirk chafed my pride.

"Does your brother know where you are?" I retorted, shifting the focus back to him.

"Yes, actually."

"Which one?"

"Both, though one is still somewhat confused by the entire concept." His lips tipped down in his backward, sheepish version of a smile.

"Really? The mutton-headed ignoramus isn't having a snit?"

"You really shouldn't speak about Hugh like that."

"Ah, but you knew who I meant. And besides, I outrank him now." It was a cheerful realization. I wondered if his title-hungry mother would die of shock when she learned of it.

"Accepted the inevitable then?"

"Unfortunately."

"Best of luck to you. I'll leave you to settle in. Will you join us for supper?"

"Yes, thank you."

The door rattled in the frame after he shut it. I collapsed onto the bed, elbows to knees as I dragged a hand through my mussed curls.

Rosehill hadn't called me out the moment he saw us. It was a better fate than I deserved.

The instinctive disappointment that he hadn't ordered Davina and I to wed that instant wasn't something I was proud of. Objectively, I knew I only wanted to marry Davina if she wanted it too, as desperately as I did. But the convenience of having the decision taken from both of us...

Was it so shameful that I wished it? Just for a second?

No, I decided. I was only a man. A man faced with the temptation presented by Davina Hasket.

∼

THE DINING TABLE, once fine, had clearly been inadvertently sawed into. I couldn't fathom having so much money that one used a fine mahogany table as a sawhorse, but I was only an earl—and a new one at that, not a duke.

I was the second to arrive to supper, preceded by a young lady thoroughly in transition from girl to woman. Her nearly black hair was wild and free, and her brow was the unmistakable dark shock that marked her a Hasket.

There wasn't a single doubt in my mind that she was Gabriel's daughter.

"Ye must be the solicitor," she said with a curious look.

"Mr. Summers," I said, gesturing to my person.

"Sorcha McAllen."

"Pleased to make your acquaintance, Miss McAllen." She surveyed me up and down, unimpressed. A Hasket through and through.

We were interrupted by the arrival of the rest of our party. Davina cradled her new nephew to her chest, bickering with Rosehill as they walked. "It was a little game of hazard. It wasn't my fault they were cheating."

"You didn't need to involve yourself," he protested.

Tom trailed behind them, wearing a bemused expression.

Davina, at last, turned her attention to the table. "Oh!" Her mouth formed a perfect O shape at the sight of the woman who was technically her niece. "Oh," she repeated, more sedately, her voice thick.

"Oh," Sorcha mocked.

Far from offended, Davina handed the babe off to her

brother before making her way to the woman's side. "Sorry, that was rude. It's just— Well, I— Thank you. Just, thank you." She caught the woman's hand and squeezed enthusiastically.

Miss McAllen looked at the offending touch with a hint of disdain. "For what? Launching a bairn? Or being yer brother's by-blow?"

Davina laughed, taking no offense to the tone or content of the words. "Both? Is both all right?"

"Neither is all right. I dinnae have a say in the second and I can assure ye, ye were not top of mind with the first."

"Oh, you must vex Xander beyond belief. Well done! It is my favorite pastime."

Rosehill sighed and settled in at the table with Tom at his side. The babe was still cradled in his arms. I took the third seat on their side, leaving Davina and Miss McAllen for the opposite. The same Miss McAllen who was staring at Davina as if she were a novelty. It likely wasn't the reaction she was used to with such a speech.

"Davina, do not encourage her," Xander said.

"I suppose no introductions are needed then?" Tom added.

"I think we're all clear," Sorcha muttered as a plump housekeeper arrived with soup. A white soup, it was creamy with the right bite of onion to balance the sweetness of the wine.

I was relieved to be seated diagonally from Davina. I doubted I could have hidden my feelings if I had nowhere else to cast my gaze. As it was, I struggled to keep my gaze on my food.

Rosehill managed to sip the soup with the babe seated comfortably on his lap beside me. The boy gnawed on his own hand, happily drooling on it.

"Mr. Summers, it seems I owe you an apology."

"Unnecessary, Your Grace."

"Xander, please. I'm just Xander here. And I do need to apologize. I knew, of course, that Davina was behind this fiasco as usual. But my worry for her clouded my judgment. I know better than most how impossible it is to get her to see reason when she's made a decision."

"I'm right here," Davina grumbled into her soup.

"Yes, and you know as well as everyone else how foolish your choices were."

"I was trying to help."

"It was no trouble," I interjected lest this supper turn into a bickering match.

"That might be the least believable lie ever told," Tom added over Miss McAllen's derisive snort.

"I'm happy to help in any way I can."

"Did you happen to have any suggestions about how to manage the legality of the situation?" Rosehill asked.

"Well, Your Grace, I had one notion, but it's not precisely — Well, it's quite a blatant fraud."

"*Xander*," he insisted again. "And go on."

I wanted the distance of his title, but I couldn't press on. Not without being considered rude. "How many people are aware of the situation?"

"The staff, the father. It's been kept relatively quiet."

"Are they trustworthy?"

"All but the father."

"Can he be bought?" I asked

Xander looked to Miss McAllen who rolled her eyes in irritation, but answered, "Yes."

I turned back to Xander. "Are you willing to give him an allowance contingent on his silence?"

"I'd like to ship him to Australia," he grumbled.

"Understandable. But in the interest of keeping this quiet,

an allowance? And perhaps a commission in order for him to be elsewhere?"

"If I must."

"I'll draw up the contracts. He'll lose the allowance if he ever breathes a word of it," I explained. "As for the rest, we're fortunate to be in Scotland. The marriage laws are much more favorable for this sort of thing than in England."

"How so?" Tom asked.

"No need for a clergyman, reading of the banns, or a license. All that is needed is a proclamation before witnesses for a legal marriage."

"I knew about the banns and license, but you don't need a clergyman?" Tom questioned again.

"No, anyone can serve as witness."

"And we can be married?"

It dawned on me suddenly and much too late, the reason for the line of questions. "Yes, Tom. *You* can be married. I wouldn't want to test its legality, but yes. Right now, if you wish."

The smile that bloomed across Tom's face was unlike any I'd ever seen before. I hadn't known him at all, it seemed, in the years I'd been joining their family dinners.

Quietly, Xander's hand found Tom's atop the table. "Tonight?" he asked, smiling at Tom's nod.

He turned to Davina with a raised brow. Her eyes were sparkling and lovely with delight for her brother.

Even Miss McAllen was hiding a pleased smile by studying the table with undue concentration.

The housekeeper returned to serve a roasted chicken, trailed by a footman with a dish of rosemary potatoes, before they dipped back out of the room.

After swallowing thickly, Xander turned back to me. "And the rest of it?"

"I think our best option is to invent a woman—possibly

someone the *ton* would deem unsuitable for a duke. That would explain why you went to Scotland and why you've abandoned London. You were wed, legally, in front of witnesses. She died, perhaps in childbirth. You tell all of this to the clergyman when the boy is baptized. You'll probably want to go to London for that—it would lend more authenticity if the boy's legitimacy is ever questioned for some reason. Though I suspect the brow will prevent any speculation."

"It's so simple," Miss McAllen stated, none of her characteristic sarcasm in her tone.

"Yes, much simpler than if we were in England or Wales. Then there would need to be a more significant paper trail and church records. I'll create some financial documents that indicate the presence of a wife—jewelry and flower expenditures, a settlement, things of that nature. And keep them in our files at the office for record purposes. You need only give me a name to use."

"Mr. Summers, I cannot thank you enough—not just for this, but for keeping Davina from harm as well."

"Kit," I replied. "Just Kit. And I may have need of your assistance." I took my first bite of chicken.

"Oh, of course. I cannot even fathom a sufficient payment for this undertaking. Do you suppose £5,000 would do it? Or is £10,000 more appropriate?"

"Xander!" Davina protested.

My stomach sank, and the chicken slid down my throat to plop in my gut like a cannon. The thought of receiving money for this week... It felt cheap and tawdry, even though the sums certainly couldn't be considered so.

"I, uh, I don't think that will be necessary. I was rather hoping for a different kind of help. I've accepted the inevitable and am planning to take my place in society as Lord Leighton. Ignoring the title has only made a muck of things. I expect I'll be in need of a great deal of advice, and perhaps a friendly face if we both happen to be in town."

"Of course, anything. I apologize if my offer was…"

"No, it was very generous."

"If he dosnae want the money, can I have it?" Miss McAllen asked, breaking the tension. I shot her a grateful look. She flushed, returning her gaze to her potatoes.

"When you solve all of my problems single-handedly and discover a way for me to marry the man I love, you may have £10,000."

"I provided ye with an heir."

I rather thought her point was a fair one.

He considered for a moment. "I've already dowered you. And you stole from me for years."

"And that dosenae do anything for me in the moment," she retorted without a hint of shame.

It was at that point that the evening dissolved into the inevitable bickering. Too many Haskets in one place was never without chaos. When Xander dropped a bite of potato on the baby's head, Tom slipped the boy onto his lap without a word as though it were commonplace.

I'd always thought Davina the argumentative sibling, but it seemed I was mistaken. Or I was until she joined into the fray with a well-placed, "Ugh, Xander!" The sound was so familiar, it warmed the still-broken pieces of my heart.

Thirty-Seven

KILMARNOCK ABBEY, EDINBURGH—APRIL
15, 1817

DAVINA

AFTER SUPPER, I'd run out to the drive with every candle I could locate. Xander's insistence on the dilapidated little shed and a half-collapsed sheepfold for the ceremony location was a little bizarre. But who was I to question a man on his wedding day? He was off changing into his wedding clothes, and I hadn't the foggiest idea what Tom was doing.

I enlisted Alfie's assistance in forming two rows of candles along the gravel path and ensuring they were evenly spaced. Then I set about lighting them one by one until there was a flickering, glowing path through the darkness that enveloped us. Rory provided droll commentary from her place leaning against the tree at the end of my makeshift aisle.

Tom was the first to arrive with a gasp. He'd changed as well, donning a bluish-green waistcoat that matched his eyes.

He caught my hand in both of his. "Thank you, Davina. For everything."

"Are you certain you wish to do this? It's not too late to escape the madness," I teased.

"You've met my brothers, have you not? And my mother..."

"You're right, there was never any hope for you."

Kit appeared behind Tom, surveying the scene with a soft expression, and my heart wrenched at the sight.

"I need to go get Xander," I said to Tom. "Otherwise he'll never be finished fussing with his hair."

"I'll be right here," he said, taking his place at the end of the aisle.

I used my thumb nail to slice off a single white daisy growing wild by the door. A little bird perched on a nearby tree chirped his approval twice.

I found my brother inside fussing with his black cravat. He wore his usual black-and-white attire, never a pop of color for him. I set the daisy aside on a table and batted his hands away. The fabric was fine but the knot was simpler than his usual style. I fluffed and smoothed until it was coaxed into that perfectly disheveled elegance he liked.

Then I snagged the flower and pulled a pin from my hair to fix it in place.

With the arm opposite the flower, Xander pulled me into a hug. "I love you, Dav. Thank you."

I flushed at the praise and pulled away. "You do not need to thank me. It's just repayment for all the times you saved me."

"With Kit's help."

I swallowed at that thought. At the understanding that I would have to rescue myself from here on out. "Come, it's time to get you married."

He put my hand in the crook of his arm and we slipped out to the garden. His gasp of delight was payment enough for my efforts with the candles. Tom waited at the end of the aisle, Kit at his side.

Kit, whose gaze found mine in the dim glow of the

candles. Down the entirety of the aisle, he didn't so much as blink. He watched me with the same expression he wore during our night together. It was love, pure and unmistakable. This time, though, there was a sad downturn to the corners of his eyes and on his lips.

When we reached the other bridegroom, Xander released me in favor of his soon-to-be husband. I was dimly aware of Sorcha at my side, bouncing the baby on her hip. On one of the listing posts of the sheepfold in my periphery, a little bird landed, black and white with a shock of yellow. I knew Alfie was somewhere nearby. Vaguely, I heard Rory acting as self-appointed officiant.

But it was all muted by the rushing in my ears. My gaze had narrowed to the point that I could see nothing but Kit. Kit, who refused to let my nonsense stand without comment but helped me anyway. Kit, who defended me from almost the very first. Kit, who lied to his own family for the sake of my reputation. Kit, who worshiped me with every inch of his body and soul. Kit, who asked for only one thing, the one thing I couldn't bring myself to give him.

"Aye," Kit said, his voice gruff with disuse and sentiment. The word snapped me back to the ceremony.

"And, Davina, do ye bear witness to this marriage?" Rory asked.

"Yes." I hardly recognized my own voice, thick and rusted.

"I declare ye forged in marriage," she said. And it was done. My brother was married to his love.

Happy tears streamed down my face, mixed with a few that were longing for Kit. When I turned back to him, I caught only a glimpse of his back as he slipped inside the house.

The celebration was moved into the house where all but Kit made quick work of a bottle of champagne, at which point the newlyweds clearly wished for their privacy.

Sorcha sat beside me on a worn chaise and took a swig directly from the bottle.

"Tell me you've done that in front of Xander."

"What do ye take me for? A simpleton? Of course I've done that in front of yer brother. He makes a ridiculous squawking sound when I do."

"Those are my favorites. He looks like a disgruntled chipmunk when you..."

I stayed awake a few hours longer, certain sleep wouldn't come were I to try anyway. I used the time to interrogate Sorcha and learn about Gabriel's daughter. She shared his sharp wit, nonchalant attitude, and dark eyes. Eventually, she pleaded a need for rest and I was forced to retire.

Against all odds, I fell asleep after only an hour or so of tossing and turning.

I WAS surprised and not at all surprised to find the breakfast table empty when I arrived. Xander and Tom would sleep late. Sorcha, too, I expected would be a late riser. And Kit was almost certainly avoiding me and had likely broken his fast in his room.

I munched quietly on a slice of toast between sips of tea, contemplating the sawed gash on the table with bemusement.

Earlier than I expected, Tom and Xander entered, hand in hand. Both were dressed only in shirtsleeves and breeches, their hair sleep-tousled.

"I didn't expect to see you two for some time."

"We needed sustenance," Tom said, filling two plates with the various offerings on the sideboard while Xander fixed two cups of tea. The easy domesticity of it made me smile.

"Have you seen Kit? Is he still abed?"

"Dav... he left at first light," Tom said with an unreadable expression.

"What?" My shrill tone, combined with the crack of my knife falling onto the plate below, startled my companions.

"Kit left at first light. I thought you knew," Xander repeated, taking the seat across from me. He was loose-limbed and unconcerned, entirely unaware of the way my heart clenched and refused to release. Even as I struggled to comprehend the words, my body reacted with instinctive agony.

"But what about our plan?" I whispered.

"The plan will go ahead. He isn't needed here for it. In fact, the sooner the documents he's creating end up where they need to be, the better. Besides, he's been away from his work, his life, for a week. He's eager to be home."

"But..."

"In fact, you abducted the man for no reason at all but to serve as companion and protector. All of this could have been managed by letter."

"But he— We..." Even through my head's numbness and my heart's crushing, I could hear the broken, tinny quality to my voice.

"Tom, could you give us a moment?"

"Of course." He set the plates down on the table and grabbed one of the teas and a saucer before leaving us.

"Davina... Is there something you wish to tell me?"

"There's nothing to tell," I insisted, my throat too thick to be convincing.

"Because if there was, you could talk to me about it." He peered at me knowingly.

"Is it worth it?" I blurted.

"Is what worth it?"

"Tom, what you two have. Because I was absolutely certain that it wasn't. Those months of watching Cee grieve... The way father dismissed everything about mother..."

A knowing expression crossed my brother's face. "What Tom and I have... Yes, it's worth it. Every single day that I wake next to him, it's worth the grief that might come someday—perhaps far too soon. He's... even a single moment would be worth it. And I know someday one of us will be left alone. And then that person will know Celine's grief truly." He broke off, swallowing. "You mourned for Gabriel. You still do. Do you not?"

"Yes."

"Would you give up the time you had with him? If it meant you wouldn't feel the hurt."

Gabriel had left an indelible mark on my youth. When Father wanted a respectable lady and Mother wanted a doll, he accepted me as I was. He taught me unladylike pursuits and encouraged my adventures. His absence still ached. But if I hadn't had him, I wouldn't be me. "No."

"I can tell you right now that Celine would say the same. She wouldn't trade a single second of her life with him to ease the pain she felt." He reached for my hand, offering a gentle squeeze. "The bad, it doesn't erase the good, Dav. You have to live for the good, otherwise you're just hiding from the bad. And I've never known you to hide from anything."

I nodded, but it was a thoughtless, monotonous movement.

"Is this why you've always insisted you do not wish to wed?"

"Yes," I croaked.

"Oh, Davina. I thought... I assumed you wanted to retain the freedoms afforded to you, living independently as you do. If I had known... we would have had this conversation years ago. Until last night, I knew with absolute certainty that I would never marry for love. Do you understand how precious the opportunity is?"

His gaze was imploring, willing me to believe him.

"He asked me to marry him." My voice was cold, hollow, belonging to someone else, someone whose chest wasn't so tight she could hardly breathe.

"And you said no."

"Yes."

"Do you love him?"

"I don't— I've spent so long fighting against the feeling. How would I even know?"

"I think you do know. I think that if you didn't feel it, there would be nothing to fight." He pressed his lips together, stacking them to one side of his face in that perfectly Xander expression of sympathy.

A sob broke free. "He's gone. It's too late."

"Is it?"

"He— I rejected him, repeatedly. I abducted him. I ruined his life. Hell, his entire family believes we're married."

His head tipped to the side, brow furrowing. "I beg your pardon?"

"It doesn't matter. He'd never accept me. Not after everything."

"We're revisiting the family-believes-you're-married issue later. That man knows better than anyone, except perhaps me, how infuriating you are. He's rescued you from ill-considered occupations and pirate whiskey. And I cannot even mention that time you snuck aboard one of His Majesty's finest vessels without nausea. He knows all that—knows you—and he still asked you to marry him. That's a man who loves you. Now that I consider it, he's probably the only man on earth I believe could survive a marriage to you. If he knew you loved him, he never would have left without a ring on your finger."

My heart froze for a breath, two, before racing ahead to compensate.

"What if he refuses me?" I whispered, breathless.

"Then he's not worthy of you and it's a problem solved in

advance. A man ought to have thick skin and very little pride if he's to be yours."

"I have to go." I shoved my chair back, scraping it against the half-finished wood. I rounded the table, making for the door.

I was halfway there before he called out, "Davina?"

"Yes?" I spun on my heel to face him.

"For the love of all that is holy, please promise to lie to me about the events of your adventure for the rest of our days."

I rushed back to his side and learned down to wrap an arm around his shoulders with a squeeze.

"I swear."

"Thank you. Now go find him."

I raced down the hall, nearly crashing into the housekeeper, and caught her about the shoulders. "The stables?"

"Turn left, just down the path," she said, not even raising a brow in surprise.

"Thank you," I called, already making for the door. I had an abduction to carry out.

Thirty-Eight

NORTH ROAD—APRIL 16, 1817

KIT

It was with a numb kind of exhaustion that I tipped my head back against the seat, willing the miles away. My only relief was the knowledge that the blasted so-called carriage we'd set off in was rotting on the roadside somewhere.

I'd left before the sun and it was barely beginning to kiss the horizon.

Up front, Rory intended to take me only as far as the first inn, where I could hire drivers for the rest of my travels. I rather thought my return journey would be lonelier and a lot less eventful than the last.

My heart gave a disgruntled thump in my aching chest at the thought. I didn't want an uneventful trip. I didn't want an uneventful *life*. Not any longer.

There were bits of Davina scattered all throughout the carriage. I found a new hairpin trapped between the floorboards. Silken strands of her hair had tangled in the velvet fabric of the seat. Every breath was filled with her earthy amber scent.

A sensible man would've opened the window, bequeathed the strands of hair to the wind, and allowed the fresh air to wipe away the essence of her. A smart man would've given the pin to the mud. Apparently, I was a self-loathing one.

I kept the window shut tight and the curtains drawn. Locking myself in this tomb with only memories of her. Hoarding each inhale like a precious jewel. Much like the one tucked on my knuckle, the one that looked and felt unnatural there in a way it never had when I brushed it with my thumb while it lived on Davina's finger.

It was a bitter kind of irony, in truth. I'd accepted the inevitable. I would fulfill my duties as an earl. As such, I could give any woman anything her heart desired. Except Davina. Wild, reckless Davina, who wanted nothing less than the life I offered.

The miles rolled by, punctuated only by an occasional jolt perpetuated by a rut in the road that had my empty stomach turning over.

What was I to do now? I hadn't been lying when I told Davina the rest of my life would seem ordinary by comparison. The thought was suddenly an unbearable prison.

And the knowledge that such a loving, vivacious soul feared love itself... The world was worse for it.

The carriage came to an abrupt stop at the same time I heard Rory cry, "Whoa!"

Presumably, another carriage passed on a too-narrow stretch. I didn't bother to open the curtain. There was nothing for me outside.

Suddenly, the handle turned on the door of its own volition. Too quick for me to react, it flung open to reveal the most breathtaking sight of my life.

Davina, bathed in morning light, hair loose and windswept, met my desperate gaze with one of her own.

And then, a teasing smile graced her sweet lips. "This is an abduction."

My heart tripped, recognizing instinctively the brightness in her gaze and the mirth in her tone before my head caught up. The expression was new on her, but somehow not. The affection, the joy were regular friends. But the crinkles in the corners of her eyes, the tilt of her lips, the softness of her gaze —*love*, this was what love looked like on Davina Hasket's face.

"It is?" I croaked as I spilled out of the carriage to join her on the rolling Scottish hills. When her smile didn't falter, I felt my own tugging at the corners of my lips.

"Yes, and a robbery," she added.

"A robbery?" My brow quirked to the heavens.

"Yes. I'm given to understand that you are in possession of a very special piece of jewelry. I'd like it back." Nothing could have restrained my smile from her in that moment.

A lock of hair slipped across her brow and I reached to brush it behind her ear without thought. The ring, still trapped between the second and third knuckles of my littlest finger caught the light, casting it into my eyes, blinding me.

"This?" I asked as I pulled my hand away only to wiggle the delicate band off my finger. Its sparkles danced in the sunlight as I held it out to her.

"Yes, that belongs to me." Her tone was all prim duchess even against her plain sun-yellow gown and wild hair. She plucked the ring out of my palm. I watched, breath caught in my throat, as she slipped it back home. Her smile bloomed ever brighter, the sight was blinding, threatening to outstrip all my senses.

My heart threatened to burst. Even overcome, I couldn't help but press her. "And where do you plan on taking me?"

"Everywhere."

"Everywhere?"

"Everywhere I go, forever. You're coming on all of my adventures with me."

She caught my hands in hers and squeezed. My chest tightened to match, stealing my breath.

My tongue darted between my too-dry lips. "Oh dear, that sounds horribly improper—an unmarried man trailing after an unmarried woman for the rest of his days."

Nothing could have prepared me for her next words.

"Good thing we're married then." She said it with such blinding confidence that my knees weakened and my heart forgot to beat.

"We are?" I asked, breathless and pathetic.

"We will be. Did you know the marriage laws in Scotland are different from England's? All that is required is for two people to claim their intent to marry in front of witnesses. And look, there are two witnesses right there." She pointed behind her to Rory, leaning back against the coach with a smirk, and Alfie beside her holding the reins of two new horses.

"Is it that easy? I suppose I have no pressing engagements today. It seems as good a time as any to wed," I teased, though the breezy, giddy quality of my voice negated the effect slightly.

"You're saying yes?"

"I'm saying yes, everywhere, always. You're my wife."

I tightened my hand around hers and caught the other. My thumb couldn't resist the desire to trace the delicate band, now at home on her third finger.

"You're my husband. And I love you."

Tears welled but I blinked them back. I couldn't risk blurring this memory, this moment. "You do?"

"Very much." Elation overfilled my body.

I turned to Rory and Alfie, finally noting the lad with two sets of reigns in his grasp. "Does this count?"

"Aye, lad," Rory called back, smile bright.

And then Davina was in my arms, clinging to my neck as our lips met for the first time as husband and wife.

The kiss was messy, sloppy, both of us smiling too wide to be very effectual. And when we pulled apart, her finger traced the curve of my lips.

"Two thousand percent," she whispered.

"What?"

"I measure your smiles, count them. This one... it blows all the others away."

"I should hope so, wife," I said, resting my forehead against hers.

"I look forward to topping it, husband."

"Come, little menace." I swung my arm over her shoulder and guided her into the carriage. "Where should we go on our next adventure?"

"I already told you. Everywhere."

Epilogue

LEIGHTON HALL—MAY 15, 1824

DAVINA

I STILL ABDUCTED my husband from time to time—only to ensure he never grew complacent.

The years had been generous, providing us with two daughters to run about the countryside like hellions. They had proven to be the greatest adventure of all.

Kit's beard may have had a hint of grey to it now, and I had more than a few laugh lines etched on my face. But my love for him had never once caused more pain than joy. And Xander had been right. I wouldn't give up this life for anything, no matter what tomorrow brought.

It took Kit less than six months to put his estate to rights and sort out Ewan's inheritance. After which we set off on a grand honeymoon, traipsing across the continent for more than a year with no hint of a plan.

Our adventures remained closer to home these days, with frequent forays north to Scotland to see Xander, Tom, Sorcha, and little Ewan. Or south, to London or Kent to see our friends and family there. Sometimes, we went west for no reason at all but to explore Wales or Ireland.

My dear husband still did, on occasion, get lost in the piles of documents in his study, particularly when Will sent some contracts for a second look. And thus, an abduction was required.

Today was one of those days.

I'd foregone stockings and boots, the waistcoat too. Instead, I wore only Kit's shirt and breeches as I beat the dust from my pirate's hat against my thigh before popping it on my head at a jaunty angle over my unbound hair.

Satisfied with my appearance, I padded down the hall, making a quick detour to snatch a bottle of whiskey from the drawing room before tracing the familiar lines of the darkened hall to his study. I had no need of a candle in this house—nor would I forsake the element of surprise for such a convenience.

The door was cracked, as usual. Kit always left a door open for me and the girls, no matter how busy he was. Peering through the gap, I saw my husband's dark curls sprawled atop the desk—asleep then.

I crept inside and set the bottle on the desk before rounding it to his side. Gently, I brushed back a dark curl that danced in front of his nose with every breath. Dark eyelashes fluttered for a moment before revealing warm eyes.

"This is an abduction," I whispered, earning a quarter smile.

Kit rose, groaning as he registered the ache in his frame. Smudges of ink lined his cheek, curved into a boyish grin. "Is it?" he questioned.

"It is."

"And how long might I expect to be gone? I would not wish for my wife to worry, you see."

"Not for long, I expect. But she should absolutely worry."

He raised a brow. "She should?"

"Oh, yes. You'll never be the same after I return you."

"In what ways?"

My grin felt wicked. "I'm going to wring so much pleasure from your body, you'll never walk straight again."

His laugh was bright and pleased. "I look forward to it. Need I pack anything?"

"Bring the whiskey," I commanded as I grabbed his half-burned candle. He snatched up the bottle and rounded the desk, following me down the hall. I may not need light to navigate, but Kit and I both liked to see during our intimate moments.

"Where are we going?"

"Slough," I retorted.

Kit chortled.

"Shh, we do not want to wake the girls."

"Or your mother," he muttered, not particularly trying to hide the words.

"Or my mother."

"I'll build the dower house with my own two hands if they don't start hammering faster."

"My hero." The addition of my mother into our lives was, perhaps, the least enjoyable adventure Kit and I had ever been on, but my husband was far too kind to do more than grumble —grumble and pray for summer when we might foist her upon Xander.

"Yes, yes."

My husband trailed after me past the dining and breakfast rooms to the darkened kitchens. There, on the counter across from the low-burning hearth, sat two unfrosted fairy cakes awaiting our attention.

I didn't bake often. I'd never mastered the activity—almost certainly due to lack of effort and not Mrs. Ainsley's instruction. But on special occasions, Kit deserved a reward for abandoning his old life and easy access to pastries. These would barely be considered a reward—I wasn't certain they were cooked all the way through, but Kit would gift me a smile all the same.

The moment I set the candle down, his hand wrapped around my waist and tugged me back against his familiar frame.

Kit's nose nuzzled my neck, his forehead jostling my hat. "For me?" he asked as he leaned forward to set the whiskey beside the candle.

"I never abduct anyone without provisions, sir. Do you think me a novice?"

I felt his smile—a full one—ghost along my shoulder before he nipped playfully, the strands of his beard catching my skin pleasantly. "I do not know. You seem sweet enough to eat. Perhaps sweeter than that fairy cake."

"Christopher... I have plans."

"Mm, so do I. And you've always so enjoyed my plans."

"But—" A broken moan rumbled from my throat as his fingertips grazed the edge of my shirt and darted below for a quick pinch, interrupting my token protest.

"Just a slight detour..." my husband teased.

"But—"

"Davina," he grumbled, his other hand working at my hip to tug the hem of my shirt free from the breeches. A little noise of triumph escaped his chest when he succeeded before his hand slid beneath the falls to test my response. His groan as he felt the dampness of my entrance left me weak-kneed. "It seems my abductress is in need of attention."

My will failed me. It was a predictable outcome—I could deny him nothing that gave us both such pleasure.

He must have sensed my submission because he immediately set to work on the buttons of my falls. "I have far more experience undoing someone else's breeches than I ever would have expected."

"And you love it."

"I don't know. There's something to be said for your pretty frocks. Easy access..."

"You love a challenge or you wouldn't love me," I retorted, then a whimper overtook me as familiar fingers slid between fabric and flesh toward the cleft between my legs.

"Loving you has never been a challenge, Davina. It's the easiest thing I've ever done."

I melted at his words and his touch. His fingers slid into my channel at the same time his thumb worked my button. My hand flew to his forearm, clutching him in place, though I knew he would never leave me unsatisfied. Kit indulged himself for a moment, moving his strong fingers in the way he knew left me breathless but not purposefully enough to bring me to a peak. His hard cock nestled into the curve of my backside with half-hearted thrusts.

"What did you have planned?" he rumbled against my ear.

"Wha?"

"You had plans... I interrupted them," he punctuated that statement with a swirl of his thumb.

Thoughts were a hazy, abstract concept—inconsequential compared to the tangible sparks of pleasure my husband wrought.

"Davina..."

"Frosting."

"Frosting?"

"I thought to..."

The smile on my shoulder was another impressive one, paired with a rewarding curl of his fingers. "Davina... Did you want me to lick frosting off you?"

"Your cock—I thought to..." My breath came in sharp pants as my cunny gripped his fingers in time to his rhythm.

His chuckle was pleased and indulgent as his fingers and

thumb found a steady—purposeful—rhythm. "Sounds sticky."

And then, my wretched husband made the worst possible choice—he pulled his hand out of my breeches.

"Kit!"

"Shh." Dexterous hands grabbed me by the waist and spun me before lifting and plopping me on the counter beside the fairy cakes.

"I have a suggestion," he whispered before his lips met mine in a desperate kiss. "If it's not to your liking, I'll fetch the frosting myself—but you will need to be the one to call for a bath after. I refuse to explain to Mrs. Reed why we're in need of a tub at this hour."

His point was valid, if annoying, but I was more curious than irritated about his plan. Soft lips found mine again as his hand slid over the damp patch on my breeches. He drew back, catching my gaze with a significant look before tugging my shirt up to trail those same fingers over the peak of my breast. Comprehension dawned at the same moment his lips found my nipple.

My whimper was drowned out by his groan, the curve of his tongue more determined than his usual distracted teasing. Even as his hand moved to the other breast—his tongue following after. Kit's groan against my nipple was an exquisite torture, sending shocks to my center.

When I was worshiped to his satisfaction, he pulled back, meeting my eyes. His pupils threatened to overtake his beautiful dark eyes. And then the corner of his lip curled up in challenge. My stomach clenched in anticipation—that expression had never once led to anything other than breath-stealing pleasure.

Kit raised his hand, the one still damp with my pleasure, to my lips. With one beautiful finger, he traced first my upper, then my lower lip before his crashed onto them. His kiss was messy, more a feast than a kiss in truth. But this taste... it was so familiar on his lips, nearly as familiar as his on my own.

When we broke apart, breathless, he chased my musk across my cheek, my jaw, my neck—wherever he'd traced in his distracted desperation.

"Kit," I whined, dragging his attention back to me with both hands on his cheeks, my shirt falling back between us. I met his gaze with a nod and a whimpered, "Yes, Kit."

His smile was pleased and bright—certainly a full one. My husband was always game for my breezy suggestions, participating with enthusiasm in all our bed sport. But his ideas were fewer and farther between, usually the result of far too much rumination and plotting. I made it a point never to deny his requests and he devoted himself to ensuring I was left boneless.

"You don't even know what I'm planning," he teased, voice low and ragged.

"Doesn't matter."

I slipped off the counter and shoved the fabric down my thighs to pool at my feet before gesturing to my husband to strip as well. He reached back with one hand, catching the back of his shirt before tugging it up and off in a way I always stopped to admire. Estate work and country living had left the lines of his chest even more refined than they were the first time I met them. I suspected at some point he had recognized my appreciation of his musculature—and hoisted a few extra hay bales as a reward. And appreciate them, I did.

My greedy hands fell to his shoulders, tracing down them to the corded muscles of his arms.

"Shirt first, then fondling," he grumbled, his own fingers landing on my thighs, rucking the cotton up my hips and waist with calloused fingers.

"*Kit,*" I whined.

"*Davina,*" he mocked. "Take your shirt off, and then you

can molest me until your heart is content." Even as he teased, he was dragging the shirt up my rib cage where it was trapped by my arms.

Reluctantly, I pulled away long enough for my husband to rip it over my head before throwing it somewhere—hopefully not into the hearth.

It seemed I was not the only one with plans to stroke and grab and, *oh God*, kiss. My fingers fell back to the strong, determined shoulders I loved, sliding along his back to feel the tendons stretch and tense, even as his lips on my breast set about driving thought from my head.

"Kit, I had plans..."

"I have better ones." The grumble of his words against my nipple set gooseflesh alight along my belly. His hand traced a teasing path up the inside of my thigh, hinting at something more.

"But..." I protested.

Wordlessly, he began to collapse, pulling me with him to the wooden floor. I landed across his still-clothed lap, his lips finally breaking with my breasts to find my mouth.

"Davina, I promise if you have the energy to reach your frosting when I'm finished with you, you may do what you wish with it."

Slowly, purposefully, he leaned back against the hardwood. One hand came up to cradle his neck while he cocked a deliberate brow. Comprehension settled and my thoughts raced ahead. He was right, his plan was better than mine. And if my legs behaved well enough afterward to stand and walk to the cold cellar for the frosting, it would be the first time.

Still, I couldn't allow him to think he'd won—not without the requisite worship of my magnificence.

"Comfortable?" I asked, infusing my tone with a bit of the haughty duke's daughter.

"Very."

I swung one leg to straddle my husband, unable to resist a slight rock against the hardness growing in his breeches. "Good, because you've made a great many promises just now. It could take some time for you to deliver on them."

He grunted when I brushed against his fabric-covered cock before coughing out, "I would never dare to rush a lady."

Warm hands settled on my thighs. "Indeed," I insisted, shifting once again, earning a squeeze from Kit.

With a sigh, he released one of my legs to press himself up to sitting, his lips catching mine. "Darling, you're overthinking this," he whispered, his lips brushing against mine.

"What?"

"I can see you thinking away. You're supposed to be riding my face until consciousness abandons your body, not fretting. What is it?" Gently, he brushed my hair away from my neck, leaving room for searing kisses along the line of my throat.

"I don't..." Kit's tongue found my nipple before my head could supply the end of that sentence.

"You don't what?" he pressed.

"What?" I asked on a groan.

"That's better. Too much planning and negotiating, not enough kissing," he murmured along the underside of my breast, his tongue tracing the lines of my rib cage. My hand tangled in his hair instinctively, pressing him closer.

"Kit!" I cried when he nipped gently at the curve of my breast before soothing it with his tongue.

"I love your sweet, mischievous mind," he mused, shifting to the other breast. My heart fluttered in response, back arching toward his mouth wantonly. "But sometimes it gets away from us both."

Kit began to lower himself down, one vertebra at a time as I chased the feel of his lips mindlessly.

"Do you remember the first time we did this? So worried

you'd suffocate me—as if I could conceive of a better death. You still get a little nervous?"

"There's nothing to grab onto here," I said, a hint of defensiveness slipping in.

"My head," he teased, settling back with his palm between his dark curls and the floor.

"Kit," I whined, even as the hand on my thigh dragged me up his torso.

"Fine." His lips quirked up in a quick smile. "Easily solved." His free hand abandoned my flesh. Stretching, he reached for the leg of a dining chair above his head. The muscles of his abdomen tensed intriguingly with the effort beneath my bare core. "Only so you don't fall so far when you swoon." He dragged it to my side—something to balance against.

"I'm not going to swoon."

"That's what you said the last time too."

And that was the crux of it. Something about this position, one of inherent power... It left Kit with a contradictory determination. Instead of remaining content to allow me to direct my own pleasure, he saw this position as an opportunity, a need really, to wring every ounce of pleasure from my body until I was nothing but a wonderstruck nerve, brainless and weak. The result was incredible, as was the journey. But I was always a little nervous to begin for reasons I could never articulate.

"Davina? Yes or no?" he pressed, gaze catching mine.

The answer had never once changed. I couldn't foresee a situation in which it would.

At my wrung-out "Yes," my husband's hand fell to my waist and dragged me up his chest. Once I hovered, needy and exposed above his too-smart mouth, the hand moved to my arse with a quick squeeze before pulling me down.

There was no hesitation, no gentle teasing touches—no, my husband feasted. Manners did not exist here. The sights and sounds had no place in polite company. His tongue slipped inside, meeting no resistance, chasing the source of my nectar with a groan.

The hand beneath his head slipped free, reaching for mine. He laced our fingers together for a gentle squeeze before directing them to his already mussed curls. My brilliant husband timed the touch of my hand to his head perfectly, shifting his attention to the source of my pleasure at the same moment.

Without permission, my fist tightened, pulling him closer. I felt his pleased smile against my soaked flesh and tugged once again in punishment. Predictably, he groaned in pleasure at my wordless reprimand. The vibrations echoed through my flesh, converging in my lower abdomen.

The beard covering his upper lip and chin prickled against my skin, a sharpened bite to my already sensitized sex. As always, the sensation ripped breath from my body, my abdomen tensing.

Seven years of marriage had left Kit with a profound and visceral knowledge of this intimate area of my form—perhaps better than my own. He used it to his advantage in this moment, guiding me closer to that inevitable peak.

No sooner had his hand slid from my waist to tease at my entrance while his tongue worked my pearl than a familiar tightening began to bloom in my belly, a matching hope growing in my chest.

Perhaps this time, this time a single climax would be enough to satisfy my husband. One glance at the heat in his gaze shattered that illusion. My husband was going to destroy me, in the best possible way. Once wouldn't be enough for my Kit, not tonight.

Anticipation tightened in my chest while his tongue swirled with the perfect pressure. Pleasure snapped through me, a blinding white overtaking my vision.

Sense returned quickly. My hand was tangled in Kit's curls, pulling rather too hard. The other was wrapped around the edge of the chair, keeping me upright. My husband's mouth was still across my sex, a comforting presence as he allowed me a moment to find breath.

One by one, I loosened the fingers in his hair. He pulled back for a quick breath.

"Chair was a good idea. Well done, you."

"It was your—"

Words abandoned me when Kit slid his fingers from my channel. And then back in. Out. In. Somehow finding an expert rhythm and a teasing twist as his lips returned to that bundle of nerves at my apex.

His free hand slid to my waist, rocking me gently against his flat tongue in time with his fingers. Slowly, he urged me onward. A little harder, a little faster with each thrust, dragging me back up that hill. My heart tripped along after my body, struggling to keep up.

It didn't take long for my fingers and toes to clench and with one quick suck of his lips, my back bowed, stars shooting across my eyelids with a cry of his name.

When my senses came back to me, he was merely breathing against my overwrought sex. From experience, he knew I would be too sensitive for more. Even this, the caress of his warm breath, sparked tiny shocks of pleasure that left me twitching.

"Can you give me another?" he whispered, dark eyes trapping mine beneath my trembling thighs, slick with our efforts "For me?"

My vocal chords refused to cooperate.

"Please, my love?"

I wasn't certain I could give him another climax. But I *knew* I wouldn't survive disappointing him. Not when he asked so sweetly.

Finally, in a tremulous voice, I croaked an affirmative. His groan was barely audible, delivered against my center as his tongue slipped inside. His now free hand pressed bluntly against my jewel, the cool gold of his wedding band, a soothing balm, steady, sure, mine.

Sweaty curls clung to my forehead and neck as he ripped pathetic whimpers from my chest, a sweet harmony with his hungry groans and the obscene sounds of his tongue in my slit.

As he caressed me impossibly softly, I could feel the pleasure rising again, soaring through my veins.

My body ceased to obey me, it was his to command. Even my breaths were not my own. Inhales came in great desperate hiccups, before air rushed from my lungs without permission.

I was a bow drawn tighter and tighter with every measured, musical thrust of his tongue, every press of his palm.

Suddenly, without the slightest foreshadowing, Kit separated his fingers, trapping my bud between them with the perfect pleasure and I snapped again, collapsing against the chair as darkness overtook me.

The world reappeared, sharpened to a bright knife edge, when his cock slid inside me. Senseless compliments and devotions spilling from Kit's mouth in a never-ceasing stream against my neck.

It took the length of one, two sloppy thrusts before my wits rejoined me in a cutting breath.

My hands found his shoulders before silently, I pushed him down, down, down until he collapsed back on the floor.

Fingers traced the elegant planes of his chest, pushing back against his abdomen when he tried to thrust up.

Methodically, pointedly, I used my palms to press my hips up before allowing them to succumb to gravity, then his cock slid home to welcoming groans from us both.

Kit's eyes flicked from mine, down to where our sexes met. Awe slid across his face, evident in his furrowed brow and panting lips.

"My turn," I whispered.

"Fuck, Davina," he mumbled back. "Goddess…"

I was still too sensitive, my thighs trembling with arousal and exertion. But I wouldn't need to last long, not if he was already cursing. Just long enough for my turn to break him.

One hand left his chest, finding my own breasts, brushing across a hyper-sensitive nipple, soft as a butterfly's wings. My husband's warm fingers squeezed my thigh, a reward for the sight.

"Davina, my love. Please, I—" An overworked tongue darted between his lips, followed by a thick swallow. "I need to—"

He bucked against the palm resting on his abdomen. Reminded of my task, I settled into an easy rhythm, tightening my internal muscles as I rocked up.

The whimpers were coming from Kit's chest this time as his gaze flicked between mine, the hand on my breasts, and our joining flesh with increasing rapidity.

"Can I— I want to touch you." The hand on my hip began to slide toward my nub.

I batted it away, knowing that as much as he enjoyed watching my hands on my breasts, he would appreciate this even more.

His gaze found mine, and I lazily slipped my hand down the curve of my lower belly, through the curls covering my mound, to the button of my pleasure.

A quick swirl finished us both, my internal muscles clenching on his cock as he spilled with wrenching gasps. Ecstasy overtook us both until we were drowning. Wave after wave threatened to pull us under until the ocean of love and lust claimed us forevermore.

When I returned to my body, I was sprawled atop my husband, jostled with each of his trembling breaths even as he ran soothing hands along my spine.

"Beautiful, brilliant menace..." he whispered. His fingers slid like silk along my oversensitized skin, dragging a shudder from me until gooseflesh pebbled along my bare skin in its wake.

It took more thought than it ought, to force my limbs to cooperate. Finally, I managed to arrange my arm across his chest so I could prop my chin on it without poking his sternum. Bemused brown eyes found mine as gentle fingers tucked a limp strand of my hair behind my ear.

"So, my love, do you require frosting?" he asked, a grin spilling across his lips, crinkles deepening in the corners of his eyes.

"Don't be smug."

"But it feels so good to be smug." Pointedly, he gave a half-hearted thrust of his hips, reminding me that his cock was still sheathed inside me. As sensitive as I was, I wasn't ready to be free of him. Instead, I merely rolled my eyes and settled my head back against his chest.

Beneath my ear, his heart trilled along, still too fast.

"Was it all right?" he pressed again, a hint of vulnerability creeping in.

My heart tugged pitifully the way it always did when my husband was a little unsure. Earlier, he'd taken on the role, but now, now, it was my turn to reassure him.

I pressed up on my hands, earning a little *oomph* for my trouble when I pushed against his chest.

He rubbed at his sternum in mock irritation before his ochre eyes met mine.

"It was perfect," I said low and assuring.

"Yes?"

"I've never regretted agreeing to an adventure with you, Kit. Your plans, even the ones that make me nervous, are more than worth it."

"They are?" he asked, cupping my cheek.

"You draft a good scheme, Mr. Summers. I think this one might be your second best."

"Second best?" A furrow settled into the crease of his brow.

"Second best. I'm afraid you'll never top the one where you asked me to marry you."

His smile pierced my soul.

"Agreed. Do you know what your best scheme was?" he asked, a grin still etched across his face.

"What?"

"The abduction."

My giggle was easy, spilling from my chest without thought. "Which one?"

"All of them. Each and every one." Love poured from every word.

"Good, because I was thinking of executing another one next week."

"I'll keep a bag packed," he promised, trying and failing to bite back the smile.

"I'll secure the carriage," I vowed, relishing in the bubble of our laughter overfilling the room, our home, our lives.

The End.

Support the author—leave a review.

Don't forget to check out some of Kit and Davina's earlier adventures here.

Keep an eye out for Ally's next series, Hell's Heiresses, featuring Michael's and Augie's daughters, set to inherit the Wayland's gaming-hell fortune.

Acknowledgments

Astute readers may have noticed my hat tip to *Schitt's Creek*. The Hasket family has always been my answer to the question, what if I plopped (some of) the Rose family into Regency-era England.

While my characters bear little resemblance to our favorite disgraced video-store dynasty, I absolutely adore Alexis's little asides about her various adventures. Crafting the Regency equivalent of "I didn't go missing, David. The FBI knew where I was the entire time," has been a blast.

∼

This book will always hold a special place in my heart.

I began my writing journey while my mother was in remission from ovarian cancer. Just before the release of my debut, *Courting Scandal*, her cancer returned.

My love of reading comes from her. And so does my love of historical romance specifically. I was a latchkey kid and before we had a reliable internet connection (ew, I'm old), I used to read from her library books after school. I was far too young to be reading the bodice rippers of the 80's and 90's, but it led me here, writing the acknowledgements on my eighth book.

I draft in the evenings, and every morning, she would read what I had written. She provided feedback, offered suggestions, and helped me plot. While *The Scottish Scheme* was the last of my books that she read (that one was written out of order), *this* was her favorite—she loved a comedy.

She passed six months ago.

Editing this book, knowing she will never read the finished novel nor any of the ones to come, has been one of the more heartbreaking tasks of my writing journey—and I did kill Gabriell, you must remember.

While I've dedicated books to other people, they're all a little bit dedicated to her. If you laughed out loud while reading this book—that was thanks to her.

∼

I must also thank my critique partner, Laura Linn, for listening to my nonsense.

Mariah deserves all the praise for taking up the impossible mantle of reading my messy chapters as they come.

Bryton for dragging me from my house on occasion.

Martha for reminding me to do other things once in awhile.

Ali for listening to me while I cry.

And Holly Perret at *The Swoonies Romance Art* for my beautiful cover.

About the Author

Ally Hudson is an Amazon bestselling author of steamy Regency romance, crafting captivating tales of love, healing, hope, and family. Her debut series, *Most Imprudent Matches*, weaves together eight unforgettable love stories spanning decades, blending humor and heart with devoted heroes and capable heroines. Ally's stories celebrate the countless forms love can take, each one deserving its moment to shine.

When she's not writing, Ally can be found embroidering, baking, or catering to the every whim of her charming dog, Darcy.

Also by Ally Hudson

MOST IMPRUDENT MATCHES

Courting Scandal - Book One

Michael and Juliet

The Baker and the Bookmaker - Book Two

Augie and Anna

Winning My Wife - Book Three

Hugh and Kate

Devil of Mine - A Prequel Novella

Gabriel and Celine

Angel of Mine - Book Four

Will and Celine

A Properly Conducted Sham - Book Five

Lee and Charlotte

The Scottish Scheme - Book Six

Tom and Xander

A Lady's Guide to Abduction (and Other Legal Matters)- Book Seven

Kit and Davina

HELL'S HEIRESSES

Coming Soon: The Viscount's Violet

Printed in Dunstable, United Kingdom